Surrender
Book One

Melody Anne

Printed and published in the United States of America.
Published by Gossamer Publishing Company
Editing by Exclusive Publishing
Cover art by Exclusive Publishing Company
Salt Lake City, Utah
Look for us online at:
www.exclusivepublishing.com
Email: Info@exclusivepublishing.com

ISBN: 10: 0615810756

ISBN- 13: 978-0615810751

DEDICATION

This book is dedicated to my Grandma Eileen. Thank you for always believing in me, for taking me into your home when I needed a place to go, and for taking such great care of me. I miss you every single day, and the only sadness I feel of this amazing journey I've been on, is that you aren't with me to share it. I love you, Grandma. I am thankful that you are looking down on me from the Heavens. I know I'll see you again someday..

Note from the Author

I have to admit I had a lot of fun writing this book. I love strong, take-charge men. I tend to write most of my books with that personality, but I got to take Rafe's character one step further. This story shocked me, though. Originally, there weren't nearly as many family scenes. I guess I can't help myself. In my personal life, family comes first. That has become very apparent in my writing. I just can't seem to leave family out.

My life has changed so much over the last two years. I am so unbelievably thankful to have achieved what I have. When I wrote my first book, I hoped a few people would be interested. I never expected the response I got and the love you all have for the Andersons. It humbles me. I say it often, and I'll never stop saying it; I have the most amazing fans in the world. Many of you I consider friends. You make me smile, laugh, and cry tears of joy. I love speaking with you. I love all the wonderful things you share with me.

A special thank you goes out to Denise Bush and Jane Bowen who make me the most wonderful advertisements for my Facebook wall, and more. Thank you for the quality and time you put in. Thank you to my Street Team, Melody's Muses. Each one of you truly does inspire me. Thank you for sharing my books, for encouraging me in all I do, and for being such a support system. There are way too many names to put in here, and I don't want to hurt any feelings, but a couple of people from the beautiful UK are very close to my heart. I don't always manage to comment on everything I see on Facebook, but I read it all and I love your comments and encouragement. One of my fans still has a sexy cop to get a pic of. ;) You are all amazing!

This book also has a special character in it that the fans helped to create. He was in the first draft as a generic character until I ran a contest on Author Ruth Cardello's street team page. I want to thank Jane Bowen, Julie Brewer, Jenny LaMere and Natalie Townson for their suggestions. You created Shane Grayson, who'll we'll meet in this book and get to know a lot better in book two.

Thank you Nikki, who I couldn't do this job without. You are there to listen to my panic when the books aren't going right. You lead me back in the right direction when I truly suck (which is often) and you create the most stunning book covers that are out there. I love your work! I dislike you a bit when I have to revise half the book, but then I love you again when the book is so much better because of it. Thank you for continuing to be my best friend. Without you and Stephy in my life, I would only be a third of a person.

As always, thank you to my family for not nagging me too much when I'm in my office from afternoon until dawn, for understanding my desire to make these books, and for standing by me every step of the way. Family always comes first – always! I couldn't do any of this without my beautiful daughter, my amazing son, and my husband. I have so many other family members who help me in so many ways that I can write a book just about that. My life is so much brighter because of all those who surround me.

A final note goes out to a few other authors. I've been reading since I was in Kindergarten (We won't say how long that has been) and I have so much love and respect for authors who have opened my eyes to so many adventures. Because of this journey I've taken, I've gotten to meet the most amazing women, and a few men, who inspire me, and help me strive to be so much better than just mediocre. Ruth Cardello has taken me under her magical wing and makes me feel like I can reach the sky. Kathleen Brooks is full of energy and can make me laugh, and touches me with her humanity. Terri Marie and Randy Mixter were there for me in the beginning of my journey and I love watching their success.

I've also gotten to visit with and meet some of my heroes; Sandra Marton who has over 80 books published is so kind and helpful, and Lynn Raye Harris who's talent is an unstoppable force. Each one of you has helped me, inspired me, and makes me want to be better. Thank you. There are so many more that I hate naming names, but hopefully I'll be like Sandra with nearly a 100 books out someday, and then I'll have time to thank you all.

Melody Anne

Melody Anne

*Having everything to lose
can make a person
do desperate things.*

*Would you surrender to
help the one you love?*

Books by Melody Anne

*The Billionaire Wins the Game – Book One
*The Billionaire's Dance – Book Two
*The Billionaire Falls – Book Three
*The Billionaire's Marriage Proposal – Book Four
*Blackmailing the Billionaire – Book Five
*Runaway Heiress – Book Six
*The Billionaire's Final Stand – Book Seven

+The Tycoon's Revenge – Book One
+The Tycoon's Vacation – Book Two
+The Tycoon's Proposal – Book Three
+The Tycoon's Secret – Book Four

-Midnight Fire – Rise of the Dark Angel – Book One
-Midnight Moon – Rise of the Dark Angel – Book Two
-Midnight Storm – Rise of the Dark Angel – Book Three

#Surrender – Book One

www.facebook.com/authormelodyanne

Melody's Web Site: www.melodyanne.com

Twitter: @authmelodyanne

Coming Soon:
*Because of Honor - A new series
*Hidden Treasure – Book One –
     The Lost Andersons
*Submit – Book Two in Surrender Series

Prologue

Divorce.

His throat closed up at the mere thought of that word. He was twenty-eight years old and had conquered the universe — or thought he had.

No! He had.

Then his picture-perfect world had shattered with a single word.

Divorce.

He'd been respectable and respectful, always treating women with admiration. He hadn't jumped into marriage at twenty-one, but had dated the same woman for three years, had cherished her, had given her everything. He thought he'd found perfection, but found disillusion instead.

Raffaello Palazzo sat straight up; his eyes narrowed.

No! He wasn't this man.

Even if groveling had been in his nature, which it most assuredly wasn't, he wouldn't consider doing it now.

"Goodbye."

He barely glanced up as Sharron walked past, her five-thousand-dollar purse slung over her shoulder, and flaunted the smirk on her face as she slammed the door in all finality. She was gone, and he was grateful.

A couple of her complaints against him were that he worked too much and he wasn't as attentive as she thought she deserved.

When he'd walked in the week before with a bouquet of roses, attempting to give her the attention she'd demanded, he'd seen that she wasn't choosy about the source of the attention. She'd been in bed with his business partner. Then to add insult to injury, she'd attempted to take him for all he was worth.

She'd lost.

Rafe's eyes closed as he pictured that horrible afternoon.

"Are you cutting out on us?"

"It's my anniversary. I had my wife's favorite flower, the Hawaiian Flora, delivered express to the floral shop, and I'm picking up her bouquet, then taking her on a surprise trip to Paris. That's where we celebrated our honeymoon."

"You're the most whipped man I know, Rafe," *his assistant, Mario Kinsor, said with a smile.*

"I'm half Italian. My father learned the ways of my mother's country and how gallant the men are

and he taught me how to cherish a woman," Rafe replied genially, not offended in the least. He hoped to have as strong a marriage as his parents had, and for just as long.

"When does Ryan get back? If you're cutting out, I'll need one of the business partners here to get work done."

"He's flying in on Friday. I spoke to him a few days ago, and he said he met someone. I'm looking forward to meeting her."

"I can't take any more of this mushy talk. Get out of here before your lovesickness becomes contagious. I'll see you Monday."

"Night, Mario. Thanks for all your hard work this week."

Heading for the door, Rafe waved to his faithful assistant. Life was great — his corporation was flourishing without help from his family, and his personal life couldn't be better.

It didn't take Rafe long to breeze into the florist's and then arrive home. When he couldn't find Sharron downstairs, he smiled in anticipation. Maybe she was stretched out on their bed in a sexy nightie...

When Rafe opened the door, he did find her in bed, and scantily dressed — hell, not dressed at all — but she wasn't alone. He froze as shock filled him.

"Ohhh, Ryan!" Sharron cried out, and Rafe's illusions of happily ever after shattered.

Silently, he stood in the dim light as one of his two best friends screwed his wife. It had been Ryan, Shane and him since middle school, always sharing

— always there for one another. Rafe guessed Ryan figured Rafe's wife was included in what Rafe was willing to share. Wrong.

Rafe cleared his throat as Sharron screamed again in pleasure. The two of them froze — locked in their torrid embrace — before their heads turned and they looked at him in horror.

Rafe walked from the room and waited downstairs. Almost immediately, Ryan scurried from the house with his head down. Sharron rushed toward Rafe and started to beg for his forgiveness.

Rafe shook off the unpleasant memory as he glanced around him. For a single moment, he'd been shattered. He'd sacrificed so much of himself to please her — give her what she wanted — but none of that was enough. She'd wanted everything from him – namely all his net worth. He wouldn't make the same mistake twice; he never did.

Rafe walked up the steps and stood just inside the bedroom door, looking warily around at the room where he'd slept beside that woman night after night. Shaking his head, he left and made his way toward his luxury kitchen. No memories lingered there. It wasn't as though his wife had known the first thing about cooking.

He had a full staff, which was a good thing. Otherwise his house would have been in shambles and he'd never have gotten fed. Sharron hadn't been domestic in the least. He hadn't cared about that — all he'd wanted was to have the same kind of family life with her as the one he'd grown up with. Before this moment, he'd been under the sad delusion that marriages could all have happy endings.

A cold silence hung around him like a shroud, and Rafe was grateful he'd sent his staff away for the day. He didn't need anyone witnessing his failure.

Failure.

He rolled the word around on his tongue. It didn't sound right. How could it? Failure was a foreign concept to him. He'd been born with the proverbial silver spoon in his mouth. And his mother often teased him, saying he was an old soul in a young body.

She was the *only* one who could get away with a remark like that — he adored her. Well, to be fair, his sisters got away with it, too, and for the same reason.

Rafe had a sudden feeling that all his family members would be relieved to hear of the coming divorce, especially his mother, though she'd never admit it to him. She had tried to get close to his soon-to-be ex-wife, but somehow it had never happened. Had Sharron had any desire at all to know his family? Now that he thought of it, he couldn't recall any evidence in her favor. True, he wouldn't have noticed while the two of them were dating, because that was during the six months out of the year that his family resided in Italy. By the time his parents and sisters had returned for their six months in California, he and Sharron were already married.

And then? It hit him right in the gut. From the very beginning, Sharron had been great at making up excuses for why she couldn't visit with them. But he was in love and stupid and he just hadn't noticed. If he had, he would never have become so serious about her. He'd been raised to believe that family always came first. Upon their marriage, he'd put her first, just as his father had put his mother first. Soon, he'd cut down on visiting his family —she'd said she couldn't go, and he wanted to please her by remaining with her. He'd done a lot of things to make the woman happy.

Apparently none of it had been enough.

With a last glance around the kitchen, he lifted his cell phone and dialed. His call was picked up on the other end of the line before the phone could ring twice.

"Sell the house. I want nothing in it," Rafe said to his assistant in clipped tones.

"Yes, sir." There was no arguing. Mario had been an employee of his from the day Rafe had started his billion-dollar corporation. The man was loyal, efficient, and trustworthy. Rafe couldn't imagine how much harder his job would have become without his favorite employee.

Rafe had learned everything from his dad, Martin Palazzo, who had made millions in the stock market, and later in smart real-estate investments. Martin had met Rosabella, Rafe's mother, while traveling for business in Italy. The two of them had been inseparable ever since, but Rosabella couldn't stand to stay away from her homeland for more than six months at a time, which was why Rafe had spent half his childhood in Italy and half in the States.

Because of his multicultural upbringing, he was much more prepared to take on the global business structure he'd adopted. He was a fierce businessman and loyal to the end to those he loved. After today, trust would be something he held much closer to his heart and gave only with caution.

Rafe had decided from an early age that he needed to make his own way in life — not just have everything handed to him by his wealthy parents. He wasn't stupid, though. He'd taken his father's advice, had even done business with him, but Rafe had dreamed big — and turning that dream into reality had taken him much less time than it would have taken the average person.

Whenever he walked into his twenty-five-story office building in San Francisco, he felt a justified pride. He created jobs for hundreds of thousands of people throughout the world, gave them an income, made sure they went to bed each night with a full stomach and the security of more work to be done in the morning.

He gave so much — and unlike his soon-to-be ex-wife, his employees were grateful and regarded him almost as a king. Sharron had thrown everything he'd given her right back in his face. Except for money.

Rafe was finished with women. *Well*, he thought with an arrogant smirk, *finished with playing the good guy*. It was his turn to take what he wanted. Never again would he be used — never again would he put his heart out there to be carelessly trampled on. It seemed all women had a purpose, and it was fueled by their greed. The richer the man, the better for them. They wanted to be taken care of, they all had their price.

Walking purposefully out his front door, he'd refused to even turn around to watch the final latching of the lock. When he was through with something, it was over. He was done with this house.

Placing his hand on the cool metal handle on the door of his black Bentley, he barely heard the familiar click as the catch released. And as he climbed into the seat, he was oblivious to the fresh, pungent smell of the smooth leather upholstery.

Pulling quickly out of the driveway, Rafe began heading the short distance to the city, where he had a condo a couple of blocks from his office building. Luckily, Sharron had refused to live in San Francisco, causing him to sleep there on the many late nights he'd worked. The apartment was his — his alone.

If she'd so much as touched the doorway of the roomy penthouse, he'd have sold it as well. He wanted no reminders of the woman, nothing of her to remain in his life. He wanted a fresh slate. To have the last eight years back — that's what he wanted most of all, but since that was impossible, he'd simply have to erase her completely from his life from this day forward.

A few more phone calls and that would be done.

Chapter One
Three years later

"You're too thin."

Arianna Harlow trembled as the man prowled around her, continuously circling her chair. She felt like a caged animal just waiting for him to strike. Why was she still sitting there? Why didn't she say the job wasn't for her, that it had all been a big mistake and she'd best be on her way?

She knew why. Reality flooded her mind — why she couldn't afford to walk away — that was, *if* he offered her the job. She was barely staying above water with her bills overflowing. Her mother was about to be moved from the rehabilitation home she was in, shipped to a lesser facility, and Ari didn't have a dollar left in her bank account.

She was truly afraid. If her mother were sent to the state care facility, she'd probably wither away to nothing and in no time at all. Ari couldn't let that happen — she wouldn't.

Arianna had already dropped out of school during her last semester, her life forever changed because of one brief moment in time, because of one horrendous mistake.

If only...

Those two words had haunted her thoughts for the past six months. She had several different endings to those words, but the dominant words were *if only...*

If only she hadn't called her mom in panic that night.

If only she hadn't gone to the party in the first place.

If only her mother had left a few minutes later.

"Are you listening to me?" Raffaello Palazzo's voice rumbled through the air, causing Ari to jump in her seat. She had to think for a moment about what he'd last said to her. Oh, yeah, she was too thin.

"Yes, Mr. Palazzo. I just don't know how to respond to that."

"Hmm." His voice came out as a hum, drifting across her nerve endings. Rafe was incredibly intimidating as he paced back and forth, towering over her at a few inches above six feet. Add to that his jet-black hair and stunning eyes and she felt like a rumpled factory worker, totally out of her element in this exquisite office.

As he made another pass around the room and neared her, Ari thought back over the last week — how strange it had been. Never before had she jumped through such hoops during a job interview.

She'd applied for more than a hundred jobs in

the past month, and only three employers had called her back. One job had been at a bank; the manager had called her a few days later, saying they'd given the position to another applicant. The second was at an insurance company, and they'd told her she didn't have enough experience.

The third job…well, she didn't really know how to describe what she'd been through. The ad had said only this:

Seeking full-time applicants for Palazzo Corporation. Must be willing to work seven days a week, long hours. Must have no other commitments — no family, second jobs, or school. Salary 100k a year plus expenses. Hand-delivered applications only.

Ari thought getting the job would be a long shot, but she had nothing to lose by applying. She had immediately spruced up her résumé, which only included two years in her local pizza parlor, then almost four years as a part-time secretary in the Stanford history department. And after that, nothing — a six-month gap in employment while she took care of her mother and dealt with the fallout of that disastrous night.

With only one semester away from graduation, her life had changed forever because of the first foolish mistake she'd ever made. Why had she been so careless with only a few short months to go? Now that night would haunt her, be something she'd have to live with for the rest of her life.

With a leather notebook in hand, résumé and application inside, she had entered the large building and approached the security guard in the lobby, who'd directed her to the secretary's office on the twenty-fifth floor. In she'd walked with what she hoped was confidence exuding from her every pore, and she'd handed over her polished résumé.

"Thank you, Ms. Harlow. If you'll have a seat, Mr. Kinsor will call you in shortly."

Oddly enough only women were in the room when Ari sat down, not a male applicant to be seen. The frightening part was that all of them looked far more qualified for whatever office position was open. One by one the women had stepped into a room, the door shutting behind them. After about ten minutes they'd walked back out, their expressions confident as they eyed the remaining applicants. This business world was a sharkfest and Ari didn't know if she was up for the swim.

"Ms. Harlow?"

"Right here," she'd called. Adjusting her oversized glasses, and picking at the bottom of her two sizes too big shirt, she stood and walked purposefully toward the small man wearing a sharp business suit and gentle smile on his face.

"This way, please."

She'd followed him into a room where a blue screen was set against the wall. There was a table with a piece of paper and a pen sitting atop it and nothing more.

"Please have a seat. I'm going to take your picture."

Ari hadn't understood the need for a picture just yet. Possibly it was for an ID card or employee badge, but usually that was done after you were hired. Maybe they were running it through security to make sure she wasn't a criminal. It didn't matter. She wasn't going to protest.

She had taken her seat and waited for the flash, knowing her smile wasn't genuine, but her anticipation had been so high, it was impossible to offer anything bigger than a slight grimace.

"Please fill out this form and make sure all contact information is correct. If you've passed to the second part of our screening process, we'll call you in three to five days," Mr. Mario Kinsor had said with the same gentle smile.

He hadn't asked her whether she had any questions. He hadn't elaborated on the job. Normally, she would have just filled out the paperwork and kept silent, but her rising curiosity had pushed her with an unknown bravery to ask what the job actually was.

"Mr. Kinsor, the ad in the paper was vague. What exactly does this job entail?"

"If you make it to the next level, you'll be given more information, Ms. Harlow. I'm sorry, but Mr. Palazzo is a very private man and this position is…confidential," he'd answered with a slight pause.

"I understand," Ari had said with a brittle smile, though she hadn't understood at all.

She'd scanned the solitary paper on the table and her confusion had only worsened.

What are your hobbies?

Are you in a serious relationship? If not, when was the last one you were in?

Are you available to travel?

What kind of questions were these? Was the

second one even allowed in a job interview? Still, she'd answered as best she could and finally read a question that made sense:

What are your career goals?

The sentence had elicited a genuine smile. Before her mother's car accident, before her life had changed so dramatically, she'd been an honors student at Stanford, working toward her bachelor's degree in history. She'd planned on getting her master's, then a doctorate so she could be a university professor.

Someday...

In her heart of hearts she still held out hope of resuming her life at some point — accomplishing the goals she'd set for herself. But instant guilt filled her whenever that hope entered conscious thought. Her mother would have liked to have her life back, too, but she never would. It was only fair that Ari make sacrifices. Ari had to atone for her sins.

Her mother had sacrificed for her entire life so that Ari could have what she needed. She'd paid for Ari's education at a small private school, and then she'd scrimped and saved to send her to the best college. Ari had earned scholarships, but her mother paid for her room and board and even her beloved car.

Ari had never realized how much her mother had given of herself until the day her mom had been checked into the hospital. Circumstances now demanded that Ari grow up quickly, without having her mother to lean on. She was now responsible for her mom's care — and Ari was failing at her new role in life.

Since the day of her mother's car accident, their lives had been filled with utter trepidation and uncertainty.

Thankfully, the Palazzo Corporation had called her back. But the second interview had been more odd than the first. She'd been put through a fitness test. They'd had her run on a treadmill for half an hour, timed her as she navigated an obstacle course, and then tested her endurance.

She'd run track all through high school and continued her running at college, so the physical aspect hadn't been a problem, but with each step she'd taken in the bizarre interview process, she'd felt rising concern about what she was applying for.

All they'd offered in response at the second interview was that it was a private position with the CEO of the corporation. Maybe she was expected to dodge bullets in countries he was invading? She'd heard rumors that his businesses weren't always welcome overseas — that some of the governments thought he was overstepping his bounds.

From the research Ari had done, the people normally welcomed him, as he paid high wages and offered excellent benefit packages. A lot of the time it seemed it was other businesses that wanted to keep him out because when he came in, he conquered, no matter what industry he was pursuing. So she knew that if she got the job, she'd have security. People rarely quit when they worked for the Palazzo Corporation.

The pay for the position was high enough to give her mother good medical care and still leave enough left over for her to save up — possibly getting her back to school within a couple of years. At this point, she'd do almost anything to be hired.

"Ms. Harlow, if you aren't going to take this interview seriously, you may exit the way you came in," Mr. Palazzo said in an irritated tone, snapping her back to the present.

"I'm sorry. I truly am. I do take this interview *very* seriously," she quickly answered, hoping she hadn't missed a question.

"I won't repeat myself again — do you understand?" Before she could answer, he continued. "I asked if you're available all hours. I don't mean Monday through Friday. This job requires your availability to me seven days a week, night and day. There will be times I won't need you for extended periods, and other times I'll need you with me for several days straight. There may be travel involved. The bottom line is that you must have *zero* other commitments. If that doesn't work for you, this interview is over."

Ari felt a lump in the back of her throat as she struggled to hold in the tears threatening to spring to her eyes. She finally gazed into his unusually colored eyes, getting her first solid look at them.

She'd heard about his type of eyes before, with something called heterochromia iridis, where two colors were present. His had a deep purple center around the pupil, fading into a gorgeous midnight blue. They were mesmerizing — intriguing — capturing her gaze, even though they were narrowing intensely right then.

"I have no other commitments. I'm available," she told him, inwardly crossing her fingers. She was committed to her mother, but with this money she wouldn't have to worry about her mom's care. She'd go see her when she had those downtimes he was speaking of. If she didn't get in to see her mom for a month, she'd be devastated, but her mom would be in good hands, and, most importantly, she wouldn't notice since she was in a coma.

"What about your mother?" he asked, as if reading her mind, his gaze boring into hers. She was stunned by the question, leaving her silent for a couple of seconds too long.

"How do you know about my mom?"

"I know everything I need to know about you, Arianna," he replied with a slight lifting of the corner of his mouth.

His expression was *far* too knowing and she immediately felt the urge to flee. Something wasn't right; something was telling her to get out while she still could. She was in over her head — she could feel it. All signs pointed to jumping from the chair and rushing out his door. But no. Loyalty to her mother kept her seated where she was.

"Yes. Of course," she responded. "My mother is being well taken care of. She's not even aware of who I am at this point. It won't hurt her in the least if she doesn't see me for long stretches of time."

He circled her again, causing her foot to twitch. When she was nervous, she did one of two things — tapped her foot, much to the annoyance of everyone around her, or bit on her thumbnail. She felt the urge to raise her hand, to make contact between thumbnail and teeth, but with great mental effort she kept her hands folded in her lap.

"I can see that as a hindrance, but as she's the only family member you have, I'll let it slide for now."

Was this guy for real? He'd let it slide? Ari was taking in air through her nose in long, deep pulls to keep her temper at bay. She needed the job, she kept reminding herself as she clenched her fingers tightly and locked her jaw to keep the words she wanted to throw at him from rushing out.

"Is something upsetting you, Ms. Harlow?" he asked, his voice smooth as molasses as he came back around and looked into her eyes again. She felt as if he were analyzing her, breaking her down into parts, trying to decide whether she was a waste of his time or not. She was sure that was how he conducted all his business. It was most likely why he was where he was in life, at the top of the ladder, and why she was at the bottom.

Some people oozed pure confidence, the ability to command and conquer the universe, and Mr. Palazzo had that in spades. She'd have given her soul for just a piece of his winning attitude and unyielding faith in himself.

"Everything's fine, Mr. Palazzo," she replied, proud of how calm and level her voice sounded, especially since her nerves were fried.

"You intrigue me, Ms. Harlow. I see you try and hide beneath your ridiculously baggy clothes, and large glasses, but there's something about you which makes me want to find out what it is you don't want the world to see." He paused, making her tug on her blouse again. "I don't hesitate once I make a decision, and I've decided to hire you…temporarily. I can see that your temper might cause a problem, but then again, meek has never been my style. Obedient…yes, but not meek."

Ari gaped at him as she tried to decipher his words. What was he talking about? What did meek and obedient have to do with anything?

"You're aware you signed a nondisclosure agreement before ever setting foot into my office, correct? Whatever is said by me is strictly confidential…and that *legal* agreement highly enforced. A former employee tried to go to the media — *once*. Let's just say, she's now lost everything…and the rumors were quickly squashed. I very much play hardball, Ms. Harlow, and it would behoove you to not become my enemy," he said in a conversational voice.

Ari swallowed hard as her eyes continued to follow him intently. He spoke of a woman's demise as if he were absently mentioning what he had eaten for lunch the previous day. Did she really want to work for this man?

But honestly, what choice did she have?

"I'm aware of what I signed, Mr. Palazzo." Ari sat up straighter in her chair, the reality of obtaining the job starting to set in. She wasn't afraid of losing everything because she had nothing to lose. Besides that, she knew how to keep things private. It wasn't as though she had any girlfriends to gossip with, anyway. She'd always been too focused on school to keep friends. Few had come and gone in her life, but none had lasted the test of time, thinking she was far too boring for their liking.

Her one attempt at acting like a normal college

student…the thought made her shudder. It was the reason she was stuck in an interview for a job she was afraid to know the title of, instead of sitting in class listening to her professor.

Rafe Palazzo's searing gaze fixed her to the spot. He'd said that he didn't go back once he made a decision, but the assessing look in his eyes belied his words. She could see that he was undecided whether he wanted actually to hire her.

She said a quick prayer that she hadn't blown this opportunity. Of course, her mother's words of advice as she'd dropped Ari off at the Stanford dorms for the first time flashed through her mind. Her mom had told her that, if the situation looks too good to be true, then it probably is, and you should run like hell in the other direction. Maybe she *should* start running, Ari thought.

"Very well, then, Ms. Harlow. The job position is for a mistress…my mistress, to be exact."

Chapter Two

Rafe watched as Arianna's eyes widened at his words. He knew he should send her on her way, but from the first moment she'd stepped inside his building there was something so mystifying about her that his interest had been instantly piqued.

She possessed an almost haunting quality in her eyes, but he pushed that thought aside. He couldn't afford to feel anything more than lust for the women in his life. He respected some of his lovers, but it was only minimal. He didn't mistrust them — he just wouldn't let them in.

All of his previous mistresses had been less than intelligent. They obeyed him, was there when he wanted, and stepped aside. The moment any of them showed the slightest amount of jealousy, he'd ended their arrangement. It was best that way. He wouldn't allow another woman to get her hooks into him where she'd only try to clean out his wallet.

It was obvious that Ari wasn't one of his typical choices. The first time he'd seen her picture, he'd passed it by, but somehow it was still on his desk at the end of his perusal, and something in her livid green eyes called to him, even though she tried to hide them behind thick glass.

He needed the women for a specific purpose — that was all. They satisfied his needs, and that was a must, since he was a highly sexual man. They also accompanied him to events where he was expected to have a woman on his arm. He normally couldn't care less what the world thought about him, but he enjoyed feeling a woman's soft curves pressing up against his body while lackluster business colleagues hemmed him in.

The fullness of a woman's pale breasts peeking out of a dark satin gown, the way her thighs would flash at him with each step she took into a room — the sight of a few strands of her hair as they tumbled down around her shoulders, begging for him to release the knot at the back of her head from its tight confines to allow her thick mane to flow forth. The extreme femininity of a woman held his attention during such tedious gatherings. All those things and more were what kept him interested in having a mistress.

He liked women to be near him; he liked them to do his bidding. He *really* liked them to satisfy his needs.

Since his divorce he'd discovered he had far more needs than he ever realized. He hadn't found a woman who could keep his interest longer than three months ever since the day Sharron had left. He was fine with that.

When he got bored, he found another willing applicant. The line of women willing to serve him was a mile long — after all, he was Rafe Palazzo, and the world was his oyster, his playground. Both the women he deigned to choose and those he didn't were hoping — all of them — to have an affair with him turn into something a lot more permanent. Too bad for them it would never happen.

His mistresses were nothing more than employees and that's precisely how he treated them. They got paid very well, were offered a severance package, and in turn, he was kept satisfied. It was win-win for both parties involved. Why not cut to the chase and offer the money to them up front. That was what they were in it for anyway.

Arianna Harlow's frozen expression made him think she wasn't going to work out as his next employee, and he was taken aback by the slight stab of disappointment he felt. Though no one he'd offered a job to had turned him down yet, he expected it to happen eventually. Surprisingly, there were women in the world who felt...uneasy about this kind of arrangement.

He honestly couldn't comprehend why. After all, he was doing nothing but ditching the obnoxious *dating* part of sex. Why not cut to the chase and tell a woman exactly what he wanted for himself and expected from her? It made everything so much simpler.

Arianna held an almost broken, yet still spirited look in her eyes, as though he'd just shot her beloved puppy and she were thinking of ways of seeking revenge. Annoyance began building inside Rafe as her gaze darted in any direction but at his face. He didn't like feeling that weak emotion coursing through him. This was business — nothing more. There wasn't room for anger, annoyance, feelings of any kind, really. Emotions like that were for lesser human beings than him.

"Take this material home and read through it. I'll let you consider your options. However, I expect an answer by five tomorrow evening."

He had a lot more work to accomplish that day and needed to get on with it. He handed her a stack of papers, then held his arm out to assist her from her seat. She glanced warily at his hand as if worried he were going to strike her. His irritation spiked.

"I may be making a mistake by offering you the job. I should simply withdraw the offer, but luckily for you, I've decided not to. I hope you appreciate how fortunate you are that I'm giving you time to think about it. There's a line of women who would literally kill to be in the position you're in."

Though he could see the words registering in her brain, she was clearly trying to conceal what she was thinking. So the sooner she was out of his office, the better for him. He needed to take a few moments to decide whether she really was the right candidate.

***

Ari felt frozen to her seat. She should tell the guy to go ahead and give the *position* to one of the many women in that disgusting line of his, and then take herself from the room. She couldn't do this — no matter how much the *job* was paying.

Guilt consumed her, though — guilt over her mother, who was lying helpless in a small bed, missing her life — a life she'd always lived to the utmost until a phone call woke her up in the middle of the night.

"Thank you," Ari replied as she finally accepted the hand Rafe was offering. As their skin touched, a small current of electricity passed through their fingers, sizzling her skin and making her insides burn in a strangely pleasurable way.

She quickly pulled back from him, rattled, unhappy with the unwelcome and foreign sensation. Without anything more being said, she walked stiltedly toward the door and then made her way to the elevator.

Ari could feel him beside her, no longer touching, but keeping pace with her as she tried to make a dignified exit. Why couldn't he have just stayed in his office instead of insisting on walking her out? She felt the air weighing down on her lungs and began fighting the desire to gasp as she tried to suck in more oxygen. She knew the danger was all in her head — there was zero chance of her suffocating. Ridiculous as it was, she had to keep reassuring herself of just that.

Mr. Palazzo reached out and pressed the down button and then stood with her; her eyes focused on the steel doors before her and she counted the seconds in her head. She'd heard the expression about tension being so thick you could slice it with a knife, but until this very moment, she'd never experienced the phenomenon. There was a first time for everything, and she seemed to be hitting several firsts in Rafe Palazzo's presence.

Open, open, open, she chanted inwardly. The elevator's arrival was made known by the chiming of the bell, which seemed much louder than usual, and she fought the impulse to jump in alarm. She entered the car before the doors were fully open, then immediately stepped to the lit panel inside and pressed the lobby button, followed by the button to close the door.

As the doors began shutting — heavens, it seemed to take forever! — Ari finally glanced up, her eyes colliding with Mr. Palazzo's intense stare. As hard as she tried to break the connection, she couldn't manage to turn her head away. When the doors finally snapped shut, she sagged against the back wall of the large box and waited for its slow descent.

After the elevator made the journey without stopping along the way and the doors opened to the lobby, she stepped out and quickly made her way across the marble floor and straight through the front doors.

Ari didn't stop until she made it to the next block. Finally, with disappointed steps, she slowed down to a more leisurely saunter until she found a bench. She gratefully sank down. Only in that moment did she allow herself to take her first deep breath since leaving Rafe Palazzo's office.

She sat for a while, trying her best not to hyperventilate. She felt as if she just couldn't get enough oxygen, but she determinedly took in slow, measured breaths. She should have said, *Thank you for the offer, but no*. She should have laughed at the ridiculous request. She should have...

With a quiet, deprecating laugh, Ari cut off those thoughts. It was a waste of time to think about what she should have done. Her *what if*s were bad enough.

But...could she do it? Could she sell herself? He was asking her to be nothing more than a high-paid prostitute, right? That's what it boiled down to, like a scene right out of *Indecent Proposal*.

Forcing herself to stand, Ari began walking the three blocks to the Palazzo Corporation parking garage. Without noticing the time that had passed during her rambles, she went up the outside steps to the third floor of the parking structure, spotted her car and climbed in the front seat. She just sat there for a moment.

As she started the engine and began driving slowly down the ramps to the exit, she remained lost in thought. She needed to get home and review the papers he'd given her — reassure herself that she couldn't take the job.

Making such a colossal decision required serious consideration. A few months ago, she never would have even considered the possibility that something like this went on. She'd been truly naïve to the world around her, protected from life's harsh realities. However, all her innocence had shattered the day the police had shown up at that college party.

In her mother's last conscious moments, her only concern had been for Ari's safety. Her mom had managed to tell the officers they needed to get to her daughter — that Ari was in danger. Only then had her mother succumbed to her injuries.

Instead of her mother, it was the policemen who'd showed up at the frat house where Ari was waiting, and then who'd transported her to the hospital. She'd waited for hours in the lobby, terror helping to sober her up fast.

When the doctor eventually came out of surgery, his news hadn't been good. Her mother was stable, but in a coma. They'd done all they could do for her. Only time would tell if she'd ever come out of it.

Sandra Harlow had had severe swelling in her brain, and they'd had to operate, drilling burr holes in her skull. Along with the head injuries, she'd also suffered two broken ribs, a cracked hip, and lacerations to her face. When Ari entered her mom's room, she'd nearly passed out at the scene before her. Its image haunted her even now.

If the staff hadn't guaranteed that the person lying in the bed was her mother, Ari wouldn't have known. The woman had been unrecognizable with her swollen face and the bandages covering her. Ari had sobbed as she'd laid her head on her mother's bed and apologized repeatedly. If it hadn't been for Ari, her mom would be home, sleeping safe and sound. Ari would never forgive herself for what she'd done.

Struggling to push such heart-wrenching memories aside, Ari focused on the road and pulled up at her small studio apartment. She slowly made her ascent up the staircase, her feet dragging as her mind raced. The papers Rafe had handed her were burning a hole in her purse.

She got to her door and fiddled with the key for several moments — if she didn't get it into the lock just right, it wouldn't turn. Heck, she thought, it would probably be faster to slip a credit card into the doorjamb.

She'd watched enough movies that she could probably break into a lot of places if she needed to. The thought made her smile as the lock finally clicked and she pushed open the door. Maybe she could find a job breaking and entering. It would be a more dignified profession than prostitution.

Though the day had started only a few hours ago, exhaustion was nipping at Ari's heels. She sat down on the couch and glared at her purse as if there were a snake inside of it just waiting for the opportunity to strike. Did she *really* want to see what Mr. Palazzo had planned for her?

With great reluctance, she finally unzipped the bag and slowly pulled the papers out, her gaze a bit clouded as she glanced down. She fought the urgency to toss them, but reality — and a slight curiosity — won out.

With only a week left at the apartment before rent was due, and no other jobs on the horizon, she needed to weigh her options. The burden of knowing that her mother's living conditions would worsen without Ari's financial support made the decision about the position even more crucial.

She'd already sold her mother's home — the place Ari had grown up in. It had broken her heart to pack her mom's most valuable possessions and take them to storage. She'd prepaid the unit for a year, taking no chances on losing the items that meant so much to her mom.

Everything Ari had of any decent value had been auctioned off. She'd done everything she could do up to this point. Now, she had to find work — and it seemed no one wanted to hire a college dropout, even if she had been an A student. It meant nothing if she couldn't finish her degree.

In the end, she really had no choice but to look at the material before her. Grasping the papers determinedly, she unfolded them and started scanning the words. By the time she got to the end she literally wanted to throw up. She couldn't do this — no way.

Chapter Three

Ari was speechless. She didn't know what to think. Her bright eyes gazed at the words while her mouth hung open in shock. There was no way in hell she would do this. She wouldn't. She couldn't. There had to be another option.

The words there in cold black type circled in her head, showing her a side of life she never imagined existed. *He owned her body? He could take what he wanted — day or night?*

Ari didn't think so. She'd end up even worse off than she was because she wouldn't abide by the stupid rules he'd set forth, and then he'd prosecute her. Could he do that? If she chose not to satisfy him as much as he wanted, could he really prosecute her?

She slowly read back through the papers, and felt a smidgeon better. No. That wasn't what he was saying. He could only actually prosecute her if she broke his confidentiality clause.

What did he mean, though, by the word *unknowingly*? If she didn't know she'd done something, then how could she be responsible? As she gazed at the paper, she realized what that meant. *If* she left information about him lying around and someone got ahold of it, leading to people finding out, then she'd be at fault.

Well, she wasn't going to become his employee, or mistress, or whatever he chose to call the ugly position, so she wasn't taking chances of someone's discovering the dang paperwork. She walked to her stove and turned on the burner, then placed the edge of the papers against it, and she was consumed with overwhelming satisfaction when the paperwork began to go up in smoke.

She held on to it for several seconds, making sure every last word would burn, then tossed the remains in her empty sink, where the wretched thing finished burning and turned into nothing but ash.

Washing the ash down the garbage disposal helped relax her shoulder muscles somewhat. She could shut that door in life behind her and move forward. It was a good thing she couldn't afford smoke detectors in her place, for her little act of defiance would have set every one of them off.

Having opened a window to let out the smoke before she choked, Ari grabbed the newspapers she'd gathered all week and began fanning the smoke toward the outdoors with a wide up-and-down motion. As the smoke lifted upward to the sky, the realization that she was turning down the opportunity of *one hundred thousand dollars a year* began to sink in and her hopes of taking care of her mother were now plummeting.

She stopped fanning the air and laid the newspaper out on the table, running her thumb along the creases to make it lie flat so she could search through the ads again. She *must* have missed something. There *was* a job out there for her — there had to be. She just wasn't trying hard enough to find it.

A three-hour search and twenty-five calls later, Ari flopped back on the couch and the tears started. At first, they were just a slendertrickle, but it didn't take long for them to flow down her cheeks and drip off her chin.

It seemed so hopeless.

What was she going to do?

After allowing herself half an hour of falling apart, Ari had just brushed away the last of her tears when the phone rang. Her head spun around as she gazed at the contraption as if it were a lifeline to save her in the middle of an ocean where sharks were slowly circling closer and closer.

"Hello." Ari's voice was full of hope. It had to be someone calling her back about one of the hundreds of jobs she'd applied, someone saying the company needed her to start immediately. It was either that or one of the many bill collectors seeking money she didn't have to give them.

"Is Ms. Harlow available?"

"This is she." *It's a prospective employer,* she thought positively.

"This is the Clover Care Facility. Your mother has been transported over to San Francisco General Hospital. Can you go there immediately?"

"Is everything OK with my mom?"

"Ms. Harlow, it would be better if you could leave now and arrive quickly. They will answer all your questions when you get there."

Ari sat silently for a moment as she forced herself to take a quick breath. Something was wrong with her mom. Selfishly, she didn't want to know. After the day she'd had, she couldn't take any further bad news.

"Yes, of course," she automatically replied before hanging up.

With sagging shoulders, she gathered her purse and left the apartment. Her mom had always told her never to leave that till tomorrow which she could do today. It was a sentiment dear to Benjamin Franklin's heart, and he happened to be one of her heroes. That proverb went with the good and the bad. Even with terrible news, she might as well get it over with.

She climbed into her car and made the thirty-minute journey to the hospital, mustering as much courage as possible for the moments that would follow her arrival. Was she going to walk in only to find that her mother had given up and passed away? She knew they planned on sending her to a state facility, and if that happened, she'd never get the treatment she needed. Ari just didn't know any of it anymore. She didn't know whether she could handle whatever they had to say.

As Ari stepped from her car she heard chanting voices and wondered what was happening. As she approached the front doors of the hospital, there was a crowd of protestors lining the walk. She had to get through, but hated to pass by them as they waved their signs angrily.

"Don't support their greed. Find another care facility!" they chanted as she neared. With her head down she passed by feeling something hit her arm. She didn't dare look up, afraid if she made eye contact, they may outright attack her. "Traitor!" was the last thing she heard before she reached the safety of the hospital lobby.

"Ms. Harlow, thank you for coming down so quickly. I apologize for the entrance. The hospital has had cutbacks and there are several previous staff members who are upset about the situation. I'm sorry if we've upset you but there's news of your mother and we needed you to come right away. She's awake."

It took a few moments for the nurse's words to register. Her mother was awake. She was out of the coma. Ari felt blackness trying to overtake her vision as she gazed in shock at the woman in front of her. There was no way she could pass out. She fought it with all she had.

She was so exhausted both physically and mentally, the unexpected news was almost too much for her to handle. She wouldn't believe them until she actually saw her mom; more than anything else, Ari needed to hear that beloved voice. No one else could comfort her like her mother — she needed the woman who'd always been there through the good and the bad.

Ari finally fully understood why she was breaking apart so much. She'd been trying to do all of this without her mom. Never before had she realized how much she'd always leaned on her — never before she'd lost her and then found her again.

"Please. Where is she?" Ari asked breathlessly, the words barely making it past her throat.

"Right this way."

The nurse turned and started leading Ari down a maze of hallways, toward the intensive care unit. When they reached the door to her mother's room, Ari suddenly found herself afraid to turn the handle.

The thought crossed her mind that she'd open that door and it would all be a cruel joke. Her hopes dashed, she'd have to deal with the pain of losing the most important person in her life all over again.

"Take a few moments if you'd like before you go inside," the nurse offered before leaving Ari to sort through her overwhelming emotions.

With a deep steadying breath, Ari pushed the door open and stepped inside. She found her mother sitting up in bed, looking extremely frail, but with her beautiful green eyes open. Ari blinked just to make sure she wasn't seeing things.

"Mom?"

"Ari! Come sit with me," her mom responded weakly as a small smile lit up her pale face. Ari needed no other encouragement. She rushed to the bedside, bent down to feel her mother's warm arms wrap around her once again, and reveled in the contentment of a loving embrace.

"I've missed you so much, Mom. I'm sorry I called you that night. I'm so sorry you got in an accident," Ari sobbed as her mom stroked her back comfortingly.

"Oh, Ari. You can't blame yourself. Bad things happen to all of us. This isn't your fault."

"Yes it is. If I hadn't gone to that party and gotten drunk. If only I'd never called you, then you wouldn't have been out there," Ari sobbed.

"The doctors tell me I've been in a coma for six months. That's a long time you've been carrying this heavy guilt around. No matter what happens to me, I want you to live your life to the fullest. This was in no way your fault."

"You have to say that, Mom. It's in the parent's handbook or something, but I'm twenty-three, not fifteen. I should have been more responsible."

"No matter how old you become, you'll always be my little girl. I would be upset if you got in trouble and *didn't* call me. I was worried about you that night, but also happy to see you having a bit of fun. Life will pass you by before you know it if you don't give yourself some room for a few mistakes. You have to do things that are not planned to the very last detail. You have to *live*."

"I don't know how," Ari said, unsure this was even her mother.

"Oh, baby, you've always done what is right. You have to allow yourself to make a mistake now and then. Sometimes in our lives, the best results come from the worst mistakes. We don't know why anything happens. You can't blame yourself for my getting into that accident. It may be the thing that saves my life. You never know the reason behind it. Maybe if I'd been home the next week, a burglar would have broken in and shot me, or what if I'd been driving to the store and a child had dashed in front of my car, and I'd killed him? We can't agonize over what has happened — we can only be thankful it wasn't worse."

"I needed you so much these last months, Mom. No one can make me feel better. Please, I'm begging you, please don't leave me. No matter what it takes, don't go. I love you."

Ari flung herself into her mother's frail arms, vowing that she was never going to let go again. She could get through anything as long as she had her mom there beside her.

"Ms. Harlow, can we speak to you for a few minutes?"

Ari sat up and turned to find a doctor standing in the doorway. Her stomach clenched with anxiety when she looked at his somewhat somber expression. She didn't think she was going to like the conversation. As she looked at her mom, she found the added strength she needed. None of this was insurmountable as long as they had each other.

"I'll be right back, Mom."

"Take your time, sweetie. I've been up for a while and these pain medications are making me tired. I think I'll catch a little nap."

Ari walked from the room, a sense of dread filling her at the thought of her mother taking a nap...oh, no. What if she didn't wake again for another six months? It would probably be months, maybe even years before she wouldn't dread it when her mother went to sleep. She knew she couldn't live that way, but tell that to her irrational heart.

Since she had no choice, Ari trailed behind the doctor down the hallway and into a small conference room, where several men in suits were sitting around a table. This couldn't be good.

"Thank you for joining us, Ms. Harlow. We were pleased when your mother was admitted here after she woke up from her coma. How are you feeling? We know that this kind of tragedy can often be harder for the loved ones than for the patients."

"I've been trying to take it one day at a time. It's all been very difficult," Ari answered cautiously, wishing the man would get to the point. She didn't want to make small talk. She needed to be with her mother.

"I'm sorry about that. I wish we could put this off, but because of your mother's condition, time is of the essence."

"Put *what* off?"

"You mother's new scans show that she has stage 4 carcinoma in her uterus. We need to operate immediately if she has any chance of survival, I'm sorry to say. At this point, her chances are slim, less than a 10 percent chance, and that's with aggressive action."

The doctor paused, letting his words sink in. Were they telling her she should have the operation done, or she shouldn't? It sounded to her as though they were telling her that she was going to lose her mom after all. This was why she'd been so afraid to hope.

"We've called you in because your mother doesn't have any health insurance benefits left, and this operation is a costly procedure. Because this isn't an emergency surgery, we can't schedule it until payment arrangements are made. We're here to help you get this funded, apply for loans, grants, whatever it takes. We won't leave you in the dark, but we must have funding before we operate."

The bottom fell out for Ari. It all boiled down to money — which she didn't have. The men continued speaking, but she didn't hear anything else they had to say. She was spiraling down a long, dark hole. The only way for her to escape, it seemed, was to take the job as Rafe Palazzo's mistress.

Chapter Four

"Have you made your decision, Ms. Harlow?" Rafe had said he'd give her until the next day to make her choice. It seemed he didn't want to allow her any time. With guilt for her mother weighing on her mind, she didn't feel she had the luxury of waiting, though.

"Yes, I'll take the…position," Ari practically whispered into the receiver. She had barely sat down on her couch at home when her phone rang and she heard Raffaello Palazzo on the other end of the line.

"I'm pleased to hear that. I'll send a driver over to pick you up so we can discuss the small details," he said just before she heard the dial tone of a disconnected call.

The man didn't give her any time to argue or tell him she had other plans. She glared at the beeping handset before slowly hanging it up. She knew what she was getting into — or did she? Once she entered his employment, that's how it would always be. He'd make a command and she'd be expected to follow whatever it was he requested.

Yes, he'd said that he wouldn't beat her or make her break the law — did he honestly expect her to gain any comfort from that fact? She'd have a broken spirit, but that didn't count.

Her mother's pale face flashed before her eyes. She could do this. She could do anything for the woman who'd given up so much for her.

She didn't bother changing from her baggy jeans and loose T-shirt. If he didn't like her outfit, he could rescind his job offer. She'd at least have no guilt about refusing the job. It would be out of her hands. Just when she was about to panic and change her mind — throw on a dress and heels because she desperately needed this job — the doorbell rang.

It suddenly occurred to her that she'd never listed her physical address on her application —she had given only an old post office box number. Still, she wasn't really surprised that he knew where she lived. She was sure he'd already done a thorough check on everything about her. He didn't seem the type of man who went into anything blindly. At this point, he probably knew her better than she knew herself.

She opened her door to find Mr. Mario Kinsor, the person she'd had her first interview with, standing before her, impeccably dressed with the same kind smile on his face as before.

"It's nice to see you again, Ms. Harlow. If you're ready, I have the car waiting."

Realizing that he had to know what the job position was, Ari's face turned slightly pink as she followed him down the steps to the back door of the Bentley, which looked so out of place in her less than desirable neighborhood. He must think of her as a tramp — or a moneygrubber. The thought was mortifying.

He held open her door and she quickly climbed in, not daring to meet his eyes again. She truly didn't know how she was going to do this. It was degrading. The many employees of Mr. Palazzo had to know he hired his lovers the same way he hired the rest of his staff.

She'd never be able to look any of them in the eye. Did his business colleagues know about it, too? Would she be in a state of infinite embarrassment the entire time and every time she was beside him at business functions? Would she be mocked?

What about after he discarded her? She'd forever have this humiliating mark upon her. Even if she managed to get back to school and somehow become a professor, people would know. She could end up with students who were aware she'd once been nothing but a high-priced call girl. She didn't see the embarrassment's ever ending, but, with her mother dying, what other choice did she have?

She'd worked so hard to make something of herself, always being at the top of her class, studying hard, forgoing dating, avoiding the social scene unlike so many other high school and college students. She'd worked hard so she could be proud of herself, and now she was reduced to becoming some man's mistress.

She'd always lacked sympathy for people who didn't live up to her high standards. Whenever she looked beyond the image of them that she fashioned from her preconceptions, she never saw complexities or extenuating circumstances. Victims allowed themselves to be taken advantage of, didn't they? She was discovering very quickly that the world wasn't as black and white as she'd always seen it from her privileged vantage point.

If her mother received the care she needed and got back on her feet, it would be worth it — even if

Ari were never able to look herself in a mirror again. She could finally understand why desperate people made shocking decisions.

"We're here," Mr. Kinsor said, snapping her out of her thoughts.

"Thank you," Ari murmured as she stepped from the car and looked at the privacy glass of the exclusive restaurant. Her stomach was rolling over as she followed Mr. Kinsor inside, past the host and straight back to a secluded area.

Sitting at the beautifully set table was Rafe, looking quite devastating in his black Armani suit and brilliant red tie. As she stepped through the doorway, he stood, walking to her chair. It wouldn't be so bad being his mistress, she tried to tell herself. She could suffer through the actual act of sex; it wasn't as if she had any desire to enter a real relationship anytime soon, so she could think of it as practice for her future husband.

"Please have a seat, Arianna. I've taken the liberty of ordering."

"Thank you." Irritation covered the increasing panic as she heard the timid sound of her own voice. She was already starting not to recognize herself. Was she truly that far gone? She'd made one mistake — one! Up until that party, she'd been the dream child, achieving the highest grades in her classes, keeping to the straight and narrow through life. She hadn't sneaked out the window at night, taken drugs or become pregnant like so many others.

Even in college she'd walked the line, putting her studies first, visiting her mother often, and staying true to the course she'd mapped out by the time she was thirteen.

Her mother wouldn't want her to do this — wouldn't want her to fall at the first hurdle.

"Have you read through all of the paperwork and now have an understanding of the position? If so, we can send you to personnel to have you fill out the necessary paperwork, and you can begin immediately."

Ari sat there as she tried to force her mouth to open and give him a simple acceptance. All she had to do was let him know that she understood and could begin her new *job* immediately. They could fine-tune the details over a nice meal.

"No." Ari heard herself say the word, though she couldn't believe it. Shock radiated through her as she rose from her seat and stood there motionless, looking at him. She'd had every intention of saying *yes*, serving herself up on a platter. She was stunned to be refusing the man who offered her and her mother the chance to escape their hopeless situation.

She stood in thunderstruck silence as puzzlement crossed Mr. Palazzo's features. He was almost gaping at her as if he'd never before heard the word *no*. Stillness suffocated the two of them as a waiter came in and set dishes on the table before scurrying from the tension-filled room.

"You said *yes* over the phone. I thought this was settled," Rafe calmly replied. He picked up his wineglass and slowly took a sip of the dark red liquid while she remained awkwardly standing a few feet from him.

Ari finally moved her head, looking around for Mr. Kinsor, but he had disappeared. She'd have to find another way home. It was too long a walk.

She watched as Rafe swallowed, saw the way his throat constricted as the fluid slid smoothly down. As if looking through another person's eyes, she noticed again how handsome and self-assured he was. Why would he need to hire mistresses? As he'd pointed out in his office building, there was a line of women practically begging to be chosen to grace his arm.

He must have known she didn't want to do this even before she refused, so why go through the motions? She would understand it a little more if he were a nasty tyrant, unbearable and hideous to look at. With his olive complexion, attractive but slight Italian accent, and amazing self-confidence, she didn't see a reason behind what he did. In other circumstances, in another universe, she might have even been disappointed *not* to date him.

Of course, he wasn't asking for a girlfriend — he didn't want to date. He wanted a woman to do his bidding, be at his beck and call, fall at his knees, and perform all sorts of kinky, twisted sexual favors. She'd never be what he was looking for.

Ari's own knees grew shaky as the two of them continued their standoff, so she slowly sank down into the chair. As his gaze held hers captive, she took a steadying breath and picked up the full glass of flavorsome red wine in front of her and took a sip, giving herself a minute to think. She didn't know why it was important for her to say anything, but she needed to.

"I thought I could do this — sell my body for the sake of my mother. I was wrong. I planned to say *yes*, was determined to take the position and deal with it. I had no idea I would say *no* until the word popped out of my mouth. I'm slightly desperate at the moment, but I guess I actually have a bit of pride still intact."

Ari watched his eyes narrow dangerously. She hadn't been trying to insult him, but it looked as though she had anyway. He seemed to be the type of guy you didn't want to rile when you were precariously close to a steep cliff.

Suddenly, she didn't care. She felt exhilaration banish her ever-present fear as she took another sip and looked him dead in the eye. He might have all the money in the world, and he might even have more power than the president of the United States, but he was still just a man. The bottom line was that he couldn't force her into anything— no matter who he was.

If they'd been in certain foreign lands, he could probably have just shot her right there on the spot with no consequences, but she was here in the land of the free, where she was safe. Feeling as if she actually had a choice gave her hope. She'd made the right decision.

She refused to be somebody she wasn't. She never would have even thought of dating a man as striking and sophisticated as Rafe — not in her lifetime. She would marry an accountant, or a fireman. She'd have a small house with a yard that needed mowing and two kids splashing in a shallow pool with their puppy. She wasn't a girl who wanted to play kinky games with a jaded, worldly tycoon.

She finished her wine and felt relief that her knees had stopped shaking. It was time to leave, so she stood up again. There was no point in having their conversation continue. She'd said *no*. She didn't owe him an explanation. She'd reached down to grab her purse when his hand snaked out and gripped her arm.

"This conversation isn't over, Ari. I've learned over the years that every woman has her price. It's just a matter of time before I figure out exactly what your price is." The raw power in his tone and the controlled movement of his hand sent a shudder down her spine. What had she gotten herself into by going to that interview? She really wished she'd never seen that ad.

He was obviously jaded to the world, because not every woman was for sale. Though she'd thought she could do this, she had more value for herself than she'd realized. Let him think what he wanted, but she wasn't for sale – no matter what he threw at her.

Chapter Five

Rafe gazed in surprise at his hand gripping Ari's delicate arm. He'd been jostled out of his normal cool and he wasn't ready to let her walk from the room. What startled him most was his enjoyment of it all. To be refused by this complicated woman intrigued him.

What he should do was wish her a good day, eat his meal in silence, and go home. His assistant would simply call in the next woman on the list. It was easy — not a big deal. So why had his hand trapped Ari's arm? Why didn't he just let her go?

It was most likely because he couldn't remember the last time he'd been challenged — by a woman or by anyone, for that matter. Everyone practically bowed at his feet. Not until this very moment had he realized how bored he was by it all. It seemed he'd already achieved everything he possibly could, and now he just compounded his successes with a minimum of effort.

Obviously, he needed more challenges if a refusal from a woman caused more excitement in him than a new multibillion-dollar merger did.

Still, there was nothing he could do if she didn't enter into his employment. He would never force a woman to be with him, and he had no desire to take the time to *court* a mistress.

It wasn't so simple when it came to Arianna Harlow. He could actually picture himself throwing her over his shoulder, taking her to his car, and spiriting her away to his home, where he'd tie her to the bed and ravish her until the morning light.

A wolfish smile spread slowly across his face at the thought of doing just that. What he wouldn't give to be a pirate in that moment. Rafe had a feeling, though, that one night wouldn't be nearly enough to sate his desires — not with this woman. Maybe it had just been too long since his last mistress. Arianna's appeal was most likely nothing more than sexual frustration.

"Sit," he commanded and watched her flinch from his cold tone. Good. She had no idea who he truly was. This was all a game to him, nothing more — and he couldn't lose. It wasn't in his DNA.

He watched emotions flit across her face as she looked down at his hand. He saw the tremor in her body, knew she wasn't unaffected by him. She might not like his rules, but she did desire him. The question was — what was he willing to do to get her to admit it?

Nothing!

He wouldn't chase her. He just wanted to finish his meal. At least, that's what he told himself. It was all merely a game that he must win, not a serious desire to be with the woman.

"I guess a free meal won't hurt," she replied after the pause became uncomfortably long. She tugged on her arm to remind him that he was still gripping her.

He let go, zeroing in on the slight redness his fingers had left against her soft ivory skin. The sight caused his body to stir, the beginnings of desire trickling in low in his belly. Normally, it took a lot more than his fingers branding a woman's arm to make his pulse quicken.

She intrigued him more by the minute, though he couldn't pinpoint exactly why. Yes, she was beautiful, but beauty wasn't a rarity in his world. Every other woman he ran across was stunning.

As Ari sat cautiously across from him, she picked up her spoon and began twisting it in her fingers as she eyed her soup. It should have been tasty, but...

The waiter soon appeared with their second course, artfully prepared sushi. Rafe had to suppress a smile when her nose wrinkled at the delicate pieces of rice, raw fish, and seaweed.

"Um, no thank you," she said to the waiter, who looked at Rafe as though he had no earthly idea what he was supposed to do. Rafe was sure the young server had never had his food returned at this exclusive restaurant.

"It's fine; leave it," Rafe said, and the waiter scurried away. "Don't dismiss it until you've at least given it a try. This one here is a rare delicacy that is said to wake up a woman's...*cravings*. Have you heard of fugu before?" When she shook her head, he continued.

"Fugu is more commonly known in the States as puffer fish or blowfish. If the chef doesn't prepare the dish just right…it's fatal to consume, which is part of the thrill of eating it."

"Why would I possibly try this if it could kill me?" she asked in exasperation, looking at him as if he'd lost his mind.

He picked up a piece and slipped it into his mouth, feeling the delicate explosion of flavor wash over his tongue. He was used to great food, but watching the fright in her eyes as he swallowed the sushi made the act of eating almost erotic.

"We all seek thrills, Ari. Very few skilled chefs can leave just a tiny trace of the lethal poison on the fish, causing a tingling sensation on your lips and tongue, enough to wake up the senses, while not enough to kill you. That little bit of excitement draws people in, makes them want to try it and tempt fate…"

Each word he spoke sent her eyebrows just a little higher, made her lips a bit more pursed. Her expressive face was a thrill to watch. He assumed an almost bored demeanor, but he couldn't ignore that this seemingly innocent girl fascinated him. He enjoyed the way she wore her feelings on her sleeve, the way everything she was thinking was an open book to him.

She again declined: "I'm just fine with not living on the edge. I prefer to keep everything about my body *un*-tingly and working just fine."

Rafe didn't like being refused even once, let alone multiple times. He really should end this game and walk away. Yet he wasn't willing to concede defeat just yet. Why? Maybe it was that slight sparkle in her eyes, the way she subtly trembled when he touched her, and maybe it was just that he wanted to tame her.

He didn't know the answers yet, but for some reason he wasn't ready to let her leave. He wasn't ready for their game to end. She *would* submit to him first. Once she was willing to do his bidding, then he'd grow bored, just as he did with everyone else.

"I'm not a man to give up, Ari. It would be much simpler for you just to try the dish. You saw that I ate one with no problem. I'm still alive." The expression on her face seemed to shout that she didn't think that was necessarily a good thing. It almost made him laugh, and he struggled to hide his amusement.

He took the spoon and drizzled a touch of sauce over the delicacy and scooped up a small bite, holding the fork out to her. "The sauce brings out the rich flavor and makes the meat very enjoyable. Come on…try just one," he coaxed in a temptingly soft tone.

She gazed at him with suspicion, but he could see that she was beginning to cave. She could be more easily trained than he'd originally thought. Teaching her could be extremely pleasurable for both of them.

Though with hesitation, her lips parted, giving him just enough room to slip the small bite inside.

He set the translucent fish on her tongue, then watched as her lips closed around the fork as he slowly pulled it out. Her nose wrinkled as she bit down, but then her eyes widened in pleasure as the burst of flavor danced on her tongue. She finished chewing before picking up her wine and taking a sip.

"OK, it wasn't horrible, but certainly not something I want to try again. If I'm too afraid to eat something, then that's all the warning I need to keep away from it, even though the flavor was actually quite indescribable. I may have to try other, safer sushi dishes. The thought of eating raw fish has always kind of freaked me out," Ari said with another wrinkle to her nose, the cute expression making Rafe grin.

"Well, the fugu is the only fish on your plate that could actually kill you. Try the hamachi roll. It's made with grilled yellowtail and shrimp. I think you'll find it refreshing."

With a heavy sigh, Ari tried the delicate roll, and smiled. She didn't complain as she consumed the last few rolls. Once her plate was empty, she picked up her glass of white wine, enjoying having new bottles with the separate courses.

"This is the best wine I've ever had, not that I'm very experienced in alcohol. My mom let me have a glass at my high school graduation party, and then I've tried a few glasses when out to dinner, but I'm not a wine expert. After a terrible experience with drinking, I can mostly do without it. However, I've had friends who could tell you what year and type each of these bottles are — wine is certainly better than the horrific stuff I drank the last time I tried alcohol."

He sat back as she babbled nervously for several moments, and found that he enjoyed the sound of her voice even if he didn't understand half of what she was talking about. Their conversation centered on mundane topics for the next half-hour, but he wasn't in the least bored. If anything, he was more interested by this woman than ever.

They ate through several more courses and he enjoyed the excitement entering her eyes as each dish was revealed. She stopped wrinkling her nose as she dived into the artistic creations, and though some of them were not to her liking, she eagerly tasted each one.

"Thank you, Mr. Palazzo. This evening turned out quite pleasant. I can now say I've tried dishes I never imagined wanting to sample. I'm sorry the…um, employment didn't work out, but I can't say the evening was a total bust. It actually took my mind off my worries for a while. However, the real world is calling and I need to get back to it."

Rafe felt a small spark of irritation that she refused to call him by his first name, even after hours of dining with him, but he tamped it down as he stood to assist with her jacket.

As his hands slid against her shoulders, he felt that now familiar stirring in his body. He found himself wanting to explore her hidden curves, touch her smooth skin, and discover whether she tasted as good as she smelled.

"I've enjoyed myself, too, Ari. Maybe you will reconsider my job offer," he whispered as he bent down so his breath warmed her neck. Satisfaction rolled through him as he watched her skin react — her body unable to hide its pleasure in his touch. He couldn't resist the urge to lean in and gently bite the delicate skin of her neck before running his tongue over the spot, making her lean momentarily against him.

Before he could wrap his arms around her and press his hardening body against her soft backside, she stiffened and pulled from him.

"No. That won't be happening. Thank you again for dinner, but I really must leave," she insisted as she strode from the room.

Rafe threw several hundred-dollar bills on the table, then turned to follow Ari. She made it out the front door and a small stretch down the sidewalk before with long, measured strides he caught up to her.

"How were you planning to get home, Ari? My assistant is the one who brought you here. Besides, I always escort my date home," Rafe insisted as he grabbed her arm and spun her around, enjoying the look of awareness on her face.

"That's not necessary, *Mr. Palazzo*, as this wasn't a date. There's a bus stop just down the road, and I'm happy to use it," she fired back.

"It's not safe for a woman to be out walking at night. There will be no way in hell that I'll allow it to happen."

"I've lived in the city for a while now and I'm fine on my own. I know how to take care of myself," she said as she tugged against his hold.

"I'm sure you do, Arianna, but why not let someone else take care of you for a while? I'm *very* good to my women," he said as he backed her up against the brick wall of the restaurant.

"I've made my decision. You need to let me go." Her voice trembled as her gaze dropped to his lips.

Rafe had a strict no-kissing rule, but he found himself wanting to devour her naturally plump pink lips. He felt himself bending down as his will began to break.

Right before their lips connected, a drunken crowd of teenagers stumbled by, one of the boys knocking into the two of them and breaking the moment. Ari slipped from his arms and tore off down the sidewalk. But Rafe overtook her as she made it to the barely lit bus area.

"I'm beginning to tire of chasing you, Ari. I said you won't be taking the bus, so that means that you won't. I really have no qualms about causing a scene, but since you've been hissing at me only beneath your breath, I take it that *you* do. You can either come with me willingly, or I'm going to pick you up, toss you over my shoulder and drag you back to the restaurant. It's your choice," he said brutally.

Ari recoiled from his words. "You wouldn't dare," she gasped as she twisted away and looked around.

A few people were beginning to walk toward them. Rafe could see the bus approaching several blocks down the street. She wasn't getting on it, not on his watch.

"Not only would I dare, but I'd enjoy myself. You have until the count of three. One...two..."

"OK, OK. I'll take your stupid ride," she relented as his hands began to reach out to her. She turned back in the direction of the restaurant, grumbling underneath her breath about pompous men who needed to learn self-control.

A smirk appeared on his lips as he pretended not to listen. She could have no idea how much self-control he was actually using around her. He'd been planning to take her to her new apartment tonight, ravish her, and initiate her into his world.

If Rafe knew one thing, though, it was that plans changed. He didn't often have to adapt, but he could make exceptions once in a while. And it seemed that if he wanted to pursue this matter with Ari, he'd have to do that now. He could live with that.

When he finally got her into his car, she refused to speak to him. She didn't give him directions, and he didn't bother to ask for them. They both knew he was well aware of where she lived.

They traveled in silence, and upon reaching their destination, he slowed his car to park in the dark parking lot. Ari jumped out, but Rafe was right on her heels. He wouldn't have her walk to the door by herself. He watched her fumble with her keys and struggle to open the door. It took her a few tries, but eventually she managed to get inside. Once he heard the sound of the lock sliding into place, he left. It was going to be a long, painful night.

A mixture of irritation and excitement coursed through him as he drove home. Ari was unlike any woman he'd ever pursued, and he decided right then that she wasn't escaping him. He'd be forever haunted if he let go at this point. The two of them might have some explosions together — scratch that — the two of them *would* have explosions together.

Chapter Six

Ari waited for Rafe to drive off and then quickly walked down to her car. She needed to go to the hospital and see her mother. She was grateful the facility was only a few miles from her apartment, because her knees were shaking and her heart was pounding and she had no business being behind the wheel of a car. When she reached the hospital's parking garage, a shudder passed through her.

"You did the right thing. Having one amazing dinner with the guy doesn't oblige you to sell your body to him. Yes, he makes you think that sex might not be such a bad thing, and the paycheck he's offering is phenomenal, but that doesn't make any of it OK. Yes, you did the right thing. Just focus on that and remember that you're not for sale. You're *certainly* not willing to do the kind of stuff *he* likes to do," Ari lectured herself while resting her head against the steering wheel.

When she finished her pep talk, she stepped from the car and walked through the shadowy garage to the elevator, grateful there were no protestors at this entrance. Some of them were downright frightening. Never before had the thought of being alone at night bothered her, but Rafe's warnings had stirred up a sense of unease that made her even more irritated with the man.

The door opened and she stepped inside, pushing Rafe from her mind as she tried to silently rehearse what she was going to say to her mother. She hadn't given up just yet. She'd simply have to try that much harder to work something out. There was no way she was letting go of her mom without a fight. There had to be programs available to help her take care of her mom. The hospital administrators had spoken of something of the sort. But, heck, she'd sleep in her car if that's what it would take.

With growing determination in each step, she walked down the long hallway to her mother's hospital room, then paused outside her door to take a long steadying breath. She couldn't let her mom know there was anything to be worried about. Her mother had raised Ari right; now it was Ari's turn to take care of her mom.

She slowly opened the door, then sighed with relief to see that her mother was sleeping. It gave Ari more time to think before she had to make conversation. She sat in the lounge chair in the corner and waited for her mom to wake. With the lights turned off and the machines beeping rhythmically, Ari fell quickly asleep no closer to getting answers. She didn't stir when a nurse came in and covered her up.

*****

"Ari?"

Arianna awoke instantly at the fragile sound of her mother's voice. It was beautiful, something she'd feared she would never hear again. She couldn't imagine life without her mother being a part of it.

Ari's father had walked out on them when she was too young to remember him, and it had been her mom and her ever since. She couldn't survive without the woman who'd raised her — or at least she wouldn't want to. Whom would she share her triumphs with, and who would hold her when her heart was broken?

"I'm right here, Mom." Ari scooted her chair next to her mother's bed and gently clasped her hand.

"I'm glad, baby. I'm sure I've put you through too much worrying already. If I know you, and of course I do, then you've been chewing off your nails and stressing out since the accident. It's my job to take care of you, and I haven't been doing that these last six months."

"Mom, it's my turn to worry about you, not the other way around. I know you told me not to, but I can't help it. If I hadn't gone to that stupid party and then called you up in the middle of the night, you never would have been hurt. I know you told me to quit stressing about it, but it's still eating me alive. I can't say enough how sorry I am," she sobbed as she leaned her head down and placed it on their joined hands.

"Arianna Harlow, do you know how upset I'd be with you if you hadn't called me? I'm your mother, and it's my job to protect you, watch out for you and ensure your safety. You may be twenty-three now, but that doesn't mean you aren't still my little girl. Don't you know that I would die for you? There's nothing a mother won't do for her child."

"But I screwed up," Ari sobbed.

"Ah, sweetheart, you've been a perfect child from the moment you came home in my arms. You rarely cried, were respectful, worked hard in school, and were always the dream child. You were living your life, growing up a bit. Don't let this one small detour end with a roadblock. Must I keep telling you, darling, to live your life to the fullest and achieve your dreams, no matter what happens to me?"

"I don't know how to do *anything* without you," Ari insisted.

"Yes you do. I know this because I'm the one who raised you, and I raised you to be independent and to succeed in whatever you set out to achieve. You can and *will* do anything your heart desires. If something does happen to me, I forbid you to mourn me for too long. That would break my heart into a million pieces. Even if I'm taken from this world a little too soon, I'll always be with you, watching out for you. Just promise me that you won't give up and settle for less. Live life to the fullest, not at half measure like so many people do!"

Ari looked at her mother's pale face, not knowing how to respond. She couldn't promise her mother that she'd continue living — she couldn't make it without her. It was the first time Ari ever remembered her mom asking something of her that she couldn't do.

"I'm serious, Arianna. I want you to live your life for you. Enough of this guilt. Enough of this sadness. Let's talk about something happy." Ari's mother brightened as she asked, "How is graduate school going?"

Ari's sense of guilt nearly consumed her. She didn't want to tell her mother how dire their circumstances were. What if the news sent her back into the coma? On the other hand, she couldn't lie.

"I took some time off school. You know I can't graduate without you sitting in the front row cheering me on. It wouldn't be the same."

"Oh, baby. I'm so sorry. Well, I'm awake now, and I'm just fine, no matter what those doctors say. You go back to school and enroll. You're not a quitter, and I already had the frame picked out for your graduation photo. I'm so very proud of all you've achieved."

"Oh, Mom," Ari cried as she climbed up into the bed next to her. And her mother, though still weak, lifted her arm and began stroking Ari's hair as she'd always done when things looked bad. Somehow it made everything better.

Here I go again, Ari sighed to herself. *After all my fine words, I'm leaning on Mom, as usual, and not vice versa.* But she didn't care. At this moment, she needed to be comforted. But she promised herself that in just a few minutes she'd find her inner strength and help her mom get through her terrible illness.

Being in her mother's arms was giving her what she needed to carry on over the upcoming weeks or months. She said a silent prayer as the two of them lay there silently together.

*****

The next afternoon, Ari came through her front door and saw the flashing light on her answering machine. She tossed her purse onto the couch and forced herself to walk casually to the sink and get a glass of water, and then stand there while she slowly drank it. Her eyes kept straying to the blinking red light only a few feet away as impatience built up inside her.

"Don't get your hopes up," she lectured herself. Too many times recently, when she'd pressed the button, she heard not the eagerly anticipated job offer but the threats of another bill collector. The letdown always devastated her.

When she deemed that enough time had passed, she approached the small black box with deliberate, unhurried steps. She casually sat on the couch, lifted pen and pad of paper, and only then pushed the button.

To Ari's disgust, hope played its usual trick and gripped her heart. All her lectures had been for naught, and she knew she was going to be crushed. Once again, she was sure, no dream job would materialize to save her mother from death and keep her from living on the streets.

"Ms. Harlow, this is James Flander from Sunstream Electronics. We've gone over your application and feel you are a strong candidate for our team. Please give us a call back as soon as you get this message so we can schedule you for an early interview."

Ari barely heard the rest of the message and had to play it back twice more so she could write down the number. Her hands were shaking so badly, she could barely grip the pen.

Waiting until her voice was calm and steady, Ari dialed Mr. Flander's number, pressed in the extension and took several deep breaths as she waited for him to come on the line.

Within minutes, she was scheduled for the interview. Excited butterflies filled her stomach as she rushed into the bathroom to shower and dress. It was going to be her day — she could feel it. She hadn't settled by selling her body. There had to be some kind of reward for that.

She left the apartment thirty minutes after taking the call and climbed into her car, taking a moment to breathe deeply because her hands were shaking so badly.

"Calm down. You don't want to blow this interview. You are smart, confident and made for this job. It was meant to be," she told herself as she started the engine and pulled from the small complex.

Arriving in downtown San Francisco, Ari found parking with astonishing ease and made her way to the modest five-story building. Sunstream Electronics provided home and business security for much of California and all across the States. It was a successful company offering great benefits and job security.

The position was for an assistant, really just a glorified secretary, but she didn't care. She wasn't above taking dictation and typing letters all day long. It was a good place to work. When the elevator announced her arrival, she gave herself a few final words of encouragement: *Chin up, shoulders back, stomach in.* With that, she plastered a smile on her face and walked confidently into the room.

Chapter Seven

With a bounce in her step that had been missing for months, Ari practically waltzed down the hallway at the hospital. She was now officially employed as a personal assistant to the vice president of Sunstream Electronics. She was getting a great salary, allowing her the financial freedom to pay her mother's medical bills. She could feel her life turning around. She might even manage to make it back to school and finish her degree.

A smile parted her lips as she turned a corner and hit a solid body with enough force that she bounced off and went flying to the floor, landing hard on her butt. The fall sent a sharp pain up her spine and her glasses went flying. Before she got her bearing, she leaned over and felt them smash beneath her hands.

She cringed as she lifted them, to see if they were fixable. They weren't. It wasn't that she needed them, they were only a piece of her armor to hide behind, but she was so used to the things that she felt naked without them.

"I'm so sorry," she gasped as she attempted to stand, struggling because the pain in her back rendered it a difficult maneuver.

"Are you OK?"

Ari's body froze as her eyes traveled up the exquisitely encased legs of none other than Rafe Palazzo. What was he doing at her mother's hospital? Had he followed her there? When she encountered his eyes, his concerned expression made her forget all about her bruised tailbone.

"What are you doing here?" she gasped.

"I could ask you the same," he answered as he bent down and ran his hands over her legs. "Can you stand?"

Not if you keep running your hands across me, she nearly said before stopping herself. "I'm fine."

"Are you sure? You fell pretty hard. It would be wise to get an X-ray," Rafe asserted, causing her temper to override the shock of seeing him.

"I said that I'm fine. Just back off so I can have some room to stand," she practically snarled. His lips quirked as he stood and held out a hand. She thought about ignoring it, but her tailbone was really smarting, so with reluctance she placed her hand in his and let him lift her.

"Mr. Palazzo, is everything all right, sir?" a man in a suit asked as he came skidding up to the two of them.

Ari wanted to turn to the little weasel and say, *Gee thanks, I'm just fine,* but managed to hold her tongue. Rafe wasn't the one who'd hit a solid wall of chest and plummeted to the floor. It was nice to see the staff so concerned about her! She supposed that's just how it was when a person was in Rafe Palazzo's presence — everyone else turned invisible within his wide-reaching shadow.

"I'm not the one who just got knocked to the ground. Maybe you should ask Ms. Harlow how she's doing," Rafe replied coldly.

Ari found herself thawing slightly toward this man of steel. At least he was human enough to acknowledge her being injured. As she stood awkwardly by, glancing at him from the corner of her eye, she had to admit he was a fine specimen to look upon. She wished he weren't quite so good-looking. She didn't want her gaze pulled to him.

"Of course, sir. How are you feeling, Ms. Harlow? We should take you back and make sure nothing was broken in the fall," the man said as he turned to her with fake sympathy written all over his face. She had to fight the urge to roll her eyes at him.

"I'm just fine, but thank you anyway. It was my fault. I wasn't watching where I was going. If you'll both excuse me," she said as she turned to leave.

"I don't think so, Arianna. Whether you like it or not, we're getting that X-ray done. You're limping, and I know that couldn't have felt good on your tailbone," Rafe said as he turned to the small man next to him and demanded a wheelchair.

Before Ari knew what was happening, she was being plopped down and wheeled through the corridors. She didn't appreciate the choice taken away from her like that. She was sure it was nothing more than a large bruise that would be quite colorful on her behind in the following days.

"Mr. Palazzo, the ceremony is about to start. I can take care of this matter for you."

In surprise, Ari craned her neck to look behind her at Rafe, who was pushing the wheelchair. Her glance then took in the other guy, who seemed to be doing a lot of sweating.

"The ceremony will have to go on without me," Rafe said as if the subject was closed.

"But...you're the guest of honor. We can't have a grand opening ceremony without the donor being present," the little man said in horror.

"Then I guess you'll just have to wait. I'm seeing to Ms. Harlow. Leave us," Rafe commanded as he pushed Ari through a doorway and shut the door with finality in the man's face. Ari almost felt sorry for the guy, even if he was a little creep.

"What did you donate?" Ari asked, her curiosity piqued.

"It's not a big deal," he replied in a clipped tone.

"If it's not a big deal, then why don't you want to say what it is?" she countered, sick of backing down to this overbearing man.

"Do you ever just accept someone telling you *no*?" he asked in exasperation, his arms spread wide in question.

"You're the one who practically kidnapped me. I'm just trying to make polite conversation." Ari wanted only to get away from him. He was back to being the man of steel, all traces of worry wiped clear from his face.

"I assure you, Ms. Harlow, that if I kidnapped you, it wouldn't be for an X-ray." He stopped and bent down in front of her so their eyes were locked together.

Ari could practically feel his body heat enveloping her, and she hated to admit it, but she wasn't unaffected. She almost wouldn't mind closing the gap between them and finding out whether his lips tasted as good as they looked.

"If you continue to look at me that way, I'll have to find a private room and show you exactly what

I'm talking about." Arianna wasn't sure if his words were a threat or a promise. She forgot to breathe as she looked deep into his midnight eyes, quickly getting lost.

With a growl of irritation or frustration — she didn't know which — he walked from the room.

"Ms. Harlow. I'm so sorry about your fall. Let's make sure everything is OK."

Ari turned to find a perky young woman walking in the door that Rafe had exited through. As her gaze settled on the closed door, she told herself it was relief that he was gone. She wouldn't have to see him again.

By the time the X-ray came back, showing that she had nothing more than a bruised tailbone, Ari was ready to go home and rest. She wasn't up for chatting with her mom as originally planned. The doctor told her she'd be uncomfortable sitting for about a week, but other than that, she'd be just fine.

Ari had already expected that, but she supposed it was better to be sure. She couldn't fault Mr. Palazzo or the staff for double-checking. They didn't want someone to get injured on their premises and then turn around and seek liability from the hospital — not that she'd ever do something like that. They didn't know her, though.

She was grateful when the woman left and she had a minute alone to get dressed. She hoped Rafe would be gone when she came back out. He was a difficult man to be around while trying to maintain a distance. She could see herself wanting to spend time with him — well, if he weren't so dang kinky.

*****

Rafe waited outside for Ari to emerge. He found it almost amusing that he was pacing the halls in a hospital, worrying about a woman. He honestly couldn't remember the last time he'd actually waited for anyone.

One minute he felt like strangling Arianna Harlow, and then the next he wanted to find the nearest bed and see whether all of the sexual tension was in his head or if they'd create steam together. He blamed his unusual desire for the woman on his recent stint of celibacy. Plus, the challenge she posed doubtlessly increased his libido. He hadn't planned on running into her, but it wasn't an unpleasant coincidence.

He shouldn't think of Ari as anything more than a conquest to be won. She'd turned him down, and now it was his job to make her want him so that he could return the favor — regain his control.

He was very glad his sisters weren't around. Members of his family were the only people on earth who could tame him, make him act like a decent human being. And he didn't want to be a decent human right now; he wanted to sink deep inside Ms. Harlow until she was screaming his name.

Just as he was getting ready to pace the long hallway again, the door to the examination room opened and Ari stepped out, surprise and apprehension in her eyes that he was still there. Good. He wanted her to be wary of him, concerned in his presence. He wanted a mistress filled with respect, not a girlfriend who adored him.

"Is everything OK?" he asked as he stopped a couple feet in front of her.

"I'm fine. There really was no need for you to wait for me."

"Of course I was going to wait. It's my fault you were injured. Are you sure everything is all right, or are you just telling me that you're fine to get me to go away?"

"My tailbone is bruised. Other than that, I am indeed fine. I need to leave now," she curtly told him as she turned away.

"I like how your eyes show so much more clearly without the oversized glasses. You should leave them off." Rafe was a little surprised by his words, but felt they were worth it as her face pinkened and she looked down.

Placing his hand beneath her chin, he lifted her head until she was looking in his eyes. "I've been picturing you lying beneath me while I make you scream in pleasure. You know this will happen soon, right?"

Rafe's words stopped her in her tracks. When she didn't turn for several moments, excitement began stirring in him. Was she going to accept his offer? He wasn't sure whether he wanted her to or not. If she did, then his game would end prematurely. And he wasn't ready for it to be over just yet.

Finally, she turned with a genuine smile on her face, one that nearly caused him to stagger back a step. She had a natural beauty about her that shone with innocent pleasure. This was the first time he'd seen an expression of happiness on her face.

"No. I can very happily tell you that I was offered an incredible job yesterday with a wonderful company." She took a step closer to him and poked him in the chest. He was so surprised by her surge of confidence that he didn't think to stop her.

"You can take your prostitution job and shove it up your a—"

"That's enough," Rafe interrupted as he grabbed her hand and forced her to take several retreating steps. He followed, speaking in a controlled voice barely above a whisper. "I may like the fire in you, Ari, but don't take my interest in you, my curiosity, as weakness. If or *when* I truly want to possess you, it will happen. Leave no doubt about that. You can have your small victory, but be very careful with what you say to me. There's nothing on this planet I like more than a challenge. Just remember that when you play with me — you will lose."

With those words he turned and walked away, leaving her standing in the hallway with her mouth hanging open. He'd taken her small victory and squashed it.

Chapter Eight

"I have a meeting with the board of directors today, Mom. I'm excited. I think things are going to turn around for us," Ari said with a big smile.

"That's great, darling, and I think you're right. I'm feeling much better — I even ate most of my breakfast today. How was your night?"

"I got a job, a really great job, as an assistant to the vice president of a prestigious electronics company. I may even get to do some traveling, but not for a while," Ari answered excitedly. Her mother's concerned expression confused her.

"I thought you were going to re-enroll in school, Ari. You won't be happy working as someone's secretary. You're far too talented and smart for that."

"I promise you I'll get back in school as soon as all this is over."

"Ari, most college students who drop out for one reason or another find it impossible to return to their studies. Life gets in the way. I *will* get my medical stuff figured out on my own. I want you to go to school and finish what you started."

"I give you my word that I'll go back. I can't concentrate on doing homework and attending classes when I know you need help. Think of it from my perspective, Mom. Would you be able to just go on living your life if the situation were reversed? If I were the one lying in the hospital bed needing surgery, could you just pretend it wasn't happening?" Ari challenged.

Her mother looked at her for a few minutes as if trying to come up with the correct words, then glanced down. Ari knew her mom wouldn't lie to her, so she instead chose to say nothing.

"I'll be back by to visit with you, but I have to run right now. I'm going to charm those board members and then we'll get you into surgery and back on your feet before you know it. Everything has turned around now that you're awake. Can't you feel the good karma in the room?" Ari said with another smile. She bent down and kissed her mother's cheek, then walked from the room and made her way to the elevator.

She admitted only to herself that she was shaking inside. She was intimidated at the idea of meeting with the panel of board members who could grant her pro bono surgery, but she wouldn't show that. If she gave the appearance of confidence, then they'd see that the only right decision was to give her mother the operation she not only needed, but deserved.

"I'm here for a meeting with Mr. Coolidge and the board members," Ari announced to the secretary stationed on the executive floor.

"Name, please?"

"Arianna Harlow."

"They're waiting for you now. Go through the door on the left."

Ari tightened her purse on her shoulder and made her way to the door. She stalled when she walked through, seeing all the exceptionally dressed men and women sitting around a large oval table. One chair was available at the end. She assumed it was for her, but she didn't want to sit until invited.

"Ms. Harlow. Thank you for meeting with us. Please, have a seat over there so we can get started."

"I appreciate your taking the time to see me," she murmured as she made her way to the empty chair. She should lift her head and make eye contact with each person there, but suddenly her nerves were getting the best of her.

Each member of the board was a doctor, retired doctor, or important member of the community. They had high-powered jobs and loads of cash, and Ari and her mother were nothing to them. For the first time she accepted that the outcome might not go the way she needed it to.

"We've reviewed your mother's case and we have a few questions for you."

Ari glanced up at the stern-looking man sitting at the head of the table. The name plate before him announced him as Mr. Coolidge, who was the chairman of the board. If she could get him on her side, things would go a lot more smoothly for her. She'd done her research.

"I'm willing to answer anything, Mr. Coolidge."

"Our pro bono budget has been maxed out this month. We have many cases where patients don't have enough insurance, or certain procedures aren't covered. We take pride in offering more discounted surgeries than other places, but we do have to set a limit. After all, we are a business, and if everyone had free surgery, we would go under. We've looked through your application and can see here that you aren't currently working. How do you expect to contribute to your mother's medical costs?"

"I was hired for a new job yesterday with Sunstream Electronics. I have an excellent salary and very few expenses right now. I can contribute 70 percent of my earnings each month toward my mother's care," she answered proudly.

"That's a step in the right direction, but it still won't be enough. The daily costs of a hospital stay add up quickly. Your mother has already been here for two weeks now and her bill is..." he paused as he flipped through some papers. "...a little over fifteen thousand. With the surgery she needs, we're looking at a final bill of well over two hundred thousand dollars. Even if the hospital managed to contribute funds, you'd be expected to pay well over a hundred thousand of that. Do you have a way of obtaining a loan, or possibly selling some personal property?"

Ari's throat closed. There was no way a bank would lend her that kind of money. She had nothing to back up the loan, no credit, and barely any work experience. Up until six months ago, she'd only been a college student. A financial institution would have to be crazy to give her the cash.

"I've filled out all the forms you gave me. I haven't heard back from the businesses yet, but expect to at any time," she squeaked past the tightness in her throat.

"I'm going to be honest with you, Ms. Harlow. This doesn't look good. If we don't have a solid plan within the next few days, we're going to have to discharge your mother."

"You can't do that! You can't just send her away when you know that she'll die," Ari begged.

"As I told you, this is a business, Ms. Harlow. We don't like denying treatment to anyone, but as I already told you, we can't afford to offer surgeries to patients who can't pay for them."

Ari's heart was breaking as she struggled with what to say next.

"Do you have another possible way of obtaining the funds — possibly a...*friend* who could lend you the money?"

Ari's head whipped around as she recognized that voice. Her startled glance clashed with Rafe Palazzo, who was sitting at the far corner of the table. She'd had no idea he was a part of the hospital board. She should have known, considering how wealthy he was. The man probably had his hand in just about everything in the city.

"I don't know anyone like that," she answered. "Are you *sure*, Ms. Harlow? You can't think of anyone who may be willing to help you out, maybe make a *trade*?"

Ari was stunned at his boldness. She knew exactly what he was talking about. She only hoped the other members were clueless about his game. As her gaze collided with his, she thought about it. Could she really turn down the money for her mother's surgery? Was her integrity worth more than her mother's life?

She wanted to tell him that *yes, she would do it.* But the words just wouldn't come out. All she could think about beyond the panic and defeat was her mother telling her to not sacrifice herself. What if she did this and her mom found out? Would her mother ever forgive her? Could she ever really forgive herself?

She had to breathe deeply through the blackness hell-bent on overtaking her.

"We'll meet with you again in a few days, Ms. Harlow, to find out whether you've made any headway in the matter," Mr. Coolidge said, saving her from having to answer Rafe.

"Thank you," Ari mumbled as the members of the board began rising from their seats.

Ari sat still, knowing her legs weren't strong enough to hold her yet. She didn't meet any of their faces as they filed past her and walked from the room. When she was sure they were all gone, she finally looked up and found herself alone with Rafe. She should have fled with the rest of the board. She didn't want to be alone with him.

"Well, Ms. Harlow, it seems you have a decision to make," he said with a confident smile. "Will you be accepting my very generous offer?"

Ari remained silent as he stood by just waiting for the chance to pounce. Was he right? Did all women have their price? Had she just reached hers?

Ari prayed for the floor to open up and swallow her. She'd rather be anywhere but where she was right then.

Chapter Nine

Arianna tossed in her bed, restless, unable to get comfortable. Her body was burning up, heat scorching her from the inside out. An ache filled her core — pulsing, swollen, needing something — though she didn't know what.

"Shh. You'll enjoy this," Rafe whispered.

His low, soothing tone calmed her, though her body temperature kept climbing. Her senses lit up in a blaze of eroticism as she felt his hands on her stomach, his fingers burning her flesh. They glided up the flat plains of her abdomen and outlined the mounds of her naked breasts. Where had her shirt gone?

"Trust me," he whispered, his mouth caressing her ear. His hands slid underneath her arms, and he lifted them higher, his fingers stroking her sensitive skin. Clasping her wrists together, he swiftly tied a silk scarf around them.

Tight.

Before she had a chance to resist, she was fastened firmly to the bed, unable to move her hands, unable to escape his touch. He kissed her wrists with feather-soft pressure, his tongue gliding along her beating pulse, then moving down her arms and over the top of her collar bone.

"Do you like this, Ari? Do you want me to stop?"

"No…please…" she pleaded with him. She wanted more. She opened her eyes, but saw only black and felt the gentle presence of a blindfold over her eyes. Instead of inspiring fear, her impaired vision heightened her pleasure as his hands and mouth continued stroking her body.

His hands cupped her breasts, his slightly callused fingers circling her sensitive peaks but not touching her where she ached, where she needed to be touched.

"What do you want, Ari?"

"…You…"

"Mmm. And where do you want me?"

"I want your mouth on my…on my nipples," she moaned. Embarrassment washed through her, but she knew he wouldn't touch her unless she begged. Rewarding her, his thumbs brushed simultaneously across her peaked nipples, making her cry out.

The tight buds were painfully hard as he circled them and then pinched them, drawing another cry from her. She needed more. Her legs opened on the bed, her body begging him to touch her where she really ached, end the torment she was feeling.

When she was ready to cry out yet again, she felt the wet slide of his tongue across her nipple at the same time as he pinched the other side, making her back arch off the bed from the intense pleasure.

"More!" she wailed, yearning for even more intimate contact. She pulled against her restraints, wanting to touch him, needing to pull him closer. She shouldn't be doing this, but she didn't care. She ached all over, her body shaking with a desperate need that only he could quench.

"Ah, don't get greedy, Ari, or I'll have to stop. I'll just fill your sweet mouth with my hardness and win my release *there*, leaving you here to suffer," he taunted as he pulled away from her breasts.

She whimpered in submission, willing to give him anything in that moment, as long as he just continued what he was doing.

"Are you going to behave?" he demanded.

"Yes. Yes, I promise," she gasped as his hand settled on her stomach.

"Good, Ari. That's what I want to hear. I want your obedience. In turn, I'll give you great pleasure, and you will satisfy my needs."

"Yes, Rafe. Please, more," she agreed with the scratchiness of pure desire in her voice.

His warm breath blew across her wet nipples, making them stiffen again and reach up toward his hot mouth. His lips closed over them as they swelled, and she felt him suck hard, his tongue swirling around the tight buds.

It wasn't enough.

His hand began moving down her smooth stomach, his fingers dancing across her skin as he reached her thigh. His thumb grazed the pulsing flesh over her pelvic bone, teasing her as he circled her swollen womanhood without touching its center, without relieving the burning ache inside her.

She knew better than to cry out, demand more from him — not until he asked her to beg. If he stopped, she'd die. Surely a person couldn't come to the brink of so much pleasure only to be left tied to the edge. She'd rather perish than feel such a pulsing desire but be left unfulfilled.

His mouth followed his hand as he kissed her between her breasts, then moved down her torso, slowly circling her belly button, before gently nipping the soft skin of her stomach. It was all so good, every place he touched relieved the ache for a brief moment, before the burning returned even greater than before.

He moved further down, his lips caressing the inside of her thighs, his tongue sliding out to caress the soft skin where her legs met her core *Just a little bit further*... she begged silently.

She twisted her body, trying to lead him where she desired him most. She heard a soft groan escape his lips as she felt his warm breath caress her swollen womanhood. The sound of his pleasure heightened her very own, knowing she turned him on...*he* actually desired *her*. A shocking thrill spiraled down her spine at the thought.

His mouth hovered over her aching heat, torturing her with his proximity, but not bending the last half inch and satisfying her. She tried raising her hips, but couldn't as his hands were pressing her against the bed, holding her in place — his captive — right where he wanted her.

When she was ready to give up, about to go out of her mind, he closed the gap. His hands moved inward and he parted her soft folds, his thumbs caressing her inner heat as his mouth bent down and he sealed his lips over her most sensitive area.

She screamed out in pleasure as he sucked her into his mouth, his tongue quickly rubbing over her swollen mound. When he inserted his fingers deep inside her core at the same time as his tongue swirled over her bud, she exploded with triumphant pleasure.

Her body shook against his skilled mouth as he eased her down the crest of her wave. Exhaustion overtaking her body, she sagged against the bed. Her bones felt liquid, making her unable to move — unable even to breathe.

She felt the release of his mouth, then the sensation of his body sliding up her own — the warmth of his skin searing hers. She wanted to push him away, tell him she couldn't take any more, but her hands were still bound. She couldn't move. She was all his for the taking.

"You don't think it's over, do you? Are you a selfish lover, Ari?" Rafe asked as he settled his weight across her body and his teeth bit down on the soft lobe of her ear.

She could feel the tip of his thick shaft pressing against her soft, wet opening. Lacking the energy to form words she simply shook her head. He slowly pushed himself inside her, one inch at a time. Too big!

He was going to rip her apart. He pushed deeper and she screamed. It hurt. This wasn't pleasurable. He was too large. They didn't fit together.

"Please stop. It hurts," she cried out. He laughed as his lips claimed her mouth, silencing her. He thrust his tongue inside at the same time his arousal pushed fully inside her. Ari screamed as she sat up in bed, sweat dripping off her brow. She looked around in confusion, then gasped at the ache consuming her.

"It was just a dream. You're OK; it was just a dream," she said out loud. Even her words couldn't calm her. What was that? Why was she fantasizing about Rafe? She didn't want him. She didn't. She had no business having an erotic dream about the man.

It had to be from their meeting earlier that day. She'd felt like a deer in headlights as he waited for her answer. Ari was still shaking from the strength it had taken for her to stand and walk from that room.

When he'd leaned over her, his mouth nearing hers, she'd almost arched her back, moved her body closer to him. She was finding his raw power to be an aphrodisiac. His seduction was hard to resist.

She had a great job; she had a few days to find help for her mom. It would be much easier for her to shun Rafe Palazzo if he weren't so magnetic. Her body seemed to be drawn to him, and she just couldn't allow that.

Still unable to calm her beating heart, Ari stood and walked into her small bathroom. Flipping on the light, she looked at her flushed complexion in the mirror. She was shaking as if he really had been there stroking her flesh.

"It was only a dream," she said again, furrowing her brow at her reflection, as if she couldn't believe her audacity to be so turned on.

Her one and only sexual experience had been in college and it had been horrible. The guy had only been concerned with himself and hadn't given her body time to prepare. The pain had been excruciating when he'd thrust quickly inside her. She knew sex *could* be good, but she figured she was somehow broken, maybe frigid. That's really why she didn't understand her dream.

She could understand the end, the painful part, but the pleasure before that? Wow. She'd never in her life felt something so intense, and since she didn't have anything to compare it to, confusion swirled around in her head. She wished she'd never read his stupid paperwork, never filled her mind with such ideas.

She didn't want to be tied up with silk scarves. She certainly didn't want him to take all the pleasure for himself and leave her hollow and aching. If only she were able to turn off her mind, purge him completely from her system. That would make her life so much easier. Though it was still the middle of the night, she knew it would be long before she found sleep again.

Turning on her shower, she stepped under the warm spray and washed away the sweat her erotic dream had produced. As she passed her fingers over her swollen folds, she flinched. *Never* had a dream made her body ache.

Pressing her hand tightly against her head, she tried to knead away the tension and torment that still throbbed from her very core all the way down the sensitive skin of her thighs. After a fifteen-minute shower, she was no closer to feeling relief, so she dried off and climbed back in bed.

Ari tossed and turned the rest of the night, not finding any solace in sleep. She was hungry, and when a woman craves something, there is no use in fighting it.

Chapter Ten

"Ari, would you like to join us? We're heading to the Temple Night Club for some sushi and dancing. We have got to have some girl time before heading home to the husbands and kids for the entire weekend."

Ari smiled at Miley, one of her co-workers, and thought how much she really loved her job. The women she worked with were wonderful and patient as she learned her varying tasks, and now they even included her in going out with them.

"I'd love to," she said, feeling truly good for the first time since her mother's accident. She'd received an advance from work, so she had a little extra cash in her pocket even after the rent was paid, and she was succeeding on her own. To top that all off, she had a reason to celebrate.

"Why are you in such a great mood?" Miley asked.

"I just received the best news ever. The hospital has found the funds for my mother's operation. I thought I might have to prostitute myself, but it turns out that waiting was the right decision to make. I'm sure my mother's going to be just fine, and my life will finally get back to normal," Ari answered with a wink.

Miley looked at her in shock for a moment before laughing. Miley thought she was joking, Ari knew, but her co-worker had no idea how close Ari truly had come to signing along the dotted line for Rafe Palazzo. If the funds hadn't materialized, she would have been left with no choice.

A hundred-pound weight had been lifted from Ari's shoulders that she hadn't realized was resting there. It was time to paint the town red, and the best part of all was that she could do it guilt free.

She gathered her purse and coat, then followed the three women from the building.

"I got my performance bonus today, so the first round of drinks is on me," Shelly said.

"Mine came in too, so I claim second round," Amber told them with a big grin.

"How many drinks are we having?" Ari asked with trepidation. Her one experience of getting drunk hadn't gone well — in fact, it had gone downright horribly.

"As many as it takes to start making my not-so-fit and very balding husband start looking like one of the Chippendale dancers," Shelly said, causing the group of women to laugh.

"I'd say that's at least twenty tequila shots if he looks anything like my husband," Miley piped in.

Ari stayed quiet as the other women bantered back and forth on their ride down the elevator. She didn't want to offend them by not joining in their fun, but she was terrified to try her hand at serious drinking again. A little bit of wine was different from clubbing with the girls.

The need for friends overrode her fear of alcohol, though, so she figured she might as well suck it up. It might not be as bad as last time. And it wasn't as if she could make her life any worse than it already had been over the last year.

"Did you drive to work today, Ari?"

"No. My car has been having engine trouble. I took the bus in."

"Good. We'll all take the bus over there and then not have to worry about having a designated driver. I hate pulling straws 'cause I always seem to end up with the short one."

Ari looked at Shelly with a bit of surprise. She was always the efficient one in their office, but it seemed that once five o'clock hit, her sights were set on partying versus filing paperwork. Ari had to admit she was enjoying the group of women. Her worries were quickly left behind as they exited the building and headed for the nearest bus stop.

It didn't take them long to reach the club, where they found a crowd already waiting for entrance outside in the cold night air.

"Wow. I wasn't expecting so many people to be out this early," Ari commented.

"It's Friday, happy-hour time. Everyone has the same idea as we do — to blow some of their paycheck before getting locked up with the kids all weekend. Even if my husband and I weren't swimming in debt, I'd be out working just to keep my sanity," Amber remarked.

"I don't think we can get in."

"Don't worry, Ari. I have connections."

Ari watched Shelly approach a stunningly gorgeous bouncer, who embraced her before nodding his head. Shelly gestured for them to follow her, and once inside, Ari found herself seated on a high stool at a crowded circular bar; she watched chefs prepare sushi rolls with lightning speed and supreme art.

The lights were turned down low and the noise level was high; waiters moved among the patrons while friends visited. The pulsing energy in the room helped the last of Ari's concerns float out the window. With her new friends next to her, she was determined to have a wonderful time.

"Ari, I did tell my friend, Tony, that if he could get us in, you'd head to the back room later and let him get to at least third base. I knew you wouldn't mind."

Ari choked on her drink and sent an incredulous look Amber's way. She was unable to tell whether the woman was kidding or not. She really hoped so.

Thankfully, Amber couldn't keep up the serious expression for long and soon burst into laughter.

"I wish I had my camera right now. You should see the expression you're wearing. Trust me, girl, Tony has zero problems getting dates. Just look at him. If I weren't already married, I'd be ripping his clothes off with my teeth. Heck, for that matter, if I get a few drinks in me, I might just go ahead and take him for a spin anyway."

"I have to admit that you girls frighten me a little," Ari replied, sending the women into fits of laughter.

"What are you ladies drinking?"

Ari looked up at the waiter and was more than a little grateful for the interruption.

"We'll have a round of tequila shots followed by apple martinis. Just make sure you don't take too long for our next round. We don't have a ton of time to get drunk enough to face going home," Miley said as she batted her eyes at the young and gorgeous man who was taking their orders.

"Mmm, don't worry, I'm always *very* attentive to pretty ladies," he flirted right back before sending a wink Ari's way and then taking off to the bar.

"Wow. I bet I could get wild and kinky with him. Too bad he was looking straight at you, Ari. He must have realized you're the only one available," Shelly said with a smile.

"I'm not available. Just because I'm single doesn't mean I have any desire to date. I have my mom to take care of, work to do, and more importantly, school to think about. I *will* get back and graduate."

"Yeah, well, you know what they say…all work and no play…"

"I'm just fine with all work." Her three co-workers looked at each other and rolled their eyes.

"Here you are, ladies. I brought an extra round of tequila shots for you — on the house."

"Mmm, mmm. You're a man after my own heart," Miley purred as she batted her eyelashes. "Our friend here was just saying what a nice ass you have."

Ari gasped in mortification as the waiter sidled a bit closer to her, his dark eyes refusing to release her gaze.

"My name's Chandler. You are more than welcome to look…touch…do just about anything you want with my ass…and any other part of me." Ari was speechless as he moved far too close for her comfort, his hip brushing up against her leg.

He turned, and if she wasn't mistaken, he was already a bit excited and pressing his arousal against her. Panic filled her as she looked toward her friends. She'd never had a man be so forward with her before — well, except for Rafe, but that didn't count, as he'd been trying to hire her for a sex slave, whereas she was pretty sure Chandler, the waiter, wanted her for just a single night.

"Her name's Ari. It appears she's being shy. Come back around after drink number three or four," Amber told him while flashing a heart-stopping grin.

Chandler grinned down at Ari before Shelly gave him their sushi order: Pacific Rim, Samurai, and Firestarter rolls.

"We can order more if we want later, but that will be a good start."

"See you gorgeous ladies soon," Chandler said with a wink sent Ari's way, causing her face to heat as she looked quickly down at her drink.

"All right, girls, let's get this night started in style," Amber said as she licked her wrist and shook some salt onto the wet skin. Ari was lost. The other two women followed Amber's lead, but Ari watched cautiously, trying to figure out what they were doing.

"You don't like tequila shots?"

"I don't know what they are."

"Oh, you poor, poor, sheltered girl."

"Miley, don't be so hard on her. We'll just have to teach her," Shelly scolded. "OK, Ari, lick your wrist—yeah, like that. Now, shake some salt on it. Good job. Finally, you just lick the salt off and then throw back the tequila. Watch and learn, sister."

All four of them did it at once, then her co-workers began laughing at the stricken look on Ari's face. She knew she was scowling, but the amber liquid was burning a hole in her throat, and the salt seemed only to intensify the flavor.

"OK, now grab the lime and bite into it like this."

Ari couldn't believe people put themselves through this torture. Her throat was on fire and her taste buds stinging as she reached for her glass of water. At least the lime helped a bit with the overwhelming flavor of the tequila.

"You just have to dive back in for round two and then it's time to dance," Amber announced. With a reluctant sigh, Ari licked her wrist and grabbed the salt shaker. The sad thing was that round two went down a little easier.

Chandler was quick to bring them more shots along with the apple martinis, and soon Ari didn't know how much she'd consumed. But it was enough that her head was getting quite foggy. In between rounds, the women made their way to the dance floor to sweat out some of the alcohol

At first, Ari was horrified by the men grinding up against her, but by her fifth round of shots, she barely even noticed the packed club — though she found herself smiling so much, her cheeks hurt.

The women continued drinking, dancing and laughing, and soon a couple of hours had passed. Ari was starting to fall to the other side of drunken bliss — the not-feeling-so-great side.

"Ladies, it's been a pleasure serving you tonight, but now I'm off shift. I was hoping to steal you for a dance, Ari," Chandler said as he sat down next to her at the crowded bar.

"Yes!" Shelly, Amber and Miley answered in unison.

Ari was feeling so light-headed that she didn't even think about fighting Chandler as he took her hand and pulled her into his arms. His head descended as he locked his lips on hers and his hands roamed over her backside. She knew she should pull away — knew this was moving far too fast, but her muddled head was preventing her from resisting.

"No need to stick around if you have to go. I'll make sure she gets home safe and sound," Chandler said. To Ari's amazement the women giggled and then waved their hands as if it were perfectly OK that their waiter was dragging her off to who knew where. She wanted to protest but couldn't seem to get any words past her throat.

He wrapped his arm around her waist and practically carried her to the dance floor, where he placed both arms around her and started grinding his hips into hers.

"Um, I don't feel too well. Maybe you should take me back to my friends," Ari slurred, surprised by how difficult it was to force the words out.

"Shh, you're fine, sugar. Let's just have a dance or two and then I'll take you somewhere you can lie down," he replied before his lips captured hers, preventing her from protesting any further. With her last bit of energy she tried pulling away, but it was useless. The world was starting to blacken, and she slumped in his arms as she began to pass out.

"That's right. Don't fight it..." were the last words she heard.

Chapter Eleven

Rafe walked into the club, irritated to be there, but it was where his best friend wanted to meet. The man was constantly on the hunt for new women — one-night stands being his preferred choice for satisfying his desires.

Rafe preferred to have exclusive women along for the ride — there to do anything he wanted until he became bored with them. Only Shane, a man he'd known since his early school years, could get him out to a club, and only because he was like a brother to Rafe. The two of them were good for each other, helped balance one another out.

With two sisters who drove him crazy, Rafe appreciated the way Shane helped level the insanity out. His sisters were great, but they could be too much to handle at times. Shane knew Rafe better than any other human being. He'd been there when Rafe went through the divorce, and he'd stayed by his side as Rafe did what he needed to in order to pick the pieces back up.

"I can already tell by the expression on your face that you're thrilled to be here."

Rafe turned around and shot an irritated glance in Shane's direction. Why he put up with the man, he'd never know, he thought sourly. Really, the friendship should never have survived all the crap Shane was known for pulling. If Rafe hadn't known beyond a shadow of a doubt that Shane was a good guy, he'd have cut all ties and called it good.

"Let's get this over with. I have plans this weekend."

"Loosen up, brother. You have to stop and smell the roses once in a while. We're two single guys out on the prowl and they only allow the hottest women in here. Let's have some fun first, then discuss business later."

Rafe sighed as a skimpily dressed hostess led them to a private table, then bent down to show her ample cleavage while asking them what they wanted to drink. Rafe normally would have enjoyed the view, but he still couldn't seem to get Ari from his mind.

Never could he remember being so taken by one woman. It was the reason he should cut his losses and forget all about her. She'd said *no* — that should be the end of it — except that Rafe didn't take rejection well. Not that he could remember the last time he'd actually been rejected.

"We'll take a couple shots of bourbon to start," Shane said as his hand reached out and copped a feel on the hostess's round ass.

"Sounds good, baby. I'll be right back," the woman practically purred.

"Damn, I may not need to look any further. She's hot enough to fry all my circuits," Shane said with a low, drawn-out whistle as he watched her walk away, her hips swinging hypnotically.

"I don't know how you screw so many women, then leave them in the dust and have them still thinking you're their freaking Prince Charming," Rafe grumbled.

"It's all in the attitude, man. I just make them believe it's *their* idea for us to have only one night together. Then, when I run away a free man, they just think it was an exceptional night of sex, and we're good friends."

Rafe snorted as he looked around the club. It was quite crowded for seven o'clock on a Friday night. He'd hoped to have a little peace for a couple of hours more. As his bored gaze started returning to his friend, his eyes caught on a woman being led to the dance floor.

"No," he uttered in disbelief.

"What?" Shane asked as he followed Rafe's gaze and saw a small brunette being led out onto the dance floor. "Do you know her?"

The two men watched as the man held on to the woman, her body flopping against him as he felt her up. Rafe's eyes narrowed further when it was obvious she was barely conscious.

"Son of a bitch!"

Rafe stood up so suddenly that his chair skidded out from behind him, hitting the people walking by. The customer the chair hit grumbled something, but then he continued walking past. It was smart the guy didn't stop to confront Rafe, because he was seeing red as he watched Ari get dragged away from the dance floor. He would have loved to take out his irritation on the passing customer, who was just in the wrong place at the wrong time.

"What's going on?" Shane asked as he placed his hand on Rafe's shoulder. That move nearly got him knocked out.

"She's obviously drunk, passed out on her feet, and the bastard is taking advantage of her!"

With Shane right behind him, Rafe quickly made his way across the club and followed Ari and the stranger, coming up to them just in time to hear the man speaking to his pals.

"Hey, Chandler. Looks like you got another one."

"Damn! She's smokin'."

"Yeah, if you liked the drugged-out look."

The four men started laughing as Chandler sent them a knowing glance, then headed for the back door. Rafe was right behind him. He followed them to the parking lot and saw the Chandler guy begin leading Ari to some run-down house behind the club.

Over Rafe's dead body.

"I dialed the police. I don't think this is the first time this creep has tried something like this."

Rafe turned to see Shane right next to him as they approached Chandler and Ari. Rafe nodded and then closed the gap.

"What in the hell do you think you're doing?" Rafe thundered as he grabbed the guy's arm.

"None of your damn business," Chandler snapped as he tried to pick up his pace.

"From what I overheard your friends saying, you drugged this woman and now plan to take her to your drug house to rape her."

"Who in the hell are you? You don't know what you're talking about. This is my girlfriend. She just had too much to drink tonight and I'm taking her home to sleep it off."

"Listen, jerkwad, if I were you, I'd hightail it inside without the girl and hide your sorry carcass because my friend is about to kick your ass all over this parking lot. I'm mighty inclined to give him a helping hand," Shane said with a smile of anticipation.

The guy's eyes were darting around. Rafe could see he was trying to decide whether to fight for his victim or drop her and run like hell. Fear won out when he saw the fury in Rafe's eyes and the determination in Shane's. Chandler suddenly pushed Ari toward the two of them, then took off running to the shack.

Rafe caught Ari just before she hit the hard pavement. He thought for one moment of setting her down and going after the punk, but when she groaned in his arms, he knew he wasn't leaving her.

Shane understood his friend's dilemma and reassured him. "I'll keep an eye on the place, make sure he doesn't run for it. You take care of her. Just give me a call later and let me know if she's OK," he said before he walked to the ramshackle steps of the house and leaned against the rail, intently watching the door.

"Ari? Ari, are you OK?" Rafe asked as he scooped her up into his arms and gently shook her. Slowly, her eyes came open, and it was obvious her vision was blurred as she squinted up at him. It took several moments for her to focus on his face.

"Rafe? When did you get here?"

Her hand came up and patted his cheek, her fingernails trailing down the side of his face before she smiled at him.

"Mmm, you smell good," she slurred.

"What are you doing here?" he demanded.

Her brows puckered as if she didn't have any idea and it was a very difficult question for her to answer. "I...I can't remember."

"I'm taking you home!"

Rafe was furious. What was she doing at a club on a Friday? And how had she allowed herself to get into this position? If he hadn't been there, she could have been getting violated at that very moment. This was why she should just accept his generous offer, he told himself. She clearly wasn't able to protect herself on her own.

He strode to his car and put her on the front seat, where she quickly passed out again. With an angry turn of his wrist he pulled out his phone and sent Shane a text message, asking to be informed the minute the guy was arrested. He wanted to make sure the scumbag was locked up for a while and, he hoped, never able to do this to another woman.

Rafe started driving toward his home, then changed his mind. He'd never taken a woman there and he wasn't going to start now. With a jerk of the wheel he turned down a side road and reversed the car, heading in the direction of her apartment.

When he pulled up to her address, his eyes narrowed in disgust. Why would someone choose to live in such a crappy location? She was being paid well at her job. She should have moved out by now. He knew she had expenses, but a safe place to live should have been at the top of her priorities.

Luckily, she was wearing a strappy purse, which was still hanging around her neck. He searched it and found her key, then lifted her into his arms and carried her up the unstable staircase to the second landing, where he found her doorknob despite the darkness surrounding them. It took him a few tries before he managed to get the door open.

His disgust grew at her small and shabby living area with its sparse furnishings. He laid her down on the couch until he could turn on some lights and find her bed, then picked up his cell phone and dialed his private physician. The respected doctor said he would be right over, though the man paused when Rafe listed the address.

Rafe would have paused too. While he waited for Dr. Malroy to arrive, he searched her tiny apartment, taking only a few minutes. Her fridge was pretty much empty, her cupboards bare, and her toiletries scarce. No wonder the woman was too skinny. It was more obvious than ever that Ari didn't know how to take care of herself. If anyone could benefit from being his mistress, she was that person. She'd get a whole lot more out of their arrangement than he would. He couldn't understand her revulsion at the idea.

At the very instant she agreed, he would move her into a beautiful condo, where she'd have plenty to eat and not have to worry about money — not even after he was done with her. He paid his mistresses a nice settlement when their services were no longer needed, making sure they were still taken care of and their futures secure.

His second call was to his assistant, who assured him he'd have her fridge and cupboards stocked within a couple of hours. Rafe wanted her to come to him, but he just wasn't going to leave her in her current circumstances while he waited for her inevitable submission.

Rafe sighed in relief at the knock on her door. He opened it and let in the doctor, who raised his eyebrows questioningly. Rafe didn't bother explaining, but just led the man to the couch so he could examine Ari. It didn't take Dr. Malroy long to diagnose the problem.

"I won't know for sure until the tests are confirmed, but it looks to me as if she received a dose of some kind of date rape drug. Whoever gave it to her most likely slipped it in her drink, causing her exhaustion and hypnotic state. More often than not it has an almost amnesiac effect, meaning that the victim won't remember anything from the night before."

Rafe's rage rose to dangerous levels. That man who'd had her in his arms had drugged her and planned to do who knew what with her before dumping her somewhere where she wouldn't remember a thing.

Once Rafe was done assuring himself Ari would be OK, he decided that he would make a visit to the would-be attacker. He had many friends at the police station who wouldn't have any problem turning their backs while Rafe got one good punch in — maybe two or three.

"Does she need to be admitted to the hospital?"

"It doesn't look as if she got a dangerously high level of the drug, whatever it was, but you need to keep an eye on her for the rest of the night. If she looks to have any trouble breathing, then you need to rush her to the ER, but they can't really do any more than give her the same medications that I have with me. Some victims have been known to die from a bad reaction to the rape drugs I've mentioned, but she would have been showing signs at this point."

"I'll take her there now."

"I don't see any allergic reactions. Honestly, I think she'll be fine. I've been your doctor for a long time, and I've never steered you wrong. If I felt there were a need for her to go in, I'd tell you. She just needs fluids and rest right now."

"If you think that's what's best—but if I get the slightest inkling that she isn't OK, I'll rush her in." With reluctance, Rafe took the doctor's advice and saw him out. Afterward, he settled in for a very long night.

Chapter Twelve

Ari woke up to the relentless pounding of a full percussion section in her head. She tried peeking through the narrow slits that were her eyelids, but the pain wouldn't allow even that much movement. Her body twitched on the bed and she felt aches move from her head all the way to the tips of her toes.

"Take this, Ari. It will help."

Ari froze at the sound of Rafe's voice. What was he doing here? What was she doing in the same room as he was? Where was she? For a moment, her mind was a complete blank, making the pain and panic escalate.

Searching her mind for the last thing she could remember was agonizing, but Ari tried to summon up her previous night's memories. Slowly, through a thick veil of fog, memories started trickling back in.

She'd been at the bar with her friends. She knew she was drinking too much, but she was having a great time — laughing, flirting with the waiter, acting like a normal twenty-three-year-old with no worries on a Friday night.

She wasn't just a normal person, though. She had her mother to take care of, bills to pay, and stress beyond anything a single woman should be enduring. She'd just wanted one single night to be free of thinking about any of it. It seemed she wasn't allowed even that.

No matter how much she searched her memory, she didn't recall seeing Rafe anywhere at the club. The very last thing she could remember was her friends encouraging her to dance with the waiter. She couldn't even think of his name. Everything had started to go fuzzy.

"Come on, Ari. I'm going to sit you up now. I know you hurt at the moment, but if you take these pills, you'll start to feel better. I turned down the lights so you can open your eyes."

The next minute was filled with excruciating pain as she felt Rafe's hands beneath her body helping her to sit up. Nausea rose in her throat as sharp arrows of discomfort tore into her.

She felt the edge of a glass against her bottom lip and she automatically opened her mouth, feeling a small token of relief as the icy-cold liquid slid down her throat. She felt Rafe's callused finger against her lip, and, opening up once again, she felt him place a pill on her tongue. She swallowed it down when he pressed the glass against her lip again.

She wasn't brave enough to open her eyes just yet. She'd wait until the pounding in her head settled down first.

Over the next several minutes, she concentrated on taking deep breaths in and out as she started to feel the effects from the magic pill. The throbbing in her head and excruciating bodily aches didn't cease, but they began to ease to a bearable level.

Eventually, Ari braved cracking her eyes open. The room was dim, but it didn't take her long to spot Rafe sitting next to the bed in one of her rickety kitchen chairs.

She was stunned to find the sophisticated man in her apartment. She never would have thought *that* day would come. He was far too polished to hang out in the slums of San Francisco.

She struggled to focus her eyes on his face, becoming more surprised by what she saw. Rafe had at least a full day's growth of stubble coating his normally smooth skin, and the circles under his eyes attested to lack of sleep. Her curiosity spiked; what in heaven's name had happened?

"I'm glad to see you finally awake. You've been semiconscious the last few hours, but only enough to allow me to get some liquids in you and take you to the bathroom. I was beginning to think the doctor was wrong. You slept all night and day and were going for night number two when you finally woke up."

"What happened? Doctor? What doctor? Why are you here with me?" Ari was again surprised by the hoarseness in her voice. She sounded as though she hadn't spoken in years.

"You were drugged at the club last night. I happened to be there and stopped the man before he carted you off to do unimaginable things with you."

Ari waited for him to continue. When he said nothing further, she turned her eyes back on him and looked into his anger-filled eyes. Why was he so upset when she was the one who'd almost been raped? It wasn't as if she'd done it on purpose. It wasn't as if she'd asked him to step in and save her and then play doctor.

As the two of them engaged in a stare-down, the reality of the situation set in. She'd come close to being raped. It seemed unreal — as if she were looking through a window and watching her story happen to someone else.

Leading a sheltered life had its positives, and one of those was thinking horrible things could never happen to you. Death, rape, suicide — they all happened, but they were so distant that it never occurred to her that she could ever be a victim. With her head still pounding, she pushed down the panic fighting to surface. The reality of the situation would most likely hit her soon, but for now it was much easier not to think about it.

"Wow. I guess you don't mince words."

"I don't see any point in beating around the bush."

"Precisely how long have I been unconscious?"

"It's late Saturday night, so it's been about twenty hours. You're probably hungry."

"No. The thought of food is horrible. I'm fine now. I appreciate your looking out for me, but I can take care of myself."

"You're far from fine, Ari. You were drugged and nearly raped. So I'm not going anywhere right now. I'll have food brought over."

Before Ari could say anything else, he stood, drew out his phone and gracefully left the room as he punched in numbers. She was still struggling to deal with the pain invading her body, and she felt too weak to argue. It wasn't as if he could cram the food down her throat. At least she didn't *think* he'd take it that far.

With a groan, she shifted her legs over the side of the bed until she felt her toes touch the floor. Slowly standing on wobbly legs, Ari held on to the side of the bed until she was sure she wasn't going to fall flat on her face. When the dizziness passed, she took a deep breath and cautiously made her way to the bathroom, firmly shutting the door behind her.

At Ari's first look in the mirror — even in the crummy bathroom lighting — she nearly groaned again. Her hair looked as if rats had burrowed several nests inside, her face was ghostlike, and she had reddish-brown smudges beneath her eyes, accentuating her prominent cheekbones.

If she'd happened to walk by someone who looked like that, she'd have assumed the person was dead or very nearly so. Hollywood couldn't do a better makeup job. Using the last of her energy, she washed her face, brushed her teeth, rinsed her mouth out and ran a comb through her tangles. She wasn't trying to impress Rafe; she just hoped that taking a bit of time with her appearance would make her feel a bit better.

By the time she opened the door, she was drained of what little energy she'd awoken with, but she did feel slightly more human.

Rafe had a low light burning in the corner, where he'd set up his laptop on a small desk that wasn't hers. Then she noticed the new bedding covering her mattress. Come to think of it, her back wasn't hurting the way it should have been after she'd been lying in bed for twenty hours.

There's no way she could have slept on the lumpy secondhand furniture for so long and not be feeling it in every vertebra of her back. She slowly returned to the bed and lifted the sheet, seeing a new mattress.

She didn't know whether to be grateful or feel invaded. Shopping for a bed was a little too intimate for a stranger to do. She really didn't want to be any more in Rafe's debt than his rescue had made her. She couldn't afford to pay him back for whatever he'd spent, but she'd have to. She refused to have that hanging over her head.

She'd hold off for now because it seemed petty of her to snap at the man for providing her with a comfortable bed when she was ill. Reimbursing him wouldn't be easy — he'd take it as an assault on his pride. She'd have to slip an anonymous envelope beneath his door, or something like that. She didn't need him to know she'd repaid him — she just needed to know, herself.

As Ari climbed back into bed and pulled the covers up over her legs, there was a knock on the apartment door. The sound echoed inside her head, feeling like a set of bass drums playing an upbeat tempo. So much for her headache easing.

With extremely cautious movements, she lay back down and covered her head with one of the soft down pillows, hoping to block out the sound of the next attack on her thin wood door. Luckily, there was no more pounding. Soon, though, delicious aromas drifted beneath the pillow, filling her nostrils.

After she heard muted sounds in her small kitchen, the smell of warm food became stronger, and Rafe sat down next to her bed.

"Sit up for me, Ari — it's time to eat something. I have soup and fresh bread."

"I'm not hungry," she said, not wanting to accept anything else from him. It was starting to get a bit ridiculous. She needed him just to go home.

Her stomach took that opportunity to growl loudly, as if to make sure Rafe knew she was a liar — that she most certainly *was* hungry. She hadn't realized how famished she was until the aromas from whatever had been delivered assailed her.

"Come on, Ari. Sit up and eat your soup," Rafe said, an obvious smile in his voice.

She didn't want to give him the satisfaction of seeing her do what he wanted, but her stomach decided to growl again, and she was too starved to play further games. With frustration and great effort, she tossed away the pillow and slowly propped herself up to a sitting position.

Rafe placed a tray across her lap and she practically drooled when she looked down at the bowl of soup and warm bread. Without further hesitation, Ari ripped off a piece of the soft bread and dipped it in the soup before lifting it to her lips and taking a bite.

Her taste buds exploded as she carefully swallowed and then dived further into her meal, appeasing her hunger. When she'd cleared everything from the tray, she realized her head wasn't pounding at all anymore, though exhaustion was quickly consuming her. She didn't care. She could sleep a while longer, and when she woke, it would be a new day with hopefully no pain, and definitely no Rafe.

Carefully, she lay back down and closed her eyes. Just as Ari began drifting to sleep again she heard Rafe on his phone. Just a little later, she barely heard his last words, thinking they weren't anything other than a dream.

"Ari, we have to move to my place. I have work I have to attend to, and I'm not leaving you by yourself. The pills I gave you take the pain away, but they also make you drowsy, so I don't want you shocked when you wake up in a new bed… Ari…are you listening?"

Ari mumbled something, though she had no idea what. Thankfully sleep took over and her pain slipped away.

Chapter Thirteen

Ari awoke feeling better, but not at a hundred percent. Stretching her arms above her head and arching her back, she didn't realize she wasn't home until she turned and felt the cool satin beneath her fingertips.

There was no way she was in her own bed. Had she died? Was she now feeling what heaven was like? The sheets were amazing and she felt as if she were floating in a cloud of soft cotton, the bed was so comfortable.

Opening her eyes, Ari was bombarded with natural light as she looked across the huge room and out the open curtains belonging to at least eight-foot-high windowpanes.

"I was beginning to think you were going to sleep the entire day away."

Ari jumped at the words and whipped her head around to find a young woman in her mid-twenties standing next to the bed.

"Um, where am I?"

"You're at Mr. Palazzo's residence. He said you might still be a bit unsettled when you woke up, that you'd been drugged. I'm so sorry you've had to go through this. The doctor looked at you again this morning and said your fever is down and you're almost back to full health, but he also said you needed to be looked after for another twenty-four to forty-eight hours."

"Forty-eight hours? What day is it?" Ari asked as panic began to set in.

"It's Monday, just past ten in the morning. You've been here for two full nights, but you spiked a fever yesterday and the doctor gave you a heavy dose of pain relievers. Your coloring looks much better now. "

"I have to go! My boss is going to fire me," Ari exclaimed as she jumped from the bed. The room began to spin slightly with her quick movements and she found herself falling back, thankfully landing on the soft mattress.

"Whoa, slow down. Mr. Palazzo already called in to your workplace and they know you'll be out for a few days."

"He doesn't have the right to do that. He certainly doesn't have the right to abduct me from my home!"

The woman looked at Ari as if she were mentally ill. Maybe she was, considering the mess she'd gotten herself into, Ari told herself with a mental shudder, but she was angry that he'd swooped in and taken over her life. She refused to be in debt to the man. She thought back over the events of the last few days, and the hospital incident a while before that, and she shook her head — she couldn't seem to get away from him. But she couldn't afford to owe him anything more.

"It's OK, Misty. I'll take care of Ms. Harlow now."

Ari's head turned sharply and her breath caught at the sight of Rafe standing in the doorway. Though she hadn't given her eyes permission, they drank in his massive frame. How she could despise everything the man stood for and still feel attraction for him she just didn't understand, but every time she was in his presence, she found herself fighting just a little more to keep her hormones at a respectable level, especially after that memorable dream a while back.

With a quick pep talk, she tore her gaze from his mesmerizing eyes and focused upon a button on his shirt instead. She had to remain calm, had to get back to her apartment and the real world before she began to think she could accept his indecent proposal.

"I appreciate your taking care of me the last few days, but I need to get home. I have a job that I happen to like and a life waiting for my return," Ari told him, proud of the false bravado in her tone. Inside, she was shaking like a leaf in a fall breeze.

"You're not going anywhere, Ari," he said before pausing. "Doctor's orders."

As if his doctor's giving an order was going to stop her.

"Where are my clothes?" She'd learned enough about Rafe by now to know that arguing with him was useless. She wouldn't bother with a battle she knew she'd lose. She'd simply get dressed and walk out the front door. She didn't think he'd go so far as to physically detain her.

"You have a fresh change of clothes in the bathroom — that door on the right. Why don't you take a shower and then meet me downstairs for lunch?" As if the matter was settled, he turned and left the room.

Ari really wished she were quick enough to come up with a suitably sarcastic retort, but of course she didn't think of anything witty until she had locked herself in the guest bathroom.

She looked around the space with awe. When she was younger, while watching romantic movies, how she'd dreamed of having such a wonderful bathing area! She hadn't been poor, but the modest home she'd shared with her mother prized efficiency over what little luxury they might have been able to afford.

The room she was standing in could be classified as a spa, it was so spacious and ornate. She glided across the heated tile, then ran her hand along the marble surrounding the large tub. She hadn't planned to take a bath, unwilling to follow any order Rafe issued, but the tub was calling her name. He'd told her to shower, anyway, so taking a bath wasn't exactly doing what he'd said. So there!

The gold handles of the taps were smooth and well-polished; no effort at all was required to move them. A giggle escaped her as the water flowed out of the spout, cascading down like a waterfall. Several bottles of bubble bath sat clustered in a basket on the corner of the tub, and Ari's hardest decision at that moment was which amazing scent to use. She finally settled on peach and honey, then inhaled the expensive aroma that surrounded her.

Once Ari had stepped into the tub and had sunk down so only her face appeared above the water, she allowed a sigh of contentment to escape. With a wide smile, she decided she could stay in this exact spot for the next hundred years or so. Rafe could just go ahead and wait on her to show up for lunch. If her luck held out, he'd get so frustrated that he'd just leave, making it easy for her to escape.

As she laid her head back on the soft cushion of the bath pillow and closed her eyes, she ignored the small voice inside saying that she was crazy to want to escape a secret haven such as this. But it wasn't the incredible spa bathroom she was running from; it was the rules Rafe insisted on if she were to accept his generosity.

She would be no man's mistress — not for any amount of luxury or security. Part of her wished she could just say *yes* and let him take the weight off her shoulders, but a greater part of her knew that wasn't who she was.

Her mother had raised her to be independent, to earn what she wanted in life, and never to let anyone make her feel cheap. Being with Rafe would slowly suck away her soul — everything about who she was. It might feel like heaven, but in reality, it was just a *very* disguised hell.

When she turned on the quiet jets and they began gently massaging her body, Ari's mind shut off and she drifted to sleep, fully enjoying the magical ambience of Rafe's guest bathroom.

*****

Rafe's irritation grew dramatically as an hour passed with still no sign of Ari. He knew the woman was stubborn and wanted to do the exact opposite of anything he asked of her, but he found it exceptionally rude for her not to show up when he was being so hospitable.

Never before had he brought a female to his home. It was a huge leap for him, and as his temper flared, he was beginning to understand exactly why he didn't invite women over. This was the reason he chose not to enter into "normal" relationships.

Having a business arrangement with a woman, making sure she knew the score, was far smarter than playing games and walking on pins and needles. He wanted his women to do what he said when he said it — not fight him each and every step of the way.

He should have just hired a nurse for Ari. He didn't quite understand why he'd felt the need to take care of her himself. He still couldn't believe he'd spent time in her horrific apartment.

He'd offered her a nice place to live, a great salary, and luxuries he was sure she'd never seen before. Why would she turn her nose up at all of it?

When another fifteen minutes had passed, Rafe lost his last ounce of patience. Not allowing his exasperation to show, he slowly stood up from the table and sauntered down the hallways and up the massive staircase of his large home.

It took him over two minutes to reach the guest room Ari had been given, but he didn't allow himself to speed up his steps: because he wanted to reach her quickly, he instead maintained a cool and leisurely pace.

No woman would control his actions.

"Mr. Palazzo," Misty said as she jumped from her chair in surprise. "Ms. Harlow hasn't emerged from the bathroom yet. Do you want me to hurry her along?"

"No. You're dismissed." Rafe didn't stop his progress to the bathroom door; nor did he turn to make sure his maid had done as he had demanded. Everyone who worked for him followed orders without question. He really should quit trying to hire Ari, he told himself. With her rebellious tendencies, it couldn't possibly end well.

He reached for the doorknob and found it locked. A wicked smile crossed his features. Did she honestly think she could keep him out of any room in his own house? His pulse quickened as he reached into his pocket and pulled out a master key. He now abandoned his misgivings about her from a moment before. Quit trying? Oh, no. Training Ari to surrender to him would be more fun than he could remember having in years.

The sensual fragrance of the bubble bath filled his nose the instant he entered the room. It sent his pulse racing as his eyes zeroed in on Ari in the tub. The bubbles had mostly faded, leaving plenty of her nearly perfect figure exposed for his visual pleasure.

Ari covered in water and a thin veil of bubbles was going to be the source of more than a few fantasies in the foreseeable future. He felt himself begin to harden as he stepped closer, then sat on the edge of the tub and let his hand sink into the still-warm bath.

When his fingers brushed along her rib cage, she quivered and then her eyes slowly opened, connecting their gazes. His stare was hot and hungry, and hers slowly waking, desire quickly filling her eyes' sleepy depths.

"I don't like to be kept waiting, Ari," he whispered, his fingers dancing along her slick torso.

She opened her mouth to respond, but no words drifted out as she was caught up in this strange chemistry they shared.

It was time he showed her how good it would be between the two of them if she decided to agree to his terms. Obviously patience wasn't working, and he still couldn't seem to get her from his mind. Now it was time for persuasion.

He reached into the water and pulled her dripping figure easily from the tub, setting her naked form on his lap, soaking his suit.

With a startled gasp, she pressed her hands against his chest, intending to push him away.

"What do you think you are doing?"

"What we both want."

His mouth dropped and he broke his "no kissing" rule — devouring her mouth in a seemingly never-ending hunger that tore right through him.

Chapter Fourteen

As Rafe's mouth captured hers, Ari remained stiff for several seconds, thinking that she just might be able to resist him. As Rafe's tongue slipped past her teeth and caressed the contours of her mouth, resistance became futile.

The sensation exploding inside her body wiped all thought from her mind. What was it that she was feeling? She'd never experienced anything of such magnitude before. Her stomach was fluttering, and she felt a swelling sensation in her core.

Ari pressed her legs together, trying to relieve the building pressure. As she attempted to gain the willpower to push Rafe away, his mouth slowly moved down her jaw, trailing soft, feather-light kisses along her slender neck. His tongue traced her skin and his teeth gently nipped her shoulder.

A shudder passed through her, and she was shocked when he effortlessly lifted her with the smoothness of motion only strong muscles could support and then walked into the bedroom, laying her upon the mattress, her body sinking into its comfort.

"I don't normally have sex without you first being an employee — without a formal agreement, but I can't seem to get you out of my mind. I have to have you, and I'm tired of resisting the pull. I'm not stopping unless you tell me to, so if you have protests, give them now," Rafe ordered as he slipped off his suit jacket and began unbuttoning his soaked shirt.

Ari knew now was the time to tell him this wasn't going to happen. She needed to get the words past her tight throat and demand he leave her alone. But as he exposed his contoured olive chest with the release of the last button on his dress shirt, she completely forgot what she'd just been thinking.

The sight of his ripped abs and narrow waist sent more sensations through her body. She felt a pinch in her breasts, and her nipples hardened, engendering an exquisitely pleasurable pain. She lifted her hands to her breasts, her palms squeezing over her peaked pink skin, trying to relieve the ache of desire.

The brush of her own hands sent more sensation coursing through her, and she involuntarily spread her thighs. Her eyes never left Rafe's as he shed the rest of his clothes and stood beside the bed, gloriously naked, looking like a statue of Adonis.

He was pure perfection, from the dark, slightly mussed hair on his head to the very soles of his feet. His body was covered in a fine layer of muscles, and his large erection stood proudly, ready to penetrate her. Fear should be rolling through her system, but all she felt was need.

"No regrets, Ari. It's too late," he murmured as he caught her hands and raised them above her head. Before she could protest, his mouth descended, capturing her aching nipple, sucking it deep inside the warmth of his mouth.

Her hips rose from the bed, turning in his direction, seeking the warmth of his body. He threw his leg over hers, trapping her as his mouth devoured first one taut bud and then the other.

He released her hands and she immediately moved them to his head, her fingers running through his thick hair, tugging on the short strands, trying to hold him in place as he relieved the ache in her breasts but caused new awareness to spread lower in her body.

Her stomach trembled as she felt warm heat radiate through her core. Moistness coated her insides, readying her for his entry, as his hand ran up her thigh and his fingers traced the edges of her slick opening. He easily slipped his fingers inside her, and the smoldering fire ignited into a raging inferno.

She pressed against him, not understanding the changes coursing through her, but her body instinctively took over as she sought relief. This was nothing like the clumsy fumbling of the college classmate during her only previous sexual experience. She was burning up, and she had no doubt that Rafe could quench her raging thirst.

His mouth trailed down her stomach, causing her to cry out as he touched every inch of her throbbing torso. Ari was reaching toward something she'd never thought to experience. Was something so amazing really possible? Why hadn't she tried to experience it before this moment?

She couldn't seem to get enough oxygen — breathing came only with difficulty as her heart thundered and her airways closed. Pressure built steadily in her core; she was close to tears and her head whipped from side to side as Rafe took his time devouring her body.

"Please, Rafe, please make it stop," she cried as she pressed her hips upward, causing his seeking fingers to plunge deeply inside her saturated folds.

"Oh, Ari, we're only just beginning," he murmured before he spread open her knees and his tongue swirled around her inner thighs. She moaned in pleasure as his fingers moved swiftly in and out of her swollen heat while his mouth skillfully circled the area.

When his tongue descended onto her engorged bud, the pressure spiked dangerously high. She felt a tingling sensation begin to flood her entire body as tension built higher and higher. His tongue swirled around her wet folds and his fingers pumped inside her faster and faster, making her reach for relief.

She threw her head back and let go, banishing any thoughts in her brain even hinting that what she was doing was wrong. It certainly didn't *feel* wrong. It felt like the single greatest thing she'd ever done. She wanted relief, but at the same time, she never wanted the moment to end. She wanted to exist solely in this pleasurable sliver of time.

Suddenly, his tongue pushed out against her, and she exploded. As his lips encircled her aching bud and his fingers pressed deep inside her body, she began to shake, her flesh throbbing as it contracted, pulsing over and over again.

She felt light-headed as fire ripped through her, her breasts heavy, her lower body burning. He slowed the movement of his tongue and gently sucked on her wet skin, making her spasm in his hands.

As the last of her tremors began to cease, his fingers started moving again, making her pull her thighs together. *No!* She was done. She couldn't take anything more.

"It's not over, Ari. Trust me," he murmured. She wanted to protest. She couldn't possibly do that again. The pleasure had been unlike anything she could imagine. It would surely send her into cardiac arrest to experience it twice in a row.

Amazingly, as his fingers gently penetrated her swollen folds, she felt a stirring of heat begin to return. Tiny sensations started flooding her core, drifting out through her legs and stomach. Joy filled her as her nipples responded, that pleasurable ache returning and her body immediately awakening to his touch.

Oh, she could do this all day and night!

She heard Rafe's low sexy chuckle before his mouth dropped down and he slid that masterful tongue along her dripping heat, and then nothing but moans of pleasure could be heard in the sun-filled room.

Rafe moved up her body, taking his time to cover her stomach with sweet kisses before his mouth rose over the mounds of her breasts and he gently bit down on her erect nipples. Her hands again gripped his hair, this time pulling him upward, wanting his lips on hers.

Quickly obliging her unspoken request, he slid further up her body and claimed her mouth, slipping his tongue deep inside. She flinched at the taste of her sex on Rafe's tongue, but he held her in place and soon the slight tanginess was just another part of the excitement, making her burn hotter.

"You're ready," he growled as he opened the nightstand and grabbed a foil package. Efficiently sliding the protection onto his impressive length, he leaned in closer, then spread her legs with his knees.

Her eyes opened wide as he pressed the head of his thick arousal against her opening. She tensed as he began pushing inside her, his engorged staff barely fitting into her heat.

A pinch of pain overrode the pleasure as he rocked his hips, pushing himself fully inside. She squirmed beneath him, suddenly scared, thinking she'd made a huge mistake.

"You're so tiny. Just give your body a minute to adjust," he groaned as he lay still against her. Just when she thought all pleasure was gone, he shifted. He pulled slightly back, then moved forward again. Several more times he moved a couple of inches, pulling out, then gently pushing back in.

The pain evaporated as that elusive pressure started building once more to a feverish pitch. As her body got used to his girth, she wiggled underneath him, seeking that peak of pleasure again, suddenly greedy for release.

Rafe had opened a gate she hadn't known she'd bolted shut long ago, and now there was no turning back.

"That's it, Ari — just feel," Rafe commanded in a low, seductive tone as he built up speed. She couldn't turn away from his desire-clouded gaze as his body moved perfectly in sync with hers. She wasn't even consciously moving her hips, but her body had taken over, knowing exactly what it needed to do in order to feel that mind-numbing pleasure of only moments before.

Sweat slicked his solid chest and Ari's hands drifted along the sleek muscles of his toned back. She wanted to touch him everywhere, feel every groove of his impressive frame.

A groan filled the room; she didn't know which of them it came from, and she didn't care. She was almost delirious as her body built higher and higher. She felt every single inch of his thick erection penetrating her damp folds — a delicious sensation.

"Ohh," she cried as her orgasm hit her with more force than the last one had. As he moved inside her, the contractions drew out, sending her to another realm of satisfaction.

"Yes, Ari, don't hold back. Let it all go. Yes…you're so tight, so hot. I can't hold out…" he groaned, and she felt him tense, his throbbing staff pulsing with his release.

A fog seemed to be engulfing her in delirious pleasure, making her unable to process even the smallest of thoughts.

Desire-filled moans continued to erupt from Rafe as his hips thrust steadily inside her, though he began slowing down his frantic motion. She felt unbelievable joy at the depth of her own fulfillment, and at the knowledge she'd been the cause of Rafe's losing control. It was an intoxicating feeling.

As Rafe's body collapsed against hers, Ari's mind could take no more and she surrendered to a blissful slumber.

Chapter Fifteen

A smiled flitted across Rafe's face as Ari snuggled deeper against his side. His arm flexed and he pulled her closer to his body; he felt the strong beat of her heart against his ribs, and the soft cushion of her full breasts pressing into his skin.

A soft orange sunset cast its colors across the walls of the room, and for a single moment Rafe felt nothing but contentment.

As his sleeping mind fully awoke, he tensed. What was he doing? He didn't allow himself to get comfortable with women. He was acting like a fool, and this road led to nothing but heartache.

He looked toward his window, shocked that he'd fallen asleep with Ari after their intense afternoon — and not simply fallen asleep beside her. It had been no light doze. He must have slept for about four hours if the sun was now going down. He hadn't slept beside a woman since his marriage ended, not even for a short nap. It was one of the rules that he never broke.

Intimacy was strictly out when it came to relationships. He wanted nothing but sex — pure pleasure. No feelings, no emotion. A controlled environment.

With a firm resolve, he started pulling away from the warmth of Ari's sated body. He barely stopped the frustrated groan from escaping his closing throat when her grip around him tightened as her unguarded, sleeping body sought his.

Digging deep within to find his iron strength, he pulled her hand away from his side and slid out from beneath her. She softly cried out in her sleep while she squirmed on the bed, seeking out his warmth. His eyes were glued to her half-covered figure as she stirred and began to awaken.

His pants were pulled up and buttoned before her eyes opened, and she looked around her in confusion as the sleepy smile fell from her lips. Before he locked away the emotion, desire began to climb, returning once again inside him.

The sheet slipped down her smooth curves, exposing her perfect breasts to his view. Evidence of their lovemaking — *no* — sex, just sex — covered her body. Small red marks were easy to see on her alabaster skin, and her pink nipples were partially peaked as if she were ready for him to run his tongue across their delicate surface again. Such femininity, such perfection.

Rafe turned away to gather the rest of his clothes. He heard her sitting up in the bed, and when he turned back around, his fingers methodically buttoning his shirt, she was gazing at him in surprise, gripping the blankets tightly across her body.

"Don't act like a prude, Ari. I've touched and tasted just about every inch of you," he said with a mocking tone, and then smirked at the narrowing of her eyes.

"Get out," she said, her voice controlled, surprising him and oddly raising his opinion of her at the same time. He'd expected hysterics or crying. He hadn't expected her cool detachment. He should feel a smidgeon of insult, but he knew he could make her body go up in flames with a single touch of his hand. He had nothing to prove.

"Meet me in the dining room in twenty minutes…unless you want me to come up here and find you again." He waited to smile until he left the room. He nearly laughed when he heard the thud against the door, wondering what she'd thrown at it.

Since meeting Arianna Harlow, his life hadn't been boring. She was constantly surprising him, not only by her reactions, but by his to her as well. She sparked a flame in him that had lain dormant for such a length of time, he hadn't thought it capable of stirring to life again.

She would be his for as long as he desired her to be so. Until she fully submitted to him, he was certainly enjoying the journey the two of them were taking. He almost dreaded the day he grew bored of her. He couldn't imagine another woman stirring his damaged soul so much.

As Rafe sat at the dining table, watching the clock, he almost hoped she would try to defy him again. He wouldn't mind hunting her down and teaching her the first real lesson in what happened to those who displeased him.

When nineteen minutes hit, his feet twitched. At exactly twenty, he was going to stand up and begin his lesson.

"I'm here, master."

"Master?"

"I figure you think you're the lord of all, so you'd want to be called by a name appropriate to a dictator," she snapped as she sat across from him.

"*Sir* is just fine," he mocked.

"How about *ass*?" she asked with an innocent air.

"Careful, Ari. I'll be pushed only so far," he threatened.

"Do you honestly think that you frighten me, Mr. Palazzo? I'm actually curious. If you so much as lay one finger on me, I won't hesitate to have you thrown in jail. You may get back out very quickly with your vast fortune, and what I'm sure is just about everyone in your back pocket, but still I'd get the satisfaction of seeing you cuffed and taken in," she said while looking him squarely in the eyes.

"I laid more than a finger on you earlier, Ari, and you were screaming — but not in displeasure. Should I demonstrate again how much you like my...fingers on and in you?" he asked.

"That wasn't the most unpleasant way I've spent a boring afternoon, but you know that's not what I mean. I looked at your stupid paperwork, and though I may not be the most knowledgeable person on this planet when it comes to sex, I can read between the lines. *You* get control of me? *You* get to choose what I do, *whom* I see, *where* I go? You're a control freak and I want no part of it. I would never allow a man to hit me!"

"Is that what you think of me? Honestly? You think that I need to *beat* my women into submission?" he thundered as he stood up with his hands on the table and his body leaning toward her. He shook with fury.

"I'm just repeating what I read," she fired back.

"There was nothing in those papers that said I get off on hurting a woman!"

"Then, please tell how you exert your control!"

Rafe sat back down, his temper at an all-time high. He took in several deep breaths as he once again thought about the sanity of dealing with this woman. She'd made a lot of assumptions and he owed her no explanations. He was furious that he even wanted to have the conversation.

Instead of saying anything, he pressed a buzzer, letting the staff know he was ready for their first course. Two people moved into the room, silent as they set down plates and filled glasses with wine and water.

Rafe lifted the cup to his lips and took a sip of the dry chenin blanc as he waited for the servers to exit. His eyes didn't leave Ari's face. She glanced at him, then looked away, muttering a quiet thank-you as her antipasto plate was placed before her. Nervously, she picked up her own wineglass and took a large gulp, then swallowed half the contents before setting the glass back down.

His staff went quietly to the back of the room, ready to refill glasses and bring out new courses. They had proved their loyalty, and he didn't have to worry about his words in front of them. He wouldn't hire anyone he couldn't be himself around, anyone without absolute discretion.

"Why don't you come and work for me so you can find out?" Rafe finally spoke after ten minutes of silence that stretched out awkwardly for Ari.

She jerked her gaze up, seemingly surprised that he was still in the room. Rafe didn't know whether he should be offended to be forgotten so easily. Yes, Ari wasn't great for his ego.

"I do appreciate your saving me from the club and having a doctor look after me, but no matter how much you rescue me, or swoop in on your white horse, I won't be a part of your chosen lifestyle. My mother raised me to expect more out of life than to be some man's mistress. This entire seduction scene is pointless. I won't be yours."

For a moment her eyes held a hint of pleading in them as if she were begging him to let her go. If he had an ounce of humanity left in him, he might have done just that, but when it came to women, he chose not to be humane. He chose to seek out pleasure.

"You say you're appreciative, but you haven't shown me any gratitude. I can think of at least a dozen ways you can repay me, Ari," he countered with a smirk. "You know how this will end — you have to have figured it out by now. Why must you insist on fighting the inevitable?"

Her eyes widened before they narrowed.

"I don't know how many times or in how many ways I can say *no* to you, Mr. Palazzo. I will never be your employee, mistress or whore," she responded before spearing a piece of proscuitto-wrapped pear and forcing it into her mouth.

"Ah, Ari, you'd make a good whore. I think you're just holding out for more money. Fine. We'll make your salary two-hundred thousand," he mocked, knowing his comment would set her off.

Her face turned red; she glared at him and bit into a piece of artichoke, chomping down on it the way he was sure she'd like to be clamping down on his skin — and not in a pleasant way.

Then, her lips turned up in a smile, once again surprising him as she slowed her vicious chewing, looking at him thoughtfully. He couldn't wait to hear what came next from her plump pink lips.

"You know what, Mr. Palazzo, I think you're right. I could enjoy being a whore. Sex isn't nearly as horrible as I remember it," she said with a cool glance that started to send his heartbeat up. "I'll just never be yours," she finished as if she were talking about nothing more significant than the weather.

Rafe knew she was only trying to bait him, and it was working. The thought of her with another man sent fire pulsing through him. She was free to whore around all she wanted once he was done with her — but no man would touch what was his and right now she was, indeed, his.

"You do like to push buttons, don't you, Ari?" he asked as he signaled his staff to bring in the next course. "And don't you think it's past time you called me Rafe? After all, I've had my tongue

149

circling your nipples while you begged me for more."

He smiled as her face flamed red while soup was being set in front of her, and smiled while she looked down at her plate in horror, too embarrassed to meet his employees' eyes. She needed to learn that she couldn't win in a battle against him. He wouldn't allow it.

"What's the matter, Ari? You don't have any more witty comebacks?"

"Oh, I have plenty, *Mr. Palazzo*. I'm just not such a brash bastard as you are," she answered between clenched teeth.

He was suddenly moving around the table and lifting her from her chair before she even had time to blink. She looked at him with startled eyes and he felt her pulse quicken beneath his touch.

"I've warned you to be careful, Ari. I mean it. Do *not* call me names. I don't act so vulgar with you, and I expect the same courtesy," he threatened as his fingers gripped her hair and he held her head back, forcing her to look into his eyes.

"You don't act so vulgar? *Ha!* You just announced in front of your staff that you were upstairs with your mouth all over my body. That's as vulgar as it gets! Now, get your hands *off* me. I thought you said you didn't hurt women," she said.

Her bravado stayed in place, but he could sense the fear just beneath.

"I don't hurt women, Ari. Am I causing you pain?"

He looked into her eyes as she struggled against him. He had her held securely against him, with her head incapable of movement, but he knew he wasn't hurting her. She couldn't honestly say that he was.

"You're holding me against my will," she finally answered as she moved her hips against his in a failed attempt at escape.

"All you're doing in your struggles is rubbing that delectable body against mine, making me want to throw you over my shoulder and take you back to that nice comfortable bed. Is that what you want?"

"If you enjoy rape!"

"I've never had to force a woman, Ari, and I never will," he hummed as his mouth descended and he sucked on her neck, feeling her pulse. He felt her internal battle as she stiffened against him.

Knowing he could make her submit was enough of a victory that he released her. Slowly, he walked back to his seat, watching with satisfaction as she dropped back into her chair as if her knees were incapable of holding her up.

"You think you've won some small victory, but you haven't won anything. Obviously, you can cause a strange reaction in my body, but you have zero of my respect," she said with a determination that impressed him.

"I never asked for your respect, Ari. All I want is your body," he quickly responded, fascinated by the fire leaping to life in her eyes.

"Well, you can't have either," she muttered as she picked up her spoon and swirled it around her soup bowl.

No skirmishes disturbed the rest of the meal. With a ravenous appetite rising up all of a sudden, Rafe polished off most of his dinner, whereas she simply picked at hers. He watched as she kept darting glances at the clock. Knowing she wanted nothing more than to run away from him, he drew out the time, making her squirm in her seat.

After an hour, they sipped coffee and he debated seducing her again. He wouldn't mind taking her once more that night. He just didn't know whether it was the smartest move for him to make in their little game.

"Mr. Palazzo, your mother is on line two."

Well, that ended his debate. His family always came before any woman he was with, and even before his own pleasure.

"Thank you. Take Ms. Harlow back to her room, please."

"Yes, sir."

"I don't need to be taken back to my room. I'm ready to go home," Ari said as she stood.

"I've grown tired of arguing with you for the night. You'll stay here as the doctor ordered. Don't worry. I won't bother you again this evening," he said, letting her know the matter was closed to further discussion.

As he walked from the room, he heard her frustrated sigh, but he knew his staff would make sure that she went upstairs and didn't make any escape attempts.

*****

Ari woke the next morning to find a note on the nightstand. Relief flooded her when she read the words that released her from her luxurious prison. Rafe was allowing his assistant to take her home.

She didn't dare use his bathing facilities again, not wanting to get too used to the deluxe bath or shower. She knew she needed to get as far from Rafe as she possibly could before she did something stupid — such as agreeing to be his mistress.

With the feelings he aroused in her, she was afraid it would be entirely too easy to say *yes* to him. That would be suicide for her. She had a feeling women were never the same after being with Rafe for any amount of time.

The man inspired too much emotion — whether it was lust or hate. She couldn't imagine how a woman felt who was stupid enough to fall in love with him. One thing she realized, though, was the fact that sex needn't be a dreadful thing.

Rafe had made her feel things she definitely wanted to feel again and again. She would have to allow herself some time to date other men, because now that those doors had been opened, she didn't know if it was possible to shut them again. She really didn't think she *wanted* to shut them.

She gathered her purse and walked down the stairs, taking her time to look around his home on her way out. The curiosity irritated her, but she couldn't seem to stem it. Rafe had good taste in decorations and furniture, using bright colors and deep, rich-toned wood.

Not wanting to learn anything else about the man, Ari forced herself to head straight for the front door, where she was pleased to find a car waiting.

"I'm glad you're feeling better, Ms. Harlow."

"Thank you, Mr. Kinsor. I appreciate all the staff's taking such good care of me. I've never felt so pampered," she replied. She genuinely liked Rafe's right-hand man. True, the guy had known exactly what the position was that Rafe wanted to hire her for, and yet he hadn't warned her. But she could hardly expect him to sell out his employer.

"Do you need to make any stops before going home?"

Ari thought for a moment as he held open her door. She wouldn't feel up to leaving her house the rest of the day, and her head was already starting to throb a little. Why not take advantage of having a driver for a little while?

"If you're not in a huge hurry and wouldn't mind, could we stop by a drugstore?"

"Of course. I'm yours for as long as you need me. Mr. Palazzo was explicit in his directions to give you whatever you needed today," he answered happily as he shut the door and quickly went around to the driver's side.

Ari's confusion grew at Mr. Kinsor's words. Why did Rafe have to be so accommodating and kind one minute and then such a brute the next? Why couldn't he have been just a regular guy she'd met on Stanford's campus? She wished she could wipe him from her mind, but the more she ran into him, the more she wanted to know about this mysterious man who offered so much, but demanded more than she could bear to give.

"Just the drugstore will be fine. I need to get home and take care of things so I can be well enough to go to work tomorrow," she said when she realized she'd never responded to his last comment.

"OK. If you do change your mind, just let me know. Would you like to listen to music?"

"No thank you. I've got a headache. I'll just rest my eyes while we're driving. I'll feel better after taking a couple of ibuprofen."

Mr. Kinsor was silent as they pulled onto the road. At least they were in a comfortable car that cruised along quietly and without many bumps. It didn't take them long to stop by the pharmacy and then reach her home. Ari was suddenly struck by the thought that she would miss having other people around her. As she stepped into her apartment she realized how truly alone she was most of the time now.

Chapter Sixteen

"Rafe!"

Rafe braced for impact as his sister threw herself into his arms. A rare smile spread across his face as she held on tightly.

"How are you, Rachel?"

"I've missed you. It seems like years since I saw you last."

Rafe laughed at his baby sister's enthusiasm. She was eight years younger than he was and full of life, certainly the most vibrant young woman he'd ever known, and also one of the few females he had complete respect for. He adored both of his sisters.

"I saw you two months ago. Are you going to let me go now?"

"If you insist," she pouted as she released him. "Two months might as well be two years. Mom's a tyrant who never lets me do anything."

"You get away with far more than I'd let you get away with. You're too beautiful to be allowed out in public," he said, only half-teasing. He would slaughter any man who dared even look at his sister wrong. It was incongruous, he knew, that he was so protective of his sisters but so indifferent to the feelings and safety of other women.

"You drive your poor father and me crazy. I am hardly a tyrant, *peste*," said his mother, Rosabella, calling Rachel a brat in Italian. She approached Rafe and planted a kiss on his cheek. "How are you son? You have darker circles beneath your eyes than you had last time I saw you," she scolded.

"I'm wonderful, Mother, even better now that you're here. To what do I owe this surprise visit?"

"You sounded as if you were under more strain than usual the last time we spoke, so I told your father we must come and visit you immediately. It was about time for us to come back to California for a while, anyway. Your father grows restless in Italy if he's there for too long. I think he just misses working, though he's promised me he's retired."

"I'm all grown up now, Madre. I keep telling you that. You really don't have to worry so much about me. As for Dad, to tell the truth, I think he sneaks off to work when you're in the States. I do notice a lot of secret phone calls, and I don't think any woman is stupid enough to embark on an affair with the man."

"No, your father knows I would kill him if he ever tried something so foolish. And you tell me I don't need to worry about you? You're not a parent, obviously, or you'd never say something so ridiculous. A mother never stops worrying about her child, no matter how grown-up he insists he is. If only you would settle down and start a *famiglia*, my child, all of your stress would disappear and I'd get to see laugh lines around your beautiful eyes instead of worry lines on your brow."

"Mother," he warned, though his tone wasn't harsh.

"Don't you dare try to use your bossy tone with me," she scolded, before shifting into Italian and calling him a few choice names. He immediately backed down out of respect. No, he wouldn't fight his mother.

"If you start harassing our only boy, he'll change out his locks the next time he gets even a wisp of a hint that we're flying in to visit him — and he'll travel to another country far from here."

"Dad. It's great to see you." Rafe gave his father a hug, grateful for being rescued. They had been outnumbered from the day Rachel was born, giving his mother her second daughter. Rafe had been hoping for a little brother, but he'd been Rachel's slave from the very first time she'd gripped his finger in her infant hand. He adored Lia as well, but he'd been older when Rachel was born and was consequently more protective of her.

"Not that I want to join sides with your mother and sisters, but you do look a bit more ragged than normal, Rafe. Is everything OK?"

"Don't lump me in with Rachel. I think Rafe looks terrific," Lia said, jumping into the conversation.

He turned a grateful smile his sister's way. Lia was a stunning woman, only five years younger than he was. She'd been turning heads from the moment she'd hit puberty, and he'd thrown more punches over her than he could count. His friends had been told in no uncertain terms that they were to keep their hands off.

Times had been really tough when Shane had come home with him from college one Thanksgiving and Lia had decided she liked what she saw. Poor Shane had been between a rock and a hard place because he knew he couldn't come anywhere near Lia, but the girl had been determined. She was only fifteen at the time — young enough that she was certainly jailbait for Shane, but old enough that she was growing into her looks.

Luckily, Shane had kept his hands to himself, and therefore his and Rafe's friendship remained intact. Lia had made Shane sweat a few times when she'd come out to the pool in a skimpy bikini. Rafe still saw red when he thought about that. She was too naïve and trusting of men. She didn't realize how easily she could be taken advantage of.

"You know, you've always been my favorite, Lia," he said as he wrapped an arm around her shoulder.

"That was just mean, Rafe," Rachel pouted, her silver eyes sparkling as she punched him in the arm. Rafe laughed as he turned to Rachel.

"You're my other favorite, Rachel," he declared, and she instantly forgave him.

"Let me call the office and cancel my afternoon appointments. I'd much rather spend the day with you," Rafe told his family before turning toward the door.

"You don't need to do that, Rafe. We can entertain ourselves while you finish work," his dad insisted.

"The nice thing about being the boss is that I can do what I want," Rafe said with a wink before leaving the room.

He sat down with an affectionate smile on his face. His family was a bit like a tornado; they caused chaos all around them. But it was a happy mess. Being with them was the only thing that seemed to keep Rafe's humanity intact — if it weren't for them, he knew, he'd be more cold-blooded than a reptile. Sometimes he was anyway, especially when he'd been away too long from the world of his happier past.

He had to remind himself that he liked his life just the way it was. He just did not want the family his mother begged him to give her. Yes, he loved women, but not that way.

He would never shatter the rose-colored glasses his family wore — never allow them to see who he'd turned into, a man who conducted his love life like a business transaction. He particularly didn't want to break his mother's heart. But marriages like his parents shared weren't common. The majority of relationships ended tragically — like his marriage. "Happily ever after" was basically a myth, or a sick joke.

"OK, phone call's taken care of. Come with me and I'll show you my new baby," Rafe said as he walked into the room.

"If you had a baby to show Mom, she'd be far less grumpy, *and* she'd allow me out from under her lock and key a little more often," Rachel said with a mischievous smile.

Rafe felt like wiping the smirk off her face. He knew that his mother would now lay on the guilt with a trowel.

"While Rachel isn't kept prisoner, she *is* right in one thing. I would love some *bambini*," Rosabella stated as she placed her arm through Rafe's. "Just think of me, growing old and lonely, no little children to comfort me in my declining years…"

"Much as I hate to disappoint you, *madre mia*, I just cannot bring children into this world," Rafe said "I could never live up to your wonderful example. I'd be a miserable father to the poor creatures," he continued as he led his family outside.

"Poor *creatures*? OK, maybe you *are* better off not being a father," his dad said with a laugh.

"See, just listen to the man," Rafe told the others. "He's clearly the only one making any sense."

"You seem capable of listening only when someone is agreeing with you," Lia said as she darted ahead; she then turned around and approached him slowly, making faces at him the whole way.

No matter how old they grew, it seemed his sisters would forever act like teenagers. What surprised him was that he hoped they never stopped.

He would forever picture them with pigtails in their hair, running into the house to tell him about their latest adventure at school. And yet Lia was now twenty-six and Rachel was twenty-three. Time flew by so quickly.

"So, Rafe, what is this new toy you've acquired?"

"I think you'll be the most excited, Dad. We need to drive to the marina."

"Ah, you got a new boat. Didn't you just buy one last year?"

"Yes, and she'll always be precious to me, but I've got a new love. The latest way to entertain clients is on private yachts, so I decided to make an investment. The IRS is a little stingy, of course, about some deductions, but the new boat will still do more than pay for itself. But ultimately, she's really just an overpriced toy," he admitted.

"Ooh, Rafe, I can't wait. Are we going out today?" Lia asked as her eyes lit up.

"I've cleared my schedule and called the crew. We can take her for a spin — have dinner on the water."

"Have I told you lately that you're the absolute best brother ever?" Rachel said as she snuggled up to his side.

"Only every time you want something from me," he responded with a chuckle.

"Big brothers are supposed to spoil their sisters. It's in the rule book."

"Yeah, the rule book that you wrote when you were five."

The family climbed into Rafe's Porsche Cayenne and he cut quickly through traffic, eager to see his family's reaction to his newest pride and joy.

"Why do you always buy all of these expensive items?" his mother asked.

"I work incredibly hard, and therefore reward myself. It makes me happy."

The thought of what made him happy brought Ari to the forefront of his mind. The longer it took for her to realize their inevitable affair would happen, the more irritated he became.

"You've always wanted things instantly, Rafe. You know that poster that says 'he who has the most toys when he dies — wins' isn't true, right?"

"This from the girl who owns at least a hundred pairs of Jimmy Choo shoes, Rachel?" Rafe remarked with a raise of his brow.

"You can never own too many shoes."

The ride went silently as Rafe's thoughts returned to Ari. It had been a week since Mario had taken her home; Rafe hadn't spoken to her since. He'd allowed some time to pass for her to see reason, or for his interest to wane. But neither was happening, which meant it was about time for him to hunt her down.

They pulled into the exclusive marina, and he moved around to the back, where his vessel was parked at a huge dock. The gleaming white vessel was two hundred and fifty feet long and put every other liner then in the marina to shame.

Rafe took pride in owning only the best. Yes, there were other boats out there bigger and more luxurious, but this baby was exactly what he wanted. Not too large to keep him from going where he wanted near to home, but large enough to offer all the comforts for longer adventures.

"Is that it?" Lia asked in awe.

"Yes. That's my girl," he answered with pride.

"You sure you couldn't have gotten one a bit bigger?" his father asked with sarcasm. The smile on his face eliminated the sting of his words.

"Ha, Father, I think that's a little like calling the kettle black. Your personal jet puts my own to shame. Who do you think taught me to like only the best?"

His father winked at him before returning his attention to the boat.

Rafe's father had always been a very wealthy man, but his mother had insisted on not spoiling the children. When they spent their time in Italy, they lived in a modest home, one that was very comfortable, but not grand or showy. In the States, however, they'd had a mansion. When it had burned down a few years ago, his father had been devastated. Now, he was rebuilding, but even having all the money in the world didn't make it an easy task to recreate a hundred-year-old home.

His father had inherited it from his parents before his marriage, and that was the only reason Rafe's mother had allowed them to live in such luxury. She often said a wealthy man was a conceited man — she just made an exception for Martin. She loved him particularly because of his generous heart, his incredible charity to the poor.

As Rafe reflected on his upbringing, he knew he wouldn't want to see the heartbroken look on his

mother's face if she knew some of the things he did
with his life. But he quickly pushed the thought
aside. His parents were good people, but his mother
was naïve about the way the world worked. So he'd
kept much from her after his divorce, and he would
continue keeping most of his private life hidden
from his family.

"Rafe, I think it's time you come home for a
while. All of this money you have is making you too
egocentric. You need to remember your roots," his
mother scolded, confirming his thoughts.

"Mom, I will always appreciate our home in
Italy. It's where I go when the world starts closing
in on me. However, don't you pretend we were
peasants. Dad came in and swept you off your feet,
then flew you around the world. I wouldn't say I
grew up impoverished," he retorted as he bent down
and kissed her cheek.

"You watch your tongue, Raffaello Palazzo," his
mother warned.

"I'm sorry, Mother."

"All is forgiven, you wretched boy. Now, give
us a tour of your new toy."

"Is that a helicopter?" Rachel asked as she
looked to the back of the vessel.

"Yes. If I'm out and there's an emergency, I
need to be able to get back to the offices quickly."

"Ooh, can we go for a ride in that?" Lia asked.
She loved flying more than any of the rest of them.

"Next time I'll have my pilot take you for a spin.
I can take only today off, though, so I'd rather hear
all about what you've been up to lately than send
you into the clouds."

Although Rafe often called home, he cherished most his visits with his family. Whether his mother knew it or not, being with them did, indeed, humble him. Too bad he easily forgot those feelings once his visits were over, he told himself ruefully. His best friend got on his case about that all the time.

"As I was saying about my yacht, she's two hundred and fifty feet long, has a twin-engine format, over three thousand horsepower, and can travel up to sixteen knots an hour."

"Stop! Stop! I don't want to hear any more!" Lia cried.

Rafe laughed. "I know, I know, that stuff is boring, so you shouldn't worry your pretty little heads about it." He laughed again when his sisters stuck their tongues out at him. "You'll be happy to hear that she has six comfortable guest cabins, each with its own private bath, a game room that will make you very happy, Lia, a swimming pool, patio bar, conference rooms —though that won't interest you — and a formal dining area."

"What about a spa?" Rachel asked mockingly.

"Actually, I did include a small spa with full-time staff so you can get your hands and feet done, and then finish off with a massage."

"Oh, Rafe, I may never leave this ship," Lia said as she jogged ahead of him up the plank.

"I may just leave her with you."

"My heart couldn't take it, Mother," he said as he clutched his chest.

"It would serve you right," his father added.

"I thought I was always a good son," Rafe said as he trailed after his sisters.

"You were a wonderful boy. Now, however, I have concerns about the *man* who's before me. If only you would settle down, I could stop worrying," his mother responded.

"Mom, I'm happy. Let's just leave it at that," he answered, hoping the subject would be dropped.

"I worry about you being lonely. Your ex-wife did you great injury, son, and I don't want you afraid to try again. You need a woman in your life to take care of you."

"I'm doing just fine, Mother. I have had a number of female companions through the years," he said in self-defense.

"None that I would be proud for you to bring home. They are more like perfect mannequins, their only thoughts seeming to be how to please you."

"Is there not a more perfect woman that one whose only desire is to fulfill my every need?" he asked. If his mother knew what he really meant by that statement, he had a feeling she'd shove him overboard.

"Rafe…"

"I'm seeing a nice woman, mother. Her name is Arianna." Rafe was stunned when the words spilled from his mouth. What was he doing? First of all, Ari wasn't really with him, and secondly, he didn't want to pique his mother's interest. He just wanted her to cease her relentless pestering about his being single.

"How long have you been seeing this woman, and why haven't you said anything about her yet?" she asked with suspicion.

"It's a new relationship and I don't want to scare her off with your talk of marriage and babies," he quickly answered, hoping she'd let it go.

Rafe missed the look between his sisters, who were now on instant alert to find out about his mystery woman. He never would have opened his mouth if he'd known how much chaos his ten little words would later cause him.

Chapter Seventeen

"We've decided to stay for a week or two. Your mother and I haven't spent enough time in California the last few years and your sisters are dying to go for another spin on the new boat. I'm starting to think it's time to spend more of our time over here."

Rafe turned almost in horror at his father's words. He was instantly suspicious. His family had grilled him the night before about Ari. They'd wanted to know who she was, how long he'd been dating her, what her family was like. The list went on and on. Rafe had a bad feeling that their impromptu extended stay had more to do with Ari than his new boat.

It didn't matter what his family's reasoning was. If they wanted to extend their visit, that was fine with him. He'd just have to be on his toes and make sure he didn't slip up about anything else.

He had a lot of work to accomplish over the week, so he wouldn't be able to spend a lot of time with them, anyway. He'd just alert his crew that the ship was at their disposal as well as any of his other possessions — his staff pretty much knew that, though.

"It will be nice to see more of you. I will warn you that I'll be very busy this week. We're going into a major merger and I'll most likely be working fourteen-hour days," he said, hoping to head them off.

"Not a problem, son. I remember those days of working too many hours. Thankfully, now I get to spend my days with your beautiful mother instead. We're taking off for Ireland after we leave here. I haven't been there in years and this time of year is a good time to go. I could use some decent beer."

"Well, my house is yours, along with all the vehicles. I'm leaving for the office now, but you can call my assistant if you need to reach me. Please don't tell her it's an emergency again just because you can't find a certain bottle of wine," Rafe warned.

"That was only one time, Rafe — and it *was* our anniversary. We've had the same wine on that anniversary for the past twenty years. In my book, that does constitute an emergency," his father answered in all seriousness.

"All right. If I don't see you tonight, I'll try to get home a bit early tomorrow."

With those words, Rafe walked out the door and took a deep breath as he climbed into his vehicle. His family was wonderful, but overwhelming. It would be good to get back into the offices where he was the one in control.

*****

"I can't believe how hard it was to track down this girl!" Lia said with frustration.

"Well, we finally did it, so relax, sis. Rafe's obviously into her, so I want to know why. I had to practically sit on Shane's lap to get the information. It was fun to watch him sweat — especially when you walked in the room while I was hanging all over him. I've never seen Shane turn red before. That was entertaining," Rachel answered with a giggle.

"Nothing is going on between Shane and me. Even if I did like him, *which I don't*, it's not like Rafe would ever allow anything to happen. He still treats me as if I'm five instead of twenty-six." Lia huffed.

"I think you should just sneak into Shane's room one of these days and jump his bones. It's obvious you've been in love with him since you were fifteen."

"Focus, Rachel. We need to get to the beach and ambush Ari. Her office buddies guaranteed that they'd get her down there today. It was surprisingly easy to bribe them. They said she really needs to get laid. I found it interesting that big brother doesn't have her chained to his bed if he's so into her."

"Maybe he's into her, but she doesn't like him," Lia said before both girls erupted into laughter.

"Seriously, if there's a woman out there smart enough to resist Rafe's charm, she is definitely a keeper. I really hope that's the case. Let's get our detective gloves on."

"I like nothing better than a good mystery."

Rafe's sisters jumped into his Mercedes convertible and immediately put the top down. It was a beautiful seventy-degree day; they were looking forward to playing at Stinson Beach, and *really* looking forward to meeting the woman who seemed to be tying their big brother up in knots.

They hadn't liked any of his mistresses they'd met previously, and they'd hated his ex-wife, but a woman he wanted to hide from them had their curiosity piqued. It would be a great afternoon.

"Have we worked out the plan, yet?" Rachel asked as they stopped at a light. It was nearly impossible to hear anything over the wind while they drove.

"I have no clue. First step was in finding the girl. We're going to have to assess the situation and think quick on our feet once we're down there."

"A challenge. You know, I always enjoy that."

"Yes, because you're a meddling brat, Rachel."

"Aren't you the touchy one. Did you have a bad night? Were you just a tad upset that I was sitting on your boyfriend's lap? You know I don't want Shane. I've known he was all yours from the first day he walked in the room and you practically tripped on your bottom lip."

"I'm not in love with Shane!"

"Oh my gosh, Lia. Give it a rest. I know about the hotel incident," Rachel told her with a wicked smile.

"How do you know about that?"

"Like you're the only one who knows how to get information. I've had the employees spying for me forever. I know some things about big brother, too. If you spill the dirt about you and Shane, then I just might tell you," Rachel gloated.

Lia glared at her sister for a moment before turning her eyes back to the road. The rest of the trip to the beach went in silence while Rachel gloated and Lia pouted. Lia was dying to find out what her little sister knew.

*****

"I can't believe you talked me into this. I have so much I could be getting done this weekend. After the incident a couple weeks ago at the bar, I really shouldn't trust you guys to take me anywhere," Ari grumbled as she climbed from Amber's minivan.

"Quit being such a grump. It's a stunning day. You really need to get some color on your blindingly white skin, and we all need fun," Shelly said.

"You'll have to forgive us someday, Ari. How were we supposed to know that the hot waiter would slip you a roofie? We just thought that he was really into you. If anyone needs to have a hot night of sex, it's you. I've never seen anyone with such a stiff neck," Miley joined in.

"OK, OK. I'll drop it if you never bring up that sicko Chandler again. I can't believe he was only in jail a couple days. What is the world coming to? I'll certainly be a lot more careful about what I drink from now on," Ari grumbled as she felt her face turn red.

Her friends had no clue at all about her night with Rafe — her very hot, very exciting night. She still got goosebumps when she recalled his touch. Ari knew she was tense. It seemed that he'd opened a floodgate of hormones inside her, and she was too chicken to pursue a guy to fill her raging needs.

She really wanted to experience another night like the one with Rafe. She just didn't want to have another night with him — well, she did, but she was smart enough not to.

"Ooh, twelve o'clock. Let's go watch some beach volleyball," Amber said while practically drooling.

The three other women turned in unison, then stood with their mouths gaping open. There were some seriously sexy men wearing nothing but beach shorts and sweat, and playing a fast game of volleyball.

"There's an open spot not far from the net with a perfect view," Shelly pointed out as she began rapidly moving to a small gap in the crowds on the sand nearby. After a moment's pause the other three women hurried behind her.

"Don't be a prude, Ari. Drop the shrug and flaunt your killer breasts. You want those hot guys to notice you, don't you?" Miley asked as she grabbed the knot on the back of Ari's neck.

Before she could stop her friend, Ari was sitting on her towel with nothing on but the bikini top Amber had lent her and a skimpy pair of shorts. She felt naked as she looked around self-consciously, convinced everyone would be staring at her in horror.

"We'd better get this lotion on you before you turn into a lobster. You need some color, not a wicked sunburn," Shelly announced as she squirted some of the ice-cold liquid onto Ari's neck, instantly sending shivers down her spine.

"Thanks for warming it first, Shelly," Ari snapped as the woman rubbed in the lotion.

"Quit complaining. I'm saving you days of pain right now."

"You wouldn't have to if you hadn't ripped off my protection."

"Oh, honey, you never want to rip off the protection," Miley said with an evil grin.

"I can't believe your husbands ever allow you girls to leave the house. You're terrible."

"Our husbands know we love them more than anything, for some unknown reason. We can look plenty just as long as we don't touch. Trust me, girl, our men don't pass up the opportunity to check out a nice firm ass when it walks in front of them," Amber said as she lay back and closed her eyes.

"You're missing the show," Miley complained as she nudged Amber.

"I know, but Sean was sick last night and I got hardly any sleep. I can stare at hunky guys anytime, but a nap is something I rarely ever get the pleasure to indulge in."

"Ooh, I like your thinking," Shelly said as she lay down next.

Pretty soon Ari found herself the only one conscious as her friends dozed and soaked up the rays. She'd been sitting in the office all week and had energy to burn. More sitting around for the entire time they were on the beach just didn't appeal.

And as good-looking as the men were who kept walking past, the idea of spending the day staring at them nonstop didn't thrill her, either. Maybe she'd attempt to take a swim. The ocean would be cold, sure, but once she got used to it, she could get in a decent workout.

She stood and began moving toward the water when a couple of women stopped her.

"Hey, we need another person for volleyball. Can you join us?"

Ari turned to politely refuse when one of the women grabbed her hand and started dragging her toward the now empty volleyball court.

"Hi. I'm Lia and this is my sister, Rachel. Thanks for joining us."

"Um…I'm really not very good at volleyball," Ari said as she tried tugging her hand away.

"That's OK. You don't have to be good. We just need a full team. What's your name?"

"Ari."

"Pretty name. It's a beautiful day, isn't it?"

"Yes. I was thinking about taking a swim, getting some exercise after being cooped up in the office all week," Ari said, trying again to get out of the game without hurting any feelings.

"Oh, that water is freezing. Besides, a couple of rounds of sand volleyball and you'll be begging for mercy. It's great exercise, especially for the thighs. They'll be burning by the time we're finished."

"I guess I can give it a go, but when you find out how horrible I am, you'll want to find a new player," Ari warned.

She had no clue that she was with Rafe's sisters and that they couldn't care less about her volleyball skills. They wanted to find out all the information about her that they could.

"We found another player. We're ready," Lia said as she bounced onto the court.

"Nice. You girls ready to lose?"

"I wouldn't count on it, slim. We're pretty feisty," Rachel countered as she got into position in front of the net.

There were six of them all together, and Ari felt better when she saw some of the other bikinis the women were wearing. Their outfits made her bikini top and shorts look downright modest. One of the women was barely keeping her large breasts contained, and Ari suspected that the large orbs were going to pop out at least once during the game.

"Heads up!"

Ari turned, but not quickly enough to avoid the spinning ball that smacked her right in the forehead. Going down about as ungracefully as she possibly could, she groaned as a pair of strong calves stepped into her vision.

"I'm so sorry. Are you OK?"

"I'm fine. I think my pride is the only thing that got wounded."

"Let me help you." Before Ari could refuse, the man reached beneath her arms and lifted her into the air, letting her body slide down his before her feet touched the ground again. "I'll make sure to be more careful," he said with a wink.

Ari was shocked speechless as she realized he was flirting with her. She didn't know what to say back. He was stunning, in a beach-bum, bleached-blond kind of way, but there were no sparks flying.

Who cares? she thought. She had just been moaning and groaning about sexual frustration and here was a hot, red-blooded male practically groping her.

Before she could decide one way or the other whether to flirt back, Rachel came running up.

"Oh, Ari. Are you all right?"

"I'm fine."

"Good; let's play." Rachel dragged her away from the too tanned man, and Ari forgot about him as the game started.

Half an hour later, Ari was feeling good. She was certainly working up a sweat, and she was laughing so much her stomach hurt. Lia and Rachel were right about the sore legs, though — she could already feel a slight burning in her thighs.

"We need a break," Rachel said as she grabbed the ball and jogged over to a water cooler. Ari was right on her heels. She needed a large swallow or three of cold liquid.

"See? It's a lot of fun, huh?" Lia said as she handed Ari a water bottle.

"I have to admit that it is. I haven't enjoyed an afternoon so much in a long while. I may have to come back next weekend and try this again," she answered with a bright smile.

"I'll meet you here. You're a lot better than you said you'd be," Rachel piped in.

"It's been so long since I played that I really didn't think I'd be any good," Ari admitted.

"Time out's over, ladies. Well, unless you want me to massage your sore muscles."

Ari turned and was surprised to find one of the other guys gazing directly at her. She was even more stunned when he nodded her way. What was going on? Maybe it was the bright red bikini top that was giving them the wrong impression. Before she could say a word, Lia grabbed her hand.

"We're just fine, John. Quit trying to unnerve us by flirting. We're not that naïve," she said as she tugged Ari back onto the court. Ari was mortified. What if that's why they were flirting? It made more sense — she certainly couldn't see herself as a sex magnet.

"Oh, that wasn't game-playing. How about I take you ladies out for a drink after the game?" he offered, soothing her ego.

"Can't. We have dinner plans, but thanks anyway," Rachel said. She then addressed Ari.

"You should come with us tonight. We're having a late dinner on my brother's boat. The thing is absolute heaven to ride on, and there's even a small spa onboard so you can get a massage. Your legs are going to need it."

Ari didn't know how to respond. These women were strangers. She really should decline the invitation graciously and return to the safety of her friends, but she found herself unable to say no.

She'd never been on a boat before and it sounded like a lot of fun.

One thing she'd discovered since starting her job and getting away from the college campus was that people in general were a lot more friendly than she'd ever thought. She had a cell phone if anything came up. She couldn't imagine that the two were secret serial killers.

"I promise we're not planning on chopping you up and tossing you in the ocean. We just don't get to San Fran very often, so we try to make friends fast," Rachel said as she crossed her heart.

If it was a bad idea to go, Ari would get a feeling deep in her gut, wouldn't she? Besides, she was sick of always playing it safe.

"Where are you girls from, if not from here?"

"We spent our childhood between here and Italy. Our dad's American, our mom, Italian, so they compromised. Six months in Italy and six months in the U.S. The last few years we've been in Italy a lot more, though. I just finished with college over there, so freedom is mine now. I think my parents are going to dump us off on my brother and go travel the world."

Ari was puzzled. They looked over twenty-one, certainly over eighteen, so why did they need to have someone take care of them? Was something wrong — like maybe a mental disorder? It would hardly do to pry, however.

"I see you look confused, Ari. It's OK. When you meet our father, you'll understand. I'm twenty-six, and Rachel is twenty-three, but to our dad, we're still twelve. Our big brother pretty much feels the same way. I've moved a few times, but then Dad either has security on my butt or he and my mother decide to vacation where I'm living. Plus, my brother has chased away about every guy I've ever even thought about dating. If I didn't love all my family so much, I think I'd hate them a little. The bottom line is, if I truly wanted to make a change in my life, they'd let me. They may not like it, but I know they love me enough to let me go. They'd just secretly stash a tracking device in my bag," she said with a laugh.

"Wow. I thought my mom was overprotective."

"Oh, Ari. My family has *overprotective* down to a science. They are amazing, though, truly amazing. You have to come with us and meet my mom. I'll try to get her mad and then she'll start swearing in Italian. It's good entertainment."

Ari couldn't help herself. She was growing very fond of these two bubbly girls. How could she not when they talked a mile a minute and smiled constantly? She felt safe in accepting their dinner invitation.

"Sure, I'll come to dinner with you. It sounds like fun. I'll let my friends know after the game is over," Ari agreed.

They played volleyball for another hour before Ari decided she needed a quick dip. She was burning up and had a bad feeling she'd sweated off most of her sunblock. Worse, she could feel a bit of an ache in her shoulders. She'd probably pay all week for her impromptu beach visit. But ultimately she didn't care — it would be worth it because she was having a lot of fun.

After introducing the sisters to her friends and explaining exactly where she was going, she hopped in the car with the two women and enjoyed the breeze blowing through her hair as they made their way to the harbor.

When they pulled up to the marina and approached the boat, Ari was stunned. She'd expected a large vessel because the girls had talked about a massage room, but she wasn't ready for what was floating in the water before her. It seemed to take up the entire dock.

"We'd better hurry. We're really late. My brother hates it when we keep him waiting," Lia said.

"Is he going to have a problem with your inviting a stranger aboard?" Ari asked, suddenly nervous. She wasn't used to hanging around people with the kind of money it took to own a boat like this one.

"He won't mind at all," Rachel said as if she were privy to her own inside joke.

The three of them climbed aboard, then turned around and watched as the crew pulled in the plank, and the boat began moving.

"We really *are* the last to arrive. Rafe's going to kill us," Rachel said, though she didn't seem too worried.

Ari turned toward the girl, her body suddenly stiff as the boat began moving out into the water. She could still make it back to shore if she jumped now.

"What is your brother's name?" Ari asked, her voice barely audible over the sound of the motor.

"Rafe Palazzo. Do you know him?"

Chapter Eighteen

Ari began to feel light-headed and, leaning against the rail, she forced herself to inhale deep breaths of air. She turned to look as the mammoth vessel moved farther and farther from land, and she tried to gauge the swimming distance. Should she jump? she wondered. And she did jump, very slightly, when Rafe spoke.

"I see you girls are late, as usual. We've been waiting on you for an hour now."

"Oh, Rafe. We were playing a very intense game of volleyball. Plus, we met a new friend and had to bring her along," Rachel said.

Ari couldn't move. She in no way wanted to turn around and see his face. She hadn't seen him since that night almost two weeks ago. If she could force herself to move, she really would abandon ship. What had she gotten herself into?

"Welcome aboard…" Rafe began saying, then suddenly stopped. Ari could sense he'd figured out who she was. Maybe he recognized the stiff set to her shoulders. Everything in her told her to just jump and get it over with, but she managed to plaster a fake smile on her face and turn woodenly around to meet Rafe's gaze.

Everyone was silent as the eyes of the two clashed — his narrowing, hers widening. Time had done nothing to lessen the man's incredible appeal. In a suit he was gorgeous. In a skin-tight polo and attractive shorts, he was devastating.

"Ari. What a coincidence that my sisters happened to run into you today," Rafe said after a few tense moments of utter silence.

"This is *your* Ari!" Lia gasped far too dramatically. Rafe sent a glance in her direction leaving no doubt to any of them that he wasn't fooled.

"I'm not *his* Ari." She finally found her voice and directed an incredulous stare at both Lia and Rachel before turning to face Rafe.

"That's to be determined," Rafe said as he took her arm. "You didn't protect your skin. We need to get ointment on it right away or you'll be miserable by the time you lie down tonight."

He led her away, leaving his sisters behind. They were around a corner before Ari thought to protest and began tugging her arm. The pressure caused the flesh beneath her skin to absorb an intense burning sensation. She really *had* gotten too much sun. As she looked at her throbbing arm, she realized she was walking next to him in only her skimpy bikini top and shorts. She must have dropped her bag back on the deck. She felt far too exposed.

Then it hit her: the women had spoken of *his* Ari. That meant he'd said something about her before she met his sisters. Puzzle pieces started coming together. It had been no coincidence that they'd found her on the beach. Why, oh why did she have to be so naïve? Of course she wasn't just going to meet great people who wanted to whisk her away for a moonlit dinner on a massive yacht.

"You can release me anytime," Ari snapped as she tugged again, ignoring the searing pain, and too irritated by the turn of events to keep her tone light.

"I don't think so. I saw the look on your face at the railing. You might just be stupid enough to jump overboard."

Ari knew they were way too far from shore now for her to swim back. She wasn't suicidal — just desperate to get away from Rafe. She really hoped his meddling sisters had extra clothes on board.

"I won't deny that the thought crossed my mind once I discovered this was *your* boat. However, I realize we're too far out now. The gentlemanly thing for you to do would be to turn the boat around and drop me off back at the dock," she said in her haughtiest voice.

Rafe stopped and backed her against the wall. He bent his knees, aligning their bodies so his chest pressed against her breasts as his eyes devoured her face.

"Since when have I ever claimed to be a gentleman, Ari?" he asked with a seductive smile.

"I refuse to play games with you, Mr. Palazzo." She paused as a new thought occurred. What if it hadn't been his sisters' meddling? What if he'd actually planned the whole thing?

"Did you send your sisters out to bring me here?"

"No. I would rather keep you far away from my family. However, I can't say I'm disappointed to see you. I've been thinking about our evening together and I would love a repeat performance. By the quickening of your breath, and the way your nipples are hardening against my chest, I'd say you wouldn't mind another opportunity yourself," he said with utmost confidence.

Ari hated how right he was. She'd been dreaming about Rafe for two months, and the dreams had only become more erotic since she'd actually shared his bed. She'd like nothing more than for him to sink deep inside her again. She just wasn't prepared to deal with the self-loathing when he treated her like a whore afterward.

"True, my body responds to you, but that doesn't mean I *want* you. I'd rather sleep with a stranger from the beach than have your hands on me again," she bluffed.

"Liar," he whispered as his head descended and he ran his tongue along the soft skin of her neck. Ari barely managed to hold the sigh in. If only he weren't so appealing!

"I'm cold, Mr. Palazzo. Could you please allow me to use a guest room to shower and change? I don't have anything with me and I would greatly appreciate it if there were some clothes I could borrow," she said through gritted teeth. It was taking all her concentration to control her breathing as his tongue circled her reddened skin. The way he touched her made her forget all about the rapidly worsening sunburn.

"Mmm, you taste salty. I'd be glad to help you clean up," he offered as he moved back and started walking through the halls of the boat again.

"I can clean up just fine on my own," she said as he led her up a set of stairs. His laughter was her only answer.

Soon, he was pushing open a large door and leading her inside a spacious room. She looked over the couch and two chairs set around a modern cherry table. Original paintings adorned the walls, with special lighting to bring out the colors and textures of the artwork. The room as a whole was remarkably decorated with an arresting mixture of dark and light.

"Go through that door on the right. I'll have some clothes brought in — unless you want to change your mind on my offer to help you."

"I'm fine," Ari said as she raced away from him and went through the door. She was in a decent-sized room with a couch and mirrors and a couple of side tables. Another door was to her right and she walked through, happy to find a full-size walk-in shower.

A large tub sat in the corner, but she didn't dare take a bath. She was going to clean off as quickly as possible and pray there were clothes waiting for her in the dressing area when she was finished.

When the strong spray hit her skin, Ari jumped back. Yes, she was definitely sunburned, and the water wasn't helping in the least. She turned the pressure down low and adjusted the temperature to barely above warm. Even that now felt like a scalding hot shower, but any cooler and her muscles would freeze up.

She suffered through the shower, carefully washing her body as best she could; it was a relief, at least that her skin was free of the stinging sand and salt water. Once she was finished, she stepped out, grabbed a soft towel and wrapped it around her body before cracking the door open and peeking into the dressing room.

Relief filled her when she saw a set of clothes sitting on the counter, and no sign of Rafe. If he really tried seducing her again, she was sure she'd cave in record time. Her body was humming with need from their brief hallway encounter, and knowing he wasn't far away was making her desire flame hotter.

When she picked up a silky blue dress and an incredibly skimpy black lace thong, she felt her face heat. The dress would barely cover more than her swimsuit had. He was intentionally tormenting her. When she discovered no bra among the garments, she glared at the closed door, wishing thoughts could kill. If they could, Rafe would have been sinking down, down, down into the ocean depths.

She walked back in the bathroom and rinsed out her bikini top, then returned to the dressing area, found a hair dryer and dried it before putting the uncomfortable thing back on. With a gasp of disbelief, she slipped on the panties — no more than a scrap of material that barely covered her "lady parts" — and pulled the sundress over her head.

The soft fabric barely reached mid-thigh, but the dress was surprisingly comfortable; the cool material felt wonderful against her heated skin. The longer she was out of the sun, the more painful grew the burn covering most of her body. The next few days weren't going to be pleasant.

She actually smiled when she found a bottle of pricey lotion with aloe in it. Quickly stripping down again, she began coating her skin with it. The cool cream felt heavenly as she spread it across her arms and neck and then her legs. She couldn't reach all of her back, but she managed to cover enough of her skin to send relief coursing through her.

She'd at least make it through the uncomfortable dinner that loomed. Rafe, she was sure, wouldn't miss an opportunity to make her squirm. She'd try not to give him the satisfaction of showing that she felt out of place.

"I was beginning to think you weren't coming out."

Ari jumped at the sound of Rafe's smooth and cultured voice. She hadn't expected him to wait for her, not when his family was aboard the ship.

"You didn't need to stay here. I'm sure I would have been able to find the dining area," she said as she approached him.

"I wouldn't be so rude as to leave my guest all alone."

"I'm not your guest, Mr. Palazzo. I simply got railroaded into being here. I'll make the best of it, but rest assured, spending the evening in your presence will be about as pleasant for me as having a root canal would."

He slowly began inching toward her with a predatory air. She wanted to make a hasty retreat, but she refused to show him signs of weakness. That would be like baring her open neck to a lion.

"I've tired of your calling me Mr. Palazzo, Ari. You will either call me by my name or I'll find very enjoyable ways to torture you in front of my family. The choice is yours," he said as he stopped with his chest just brushing across her swelling nipples. The dress he'd given her hid nothing from his view, and he smirked at her reaction to him.

Ari would have loved to call his bluff, but what if he actually followed through? She didn't think he'd do anything outrageous, especially with witnesses, but for all she knew, his entire family was twisted. Maybe they liked to sacrifice young women at sea by throwing their bodies to the sharks.

"What? No sarcastic comeback, Ari. That's unlike you," he teased as his fingers ran through the natural curls of her hair. The slight tremor that raced down her spine was a clear giveaway of how much he was affecting her, but no matter how much she scolded herself, she couldn't control her hormones. She could hate him for the way he made her feel, but she couldn't stop desiring him.

"I'm very hungry, if you wouldn't mind taking me to the dining room," Ari spoke just above a whisper, avoiding calling him by any name at all.

"I wouldn't want to keep you waiting," he answered as he slipped her arm through his. She knew resisting him would be to no avail, so she forced herself to relax as she walked beside him, out the same door they'd come in.

At least when the two of them were around other people, she wouldn't have to battle him — and herself. If she could understand how she could hate the man while still desiring him, she'd be able to make millions. Women in droves would pay her for the secret.

"How was your shower?"

"Not too pleasant. You have a beautiful bathroom, but I did get too much sun today. The water felt like tiny knives cutting into my skin. However, the lotion on the counter worked wonders. I don't know what magic ingredient is in it, but I feel almost back to normal."

"After dinner, I'd be glad to rub it all over your body. I'll make sure to reach those hard-to-get-to places."

The soft purring sound of his voice caused her stomach to drop right from her body. Her legs were nothing but gelatin, and the fires of hell seemed to be heating her core. How could she possibly think she'd be safe in the presence of others? The man could whisper a single word and melt her, or brush against her with the lightest of touches and make her putty in his hands.

Maybe she would take her chances with the sharks. At the moment, a shark seemed the less dangerous creature.

Chapter Nineteen

Rafe should have been furious with his sisters, but he was too pleased to have Ari's arm wrapped in his and the soft curve of her breast pressing against his bicep. Even knowing it was more than a desire to break her spirit — knowing he was intrigued by her — he continued his pursuit. Ignoring his intuition, he chose to enjoy Ari.

"You have a nice boat."

Ari's compliment filled him with warmth he'd rather not feel. He thought about making a sarcastic reply, but instead something held him back.

"Thank you. Right this way," he said as he opened a door that led into his ornate dining area. A large table was centered in the room with enough seating for twenty. In addition, another seating area was to the right, where his family was chattering in a lively fashion while having predinner drinks.

"We were beginning to think you were never going to show," his father said as he stood. "Who's your beautiful companion?"

"Father, this is Ari. It seems the girls found her at the beach today and invited her aboard," Rafe replied as he sent his sisters a stern look. They actually had the decency to glance away, knowing they were busted.

"We needed an extra person for volleyball and ran into Ari. We had no idea she was the same girl as Rafe's…*friend*," Rachel said with an innocent smile.

"What a happy coincidence," Rafe replied with mockery.

"Ari, it's so good to meet you. My son seems to be quite fond of you," his mother said in her slight Italian accent. It had lessened over the years as she spent more and more time with his father in the States.

Rosabella stepped forward and took Ari's hands, then leaned in and kissed her cheek, causing Ari to blush slightly at the warm greeting.

"It's nice to meet you too, Mrs. Palazzo."

"Oh, darling, please call me Rosabella," Rafe's mother insisted.

"Thank you, Rosabella. You have wonderful daughters. I had a very pleasant day with them. I've also never been on a large boat like this before, and it's quite the treat."

Rafe noticed that Ari had no trouble calling his mother by her first name.

"My ornery son hasn't brought you aboard yet? Well, I'll just have to speak to him about his

manners. The yacht is a nice escape. I'm thinking
my husband and I need one of our own so we can
take off for a few months. I could get used to sailing
the high seas," Rosabella said with a delighted
laugh.

"I will order one tomorrow, dear, and whisk you
away to the far corners of the world," his father said
as he leaned down and gently kissed his wife.

Watching the obvious love between his parents
always pleased Rafe. If only he hadn't seen so much
devastation in other relationships…

Lia spoke up. "Mom, you guys are getting all
mushy again and embarrassing Rafe's guest."

Another blush stole over Ari's cheeks. "Don't
mind me at all," she murmured.

"I don't know about the rest of you, but I'm
starving. That volleyball game really sapped my
strength," Rachel said, saving them from the slightly
awkward moment.

"I'll second that emotion," Lia piped in.

"Yes, Ari was saying she was quite hungry
herself. You must have played a strenuous game. I
may have to join you next time," Rafe said as he
looked down into Ari's eyes, which widened in a bit
of panic. *She's really cute when she's … off guard*,
Rafe told himself. *No, not cute, but sexy as sin. I've
been giving her too much space.*

"A couple of our opponents sure wanted to
whisk *Ari* off to the high seas," Rachel said with a
mischievous grin at Rafe. He glared at his little
sister before turning to Ari, who was looking at
Rachel in horror.

"Really? Do tell," Rafe commanded.

"Oh, I think it was the red bikini. She looked hot with a capital *H*. The guys were tripping over themselves to offer her drinks and help her up when she fell, and then, of course, there was a dinner-and-drinks invitation. We were a little tempted to accept and tag along just to watch the show, but the boat was calling our names," Lia answered.

Neither of his sisters was fooling him. He knew exactly what they were doing. Knowing didn't matter, though. The thought of these unknown men flirting with Ari was causing a low burn in his gut. He needed to brand her — let the world know she wasn't up for grabs. And he had to do it soon.

"I need to speak to the captain. Why doesn't everyone get seated? I'll ask that dinner be served immediately," Rafe snapped as he walked from the room.

He decided right then that they were staying out for the night. His family wouldn't mind, he knew, and he wanted to keep Ari trapped on ship with him — where she couldn't possibly escape. He would show her who it was she belonged to.

He returned shortly and the first course was served. As she sat next to him, his temper cooled, but his desire continued to escalate.

Conversation filled the room as his exuberant family all spoke at once. Rafe enjoyed nothing better than sitting back and listening to his loved ones all clamoring to be heard, especially now. It helped soothe his easily roused temper.

"Ari, has Rafe told you yet what a hellion he was as a teenager?" Lia asked with a twinkle in her eye.

"Lia…" Rafe said in a warning tone which she completely ignored.

"I somehow can't imagine Mr.… um…*him* as a child," Ari quickly corrected herself. Rafe was rather disappointed that she hadn't slipped up. He had big plans for different forms of exotic punishment.

His hand slid beneath the table and landed on her bare thigh, causing her to jump and nearly knock her wineglass over.

"Is everything OK, Ari?" his mother asked.

"Yes. Sorry about that. I'm being a bit clumsy. I think I got a little too much sun today," Ari said as she tried to push his hand away without causing a scene. He just squeezed her leg a little tighter, letting her know he had no intentions whatsoever of letting her go.

She sent a desperate look his way before responding to a question his father asked her. As his fingers danced along her thigh, she sat tensely next to him with her legs clamped tightly shut. He had no doubt he could outlast her. She'd grow too tired to hold herself so stiffly long before he'd lose interest in caressing her.

"Back to my story, Ari. Rafe was once a child, though I do understand how that's difficult to believe, considering he rarely takes off his suits now. He was a horrible monster, always playing tricks on Rachel and me. Here's the worst thing he did, and it's a doozy. I was exhausted after a late night volunteering at our church, and the room was dark. I turned on my lamp and pulled back the covers and a seven-foot snake was slithering across my sheets. I screamed so loud that my dad burst through the doors a few seconds later with the shotgun raised. Yes, Rafe had put that snake in my bed. I was pretty satisfied when Rafe got grounded for a month. To this day if I see any snake, even a gardener one, I freak out," Lia said.

"How did he get that big a snake to stay in your bed?"

"Oh, it was his friend's pet. After that incident, Mom wouldn't allow him to have one of his own, which he was close to talking her into. I was quite pleased with that outcome."

"Snakes give me the creeps, too."

"Who actually likes them? Only other reptiles," Lia said as she stuck her tongue out at Rafe.

"You played your own share of pranks, Lia. Why don't you explain why I put that snake in your bed?" Rafe said with a laugh, not offended at all by her goading.

"It was nothing compared to what you did to me."

"Nothing! Are you kidding me? She put itching powder in my workout shorts. I started running in P.E. and then had to make a mad dash to the showers. My friends wouldn't let me live that one down for the rest of my high school career."

"Oh, that's great!" Ari said with a laugh as she looked up at him, delight dancing in her eyes.

It seemed his Ari had a wicked streak about her.

The bantering of his family caused Ari to relax, and Rafe was able to move his hand higher up her leg, his fingers drifting to the inside of her thigh. Before she realized she'd let down her guard, his fingers brushed the brief piece of lace covering her delectable womanhood.

Her legs tightened immediately again, but all it did was trap his hand flush against her heat. He took immense pleasure when he felt the warm wetness of her body through the delicate lace. She desired him — whether she was willing to admit it or not.

Suddenly, his little game turned on him, to the point of pain. Knowing her body was prepared for him to enter her caused him a pulsing erection. With an angry look his way, Ari opened her legs, and he reluctantly removed his hand. He'd never have made it through the rest of the meal while feeling her moist heat — plus it could be difficult to eat with only one hand.

Her cheeks were flushed and her breathing quick, and she refused to meet his gaze. Though she was doing her best to carry on conversation with his family, he could see the effort it was costing her.

As the meal was nearing an end, Rafe breathed a sigh of relief. Soon, he'd get her alone again. Surely it couldn't take him much longer to convince her to join in with his plans. He could offer her so much pleasure, and he had little doubt she'd provide for all his needs.

After the dessert course was finished, Rafe decided he was done conversing with his family for the night. He had to get Ari to his bed. It was beyond desire — pure need was gnawing at the zipper of his pants. *Had he really thought such a thing?* he reproached himself. *Gnawing need? Zipper? Pants? Sheesh! Talk about hopelessly horny!*

"I hope you all don't mind the surprise, but I've told the captain to keep us out to sea. I thought you'd all enjoy spending the night on board the ship," Rafe announced, not turning toward Ari when out of the corner of his eye he caught her head whipping around in his direction.

"I… uh…can't. I have to get home," she stuttered.

"Oh, do you work tomorrow, Ari?" his father innocently asked, not sensing her tension.

"No," she responded with hesitancy. "I'm not actually working then, but I have laundry to do and other stuff to get ready for the week," she finished feebly.

"Don't worry, Ari. We'll get in early," Rafe said, making it clear by his tone that the discussion was closed.

"I'm delighted with the surprise, Rafe," his father said. "It will give me a chance to see how I sleep aboard the boat. I guess I should try it at least once before purchasing one of my own."

"We're going to go get some rest," his mother said as she rose from the table with his father being the one to step up and pull out her chair. The two of them left the room practically giggling. It took his sisters a couple of minutes to understand Rafe's look; they then made their own excuses and ambled out after their parents.

"It looks as if it's just you and me now," Rafe said as he scooted his chair back and gripped Ari by the waist. He moved quickly and had her straddled across his lap before she knew what was happening.

"This is kidnapping, you know," Ari warned him breathlessly.

"All you have to do is say *no*, Ari," Rafe promised as he pulled her forward against his straining erection, ending any protest she might have had.

Chapter Twenty

Ari knew she should climb off Rafe's lap and run as fast as she could to the nearest door, shutting and locking it tightly behind her. She knew she'd regret making love to the man again. She also knew that if she were to command him to let her go, he'd do just that.

Knowing he'd let her leave made her want to stay even more. Why, oh why, was this happening to her? But it was, and he was so hard to resist.

So what? She could handle one more night in his bed, or at least at his dining table. She forgot about his staff, who could just wander in, as well as his family members, who were somewhere nearby. She practically forgot her own name as his lips overtook hers, and his tongue thrust inside her mouth.

Rafe's hands slid through her hair, untying the band at the base of her neck and releasing the dark strands. He moved his hands gently across her shoulders, grasped the straps of her sundress and pulled them down her arms.

The material rubbed against her sunburn, making her gasp, but the pleasure warming her body far outweighed the discomfort.

She felt the air hit her breasts, the bikini top barely covering her now. When Rafe stopped moving the straps as they reached her elbows, she struggled against him. She wanted the dress taken all the way down; she was desperate to pull her arms up and clasp his head, but he was trapping her arms against her body, making it impossible for her to move them.

"What's the matter, Ari? Are you feeling trapped?" he whispered as his mouth moved across her cheek and made contact with her ear.

"What are you doing?" she gasped as he sucked her lobe into his mouth.

"Pleasuring you..."

His hands next ran up to the front of her neck and splayed across her chest bone, before his fingers slipped inside the material of her bikini top. He edged first one side over, and then the other, causing her breasts to slip free of the material and press together.

As the cool air hit her nipples, a stinging sensation rushed from the dusky pink peaks all the way to her core. They tightened even further when she opened her eyes and saw the lust burning in his expression as he gazed at her body's charms.

She moved on his lap, arching her back, silently begging him to take her breasts into his mouth and ease the ache throbbing inside her.

"Patience, Ari," he teased as his fingers circled the dusky peaks but didn't touch her the way she needed.

She didn't like this new game. She wanted satisfaction, and he wasn't giving it to her. Almost panting, she struggled to move closer to him, need burning her, impatience evident in her every action.

"Don't you know that it's the anticipation of what's to come that heightens the pleasure when I eventually do touch you…just…like…this…?"

Finally, he bent his head forward and licked her nipple, pulling back quickly to blow his warm breath across the wet surface. She cried out at the exquisite pleasure, but still he took his time, slowly moving his tongue up her breast and across her neck, swirling its moist tip around her quickly fluttering pulse, and scraping her skin lightly with his teeth.

Every place he touched soothed her for the barest of seconds before the raging fire within her leapt higher, making her squirm on his lap, her core pressing against his rampant manhood.

Knowing how badly he desired her sent her own passion through the roof. The sight of her, not her touch, had caused his incredible erection, and that made her dizzy with euphoria. If she could have spoken, she'd have demanded that he take her, but no words came out, only heated gasps of pleasure.

Rafe trailed tender, light kisses down her neck to the top of her swollen breasts, then circled his tongue around one of her nipples. With a gentle pressure, his teeth gently bit the sensitive skin before he moved to the other side to offer equal attention. She wriggled her back, trying to lead him to take her tight buds into his mouth, but he was in no hurry, and no amount of whimpering seemed to have an effect on him.

Just when she was ready to scream out in absolute sexual agony, he latched on to one tight nipple, and the sensation that traveled through her made it all worth the wait. The sensual peak he'd brought her to nearly sent her over the edge.

She shook in his arms as his tongue laved her nipple, then his teeth lightly nipped the swollen bud. He feasted on her breasts, making her head light with the pleasure, before he eased back up her throat and once again connected their mouths.

"You taste so good, Ari. I could dine on your body all night long."

Ari moaned into Rafe's mouth as his tongue caressed every crevice. Her throat caught when his hands moved down her sides, brushing against her still-bound arms and then moved to her exposed thighs. Quivering with excitement, she opened her mouth again, trying to get the words out.

"Please, Rafe. Please take me."

"Say my name again," he commanded as he sipped from her lips in reward.

"Rafe…Rafe, I need you…"

Another moan escaped her as his hands slid beneath the fabric of her dress and caressed her backside before he plunged his tongue deep into her mouth, seeming to reach her very soul.

"I've been picturing your sweet little ass in nothing but this sexy lace thong since the moment you stepped from my bathroom."

The remaining breath still in Ari's lungs whooshed out at Rafe's words. She struggled in his arms, trying to get free, crying out when he only shifted, moving the fabric farther down her arms and making the material bind her even tighter.

"Rafe, please…"

"Yes, Ari. I love to hear you beg. I plan on making you do it a lot more."

"Release me from this dress!" she growled, her frustration mounting.

"Not until I'm ready to. You should already know I don't do anything until I'm ready. I happen to like looking at you ensnared. I think I'll leave you that way."

Ari's frustration grew at Rafe's refusal. She struggled against the binding of the tight fabric, which seemed to do nothing more than excite him further.

Rafe suddenly stood up, gripping her butt in his hands, and almost made her fall backward. He set her on the table, the cold wood sending a shiver down her legs. Before she could utter a word, he pushed her back and spread her legs wide.

She felt open, vulnerable, and too exposed, but as his fingers slipped beneath the lacy fabric covering her core, heat stole through her and her anxiety disappeared.

His fingers dived inside her body, making her back arch off the table, and a cry erupted from her lips. She was more than ready for him and wanted an end to these power games.

He pulled her forward and pushed his still-covered arousal against her wet and exposed opening, grinding his hips into her, the material of his trousers scraping against her wet flesh, making her burn

"I should punish you, Ari, for the torture you've been putting me through. I should bind your legs apart, and let the air stroke your heat, igniting your flames so high you feel like bursting. I shouldn't bury myself deep inside your body and offer you relief," he growled as his hand gripped the sides of her string thong.

"Noo... Please take me. Now" she sobbed as she writhed and twisted on the table in front of him. Her body was his — there was no fight left in her.

Just when she thought he was going to leave her there in unbelievable agony, he tugged against the delicate material, tearing the thong from her body. Excitement filled her when she heard the telling rip of a foil packet.

"Yes, please…"

With one fluid motion he thrust his engorged manhood into her core; light exploded behind her eyes. He pushed her legs wider apart, baring her body to his view as he pushed deep inside, over and over again.

The table shook as he buried himself deep within her swollen folds. He was pushing so fast — so hard — that she should be in pain, but she could only feel ecstasy as she reached for the edge of her abyss.

"Don't stop, please don't ever stop…"

"I can't stop — not ever," he cried out as he moved even quicker, the muscles in his legs quivering as he rocked into her. The complete haze of lust covering his eyes sent her flying beyond the realm of sanity. His thick staff ripped into her, his body taut and filled with desire — for her, only her. She was heady with the surge of power coursing through her blood.

"Oh, Ari, you feel so good. Yes, baby, grip me tight…" he cried as he slammed against her, his pelvis hitting her throbbing womanhood, causing an explosion. She shattered around him, gripping his throbbing erection tight with the spasms of the strong yet swollen walls of her femininity.

Rafe froze against her as his body shook, his manhood pumping repeatedly inside her while he groaned in pleasure. She felt every motion as he began easing gently in and out of her, drawing the moment out for both of them.

Neither spoke as they began to breathe more easily, both lost in the exhilaration they'd just created for each other. For those few silent moments, Ari could pretend they were like any normal couple who'd just come together in an burst of color and light.

"Come work for me, Ari. We're good together. You know you want to. What price will it take?"

Ari's bubble popped at his words. She wasn't with a typical man. She was with Rafe — control freak extraordinaire. She could never have a regular relationship with him.

"It will never happen. You may set me on fire, but once I've come back down to earth, I remember you for the monster you are," she calmly answered. She heard Rafe's sharp intake of breath.

"I'm still buried deep inside you, Ari. Am I really such a monster?" he mocked as his hips moved, stirring her heat against her will.

"You've been with a lot of women. You obviously know how to pleasure one. Just because a chicken dances on a hot plate doesn't mean he wants to be there. I can feel pleasure while still despising you. I can come while wanting to be anywhere but underneath you. Don't think too highly of yourself just because you know how to touch me in the right places," she said bravely, praying he wouldn't call her bluff.

She was falling for him — falling in ways that terrified her. If she submitted to him, he'd own her, body — heart — and soul. She would never be free again. Her goal now was to anger him enough that he'd walk away before he destroyed her.

"You will push me too far someday, Ari," he warned as he pulled from her, leaving her with a feeling of emptiness as he sat her up and moved the straps of her dress back to her shoulders so she could once again move her arms. When he was finished, he looked her deep in the eyes.

She cringed as the blood rushed down her arms, sending a throbbing sensation through her upper torso. As her body relaxed, the pain from her sunburn and from being bound rose to the surface. Yet she refused to rub those areas in his presence —

she had no wish to give him that sort of satisfaction. She'd wait to whimper when she was by herself.

"I don't care. If you don't like what I have to say, then quit pursuing me."

"I'm not pursing you, Ari. You happened to show up on my boat, remember? Needless of who came to whom tonight, you'll be mine — in just the way I owned you only moments ago. It's only a matter of time. As long as you keep fighting me, you're only denying both of us pleasure we could be feeling every single night. I'm not the monster you think I am. I just have certain rules. Doesn't everyone feel the same when they go into a new relationship together? I just happen to be honest about myself, and I expect the same from my business partners," he said as if he were the most reasonable man ever to live.

"If you're so honest, does your family know about your affairs?"

He glared at her and she knew she was pushing all the wrong buttons with him that night. His hand lifted and she was afraid for a moment that he was going to strike her.

He glared when she flinched.

"I've told you before that I don't need to use pain, Ari. You'll learn that. There are much more pleasurable ways for me to punish you," he threatened as he stepped back.

She slowly scooted off the table, finding her legs weak as she stood. She didn't know what to do next. She was stuck in the middle of a large bed of water on a boat with a man she didn't know if she wanted to kiss or kill.

"I'll escort you to your room. You know where mine is in case you change your mind," he said stiffly as he turned and started walking toward the door. She had to jog to keep up with him as he led her down the hallway.

No more words were spoken between them as he directed her to a door and opened it for her. She shut it in his face, then leaned against the solid wood and fought the urge to cry. She was really in the deep end now. She walked to the bed and sank slowly onto it, but with no expectation that sleep would claim her that night.

She was wrong. The soothing motion of the boat rocking gently on the waves lulled her to sleep in no time — clearing her mind of stressful decisions, and allowing her body time to heal.

*****

Anger consumed Rafe as he walked away. His face was stone cold, not a single feeling apparent, but his insides were boiling.

He wanted her to be with him. He needed her to do it willingly.

Doubt flooded him for the first time, and the foreign emotion moved him to near panic. He didn't like any weak emotion to penetrate his thick skin. He was too strong for weakness — he was too good for that.

Rafe turned down the hall and walked into his room, quietly shutting the door, not allowing his anger control over him. He wouldn't slam the door;

he wouldn't smash his fists into the walls. He'd have a drink and figure out his next move.

He would get what he wanted — he always did. It was just a matter of time.

Chapter Twenty-One

Guilt consumed Ari as she slowly opened her mother's hospital room door. She hadn't been to see her in two weeks, because she'd come down with a cold that refused to end. It didn't keep Ari from work, but it was bad enough that the hospital staff said she shouldn't visit her mother, whose immune system was still too weak from her last surgery for her to be exposed.

Ari's co-workers had wanted her to go to dinner with them, since it was Friday, but she had turned them down. Seeing her mom was much more important.

She'd rushed from work straight to the hospital, not even calling ahead. She'd spoken to her mom on the phone a number of times over the past two weeks, but Ari wanted to be with her in person.

Her need to spend time with her mother was another reason she couldn't even think of agreeing to work for Rafe. He'd made it clear that being with *him* was the only priority she was allowed to have.

If she became his mistress, she couldn't see her mother when she wanted to. That would never work for her. And on top of all of that, the man had her tied in so many knots that she didn't know what was up or down anymore. How could she continue living that way?

Two weeks ago when she'd awoken on the yacht and found it at the dock, she hadn't thought about anything other than escape. She'd made it from the ship without running into Rafe or any of his family members, and counted her blessings. She'd gotten as far from there as possible, and hadn't looked back.

OK, OK, she had looked back, to her disgust. She was angry with herself for being disappointed when she didn't hear from him. That was what she wanted, wasn't it? She'd been well aware that he would grow bored with the game of chasing her, and she should be shouting from the rooftops with joy at being free. She didn't have to worry about her weakness around him if she didn't have to see him. It was a win-win situation. Of course it was.

"Ari! It's so great to see you, darling."

Ari jumped at the sound of her mother's voice. She'd been so lost in her own thoughts that she hadn't realized she'd pushed the door open all the way.

"I'm so sorry I didn't come sooner, Mom. I feel terrible about it, but the doctors said I could cause you an infection," she replied as she rushed to her mother's bedside.

"Oh, posh. You have a life, dear, or I certainly hope you do. Young women have much more important things to do than to hang around an old woman's bedside day and night — whether you're sick or not."

"There is nothing in my life that's more important than you, Mom. Dr. Morgan said there were some complications from the surgery. He said it was an infection that turned septic, and they have to keep a very close eye on you or you could have organ failure. Why does one bad thing keep happening after another?" Ari sobbed.

She wanted to take her mother home, though she still hadn't told her that she'd had to sell the house. She didn't know how she was going to put her mother through that when she'd been through so much already. It was going to be a very bad day, indeed.

"I'd hoped the doctor wouldn't tell you any of that," Sandra said with some annoyance.

"I'm not stupid, Mom. You should've been out of here weeks ago. I knew something was going on. What was he supposed to do — tell me he had a big crush on you and refused to let you leave?"

"Mmm, he is quite handsome, isn't he?"

"Mom, this is serious!" Ari scolded.

"Oh, Ari, you mustn't worry so much. There's nothing we can do about any of this, and I tire of constantly discussing it. Please, *please* tell me anything to get my mind off it. I would even be happy if you start discussing the weather, or what you ate last."

Ari looked at her mom for several seconds, noting how pale she looked, how much weight she'd lost. Ari was beyond worried, but her mom was right — talking about it over and over again wouldn't help her mother heal. All she could do was give her mom what she asked for.

"I met these three wonderful women at work. They are very pushy, but they make me smile when I think I have nothing to smile about. They are a little crazy and I think you will adore them. Shelly, Amber and Miley are completely your type of women and like to try to find me brainless men, but they also make me laugh. I didn't think that was something I'd ever do again after your accident."

"Oh, Ari, I'm so happy to hear about your friends. You have always been too serious. You studied all through high school when you should have taken a bit of time for a social life, and then you did the same during college. I'm proud of you, as I always have been and always will be, but I want you to stop and smell the roses once in a while. I want you to have fun. Getting good grades is important, but I think you can do that with one eye closed and half your brain shut down. Having fun once in a while is just as important — to good mental health."

Ari smiled fondly at her mother's familiar speech. She'd heard it often in her late teens when she'd chosen to stay home each weekend studying instead of going out. It wasn't that she hadn't wanted to make friends. It was just that she hadn't connected with anyone who became more important than her schoolwork.

If she'd found something to do that was more interesting than getting lost in a favorite book, then she'd gladly have put away her reading glasses for the night and gone out on the town. But the recent past didn't support the value of socializing — just thinking about that fateful party and what had happened to her mother was a lot worse for her mental health than not having fun… And then there was…

Rafe.

Yes, Rafe made her want to put away her books. He made her want to star in her favorite romance movie with him as the male lead. He made her want to rip off her clothes and cry out for him to take her. He frightened her because he made her want to change everything about herself.

The word *dangerous* didn't begin to describe him.

She needed to remember that and just stay away.

"Did I lose you, darling?"

"I'm sorry, Mom. I haven't gotten enough sleep this week, so I'm a little on the spacey side. Tell me honestly how you're feeling today."

"I'm feeling wonderful. I was going to call you this evening. Dr. Shepp's last scans showed that most of the cancer was removed. He thinks he'll be able to get the rest through chemo. I just can't begin that treatment until this infection goes away. I may have to go in for another surgery, but you can wipe off that frown because it won't be as bad as the last one."

"I thought the money we got only covered the first surgery. Did we get more money?"

"I don't know. He said not to worry about any of the red tape, that it was all taken care of. I'm not going to look a gift horse in the mouth. I know I filled out a heck of a lot of forms. There are several organizations that step in to help in cases like mine. My best guess is that one of them said *yes*."

"That's wonderful, Mom. I'll call my boss and take Monday off work. I'm staying here with you all weekend to make sure everything goes right."

"You most certainly will not, child. You will go insane sitting in this room all day and night. I'm going a bit insane myself."

"You're too weak to stop me, so it looks like it's just you and me and a full box of Yahtzee cards. I'm going to run home and grab a few things, and I'll be back in an hour. It will be just like old times, when we had all-nighters. I would get so mad at you for making me leave my books in my bedroom, but now, those are my favorite memories."

"How can I fight you when you're making me all sentimental? Fine. You can stay with this old lady if you like, but be warned, I'm not against a little cheating to win each game."

"Even if you're cheating, I'll kick your booty. I love you so much, Mom. I'm so glad you're feeling better. I also think you're right — I have a feeling that everything is going to work out."

Ari leaned down and hugged her mother. Although terror was clutching at her heart — could this be the last weekend she ever spent with the most important person in the world to her? —with a hard swallow she pushed the fright down.

She hated that she'd been sick so long with that miserable cold. What if something did go wrong and these days were the last she had with her mom? It would haunt her forever.

No! Ari stopped her guilt-ridden thoughts in their tracks. She wouldn't allow fear to ruin her time with the woman who'd given her life — who'd always been there for her — who was her best friend. Ari couldn't change the past, but she could make sure their present was as perfect as possible.

She quickly ran to her apartment and gathered a couple of changes of clothes, then stopped in at a local store and picked up a few games. Of course, she sneaked in a couple of books, just in case her mother got too tired and fell asleep for a while. Ari wasn't leaving her mom's side all weekend.

If these truly were their last few nights together, she needed to pile on the memories. Losing her mother would be worse than anything she could imagine. The world would simply stop spinning. What reason would she have to go on? She'd smile and lie to her mom, telling her it would all be OK, but Ari knew that if her mom died, it wouldn't be OK. Nothing would ever be OK again.

Chapter Twenty-Two

"If you see a bright light at the end of a long dark tunnel, then you run like heck in the other direction. Do you understand?"

"Surgery will be fine, Ari. You need to quit worrying about me, OK? How many times do I have to tell you this? I'm your mother and it's *my* job to worry about *you*. You just take care of yourself. The doctor said surgery will last for several hours. I'd tell you to go outside and enjoy some of this beautiful sunshine streaming through the windows, but I know what a worry wart you are and I realize you won't leave this hospital. Instead, I need you to do your best to stay calm, and know I'll be as good as new in just a few hours."

"I love you so much, Mom. Don't you dare leave me. I mean it."

"I promise you I won't."

"Ms. Harlow, it's time to go now."

Ari's jaw tensed in frustration. Knowing that the nurse was only doing her job didn't help because Ari had a horrible feeling in her gut and she didn't want to let her mother out of her sight. All she wanted to do was keep holding her hand. If there was a way for her to go into the surgical room with her, she would. She wasn't ready for this — not that any amount of time would prepare her for her mother's possible death.

"Quit trying to intimidate these nice medical people, Ari. You are far too petite to scare anyone."

Ari hadn't even realized she'd growled at the nurse when the woman had stepped up to the bed.

"You raised me, Mom. I'm tougher than I look," Ari joked as she bent down and kissed her mother's cheek with tenderness.

People not much better than strangers wheeled her mom from the room, and Ari slowly sank down into her chair, finally allowing the tears that had built up all weekend to fall. Her mother was tough — she'd make it through this just fine. Why be pessimistic for no good reason?

After about an hour of sitting alone in the room panicking, Ari decided she had to get up and walk around. Driving herself crazy wasn't helping and sitting there all by herself was only fueling her pessimism. She wandered from the room and found herself in the spot where she'd collided with Rafe so many months ago.

It seemed like a different time. She'd grown so much in the last nine months — dropping out of college, losing her family home, finally finding work and, of course — meeting Rafe. She almost wished she'd taken up his offer just so she could lean on his shoulder at this moment.

She immediately snapped herself out of those kinds of thoughts. Even if she had taken his offer, it wasn't as if he'd be there for her. The whole point of his kinky arrangement was to have his women at *his* beck and call. He wouldn't be her boyfriend and he certainly wasn't the type of guy to hold her hand while she worried about her mother.

Moving down the hall and finding pictures lining the handsome tan walls pulled her thoughts in a different direction. She admired the work of the photographer, seeing beautiful images of historical homes, blooming flowers and important members of the community in a range of different outfits, most of them volunteering at various functions.

When she got to the end, she found a picture of Rafe wearing a hard hat and with a hammer in his hand and a big smile on his face. She was stunned at how human he looked without his custom suit on.

She read the words beneath: *Our deepest thanks go out to Raffaello Palazzo, who donated the funds for this wing to be built. A dedicated member of the community, he can always be counted on to lend a helping hand.*

Ari rolled her eyes at the words. She was sure the picture had been nothing more than a publicity stunt. He most likely had dressed in a pair of jeans, had the paper come out and take his picture, then ran as fast as he could to his air-conditioned limo.

"I've never been very fond of that picture. I always photograph so much better on my left side.

My assistant insists that it's her favorite image, though, and I've learned over the years that it's a losing battle to argue with her."

Ari jumped at the sound of Rafe's voice. By the teasing quality of his tone she knew he was once again trying to rile her — she refused to bite.

"Hello, Mr. Palazzo. It seems to be an unfortunate occurrence that I continue running into you here. Hopefully this time I don't end up needing an X-ray," Ari said as she turned to see his eyes narrow.

"Ari. Ari, Ari. Did you not listen the last time we spoke? I warned you that you'd be punished the next time you called me by my last name."

"As we're in a public building, I don't see that there's anything you can do to me," she smarted off, secure in the knowledge that not only were they surrounded by patients and visitors, but there were also armed staff members throughout the building.

"I see that you think you're safe, but never underestimate me, Ari. Once I decide on a course of action, nothing…and no one…can stop me," he threatened as his hands came up on either side of her head and he boxed in her against the wall.

"Normally, I'd love to prove to you how wrong you are, but today's not the best day. I need to get back soon."

His eyes assessed her face, and though she tried to keep a neutral expression plastered on, she knew he could see right through her. She had dark circles, edged by red from the tears earlier shed, and she'd lost another five pounds. She looked terrible, and she knew it.

"What's wrong?"

"None of your business."

"I thought you said you didn't want to play games. If you don't, then just answer my question," he said firmly.

"Fine. It's not like you can't figure it out. With most people, you barely open your mouth and they're spilling everything to you. My mom's in surgery. It's just been a little stressful. She had complications from her last surgery and they had to go back in. She should have been out of here weeks ago, but her body is fighting her every step of the way. I know she'll be fine but I can't stop worrying.

"I wasn't sure if you'd tell me or not. Thank you for sharing this with me. I'm going to help you take your mind off the surgery while we wait for information from her doctor."

Rafe moved his hands from the wall and gripped her arm, sliding it through his. He started tugging on her, causing her nearly to trip as she tried to make a stand against him. Since she could either crash to the floor or go along with him, she finally started to move. What else could she do? She didn't want to cause a scene and have people staring.

"I don't need your pity or your attention. I've been doing just fine all morning on my own."

"Obviously you aren't doing fine. You've lost even more weight that you can't afford to lose, your cheeks are sunken in, and you look like you haven't had a decent night's sleep in ages. You, more than anyone I know, should be working for me. You obviously need a keeper."

Ari was almost grateful for his words. For a brief moment, her worry over her mother was pushed aside as irritation with Rafe jumped to the forefront. What an overbearing, tyrannical…

"I'm taking care of myself just fine. I *absolutely* do not need a keeper. And as a matter of fact, I had a large breakfast this morning."

"Liar. I bet you've barely pecked at your food over the past few days, and had absolutely nothing today. You're worried about your mother and I can understand that. But you're being selfish, Ari. How do you think it makes her feel to see her daughter taking such poor care of herself? Your mom will need to concentrate on getting herself better when she comes out of surgery, not spend her time fretting about you."

Ari took in a sharp breath at his words. He was so arrogant and rude! But it *really* infuriated her that he was also right. The thought of food turned her stomach. How could she eat when her mother could possibly be dying? It just seemed wrong.

"Where are we going?" she finally asked as he turned a corner.

"To get lunch."

"I'm not hungry. I already told you that I ate."

"And I already called you a liar. How many arguments have you won with me, Ari? None. You may not be mine to control yet, but that's just a formality. I plan on having you; therefore, your health is of importance to me. You can either sit here in this cafeteria and eat a decent meal, or I won't hesitate to throw you over my shoulder, take you to my place, and force food down your throat. Your choice."

Ari stopped outside the cafeteria's doors and stared at him incredulously. The outrageous things he said to her in a normal, everyday tone of voice never ceased to amaze her. She really, *really* wanted to call his bluff, but by the look in his eyes, she had no doubt he'd follow through on his threat.

Even though the building was filled with security, Rafe was a major donor to the hospital. She was beginning to doubt that they'd stop him from kidnapping her even if she were screaming her head off. Ari couldn't take the chance that he'd take her away and that her mother would come back from surgery without her there.

With a growl of frustration she turned from him and walked into the quiet cafeteria. Thankfully, there weren't too many people around. She didn't want to listen to their conversations or squeeze past a line. She was going to have to concentrate fully on trying not to choke on horrible hospital food while her stomach was already heaving at just the thought of cramming anything down her throat.

"Ah, Ari. I'm a bit disappointed you didn't choose option two. I like the thought of you thrown over my shoulder with your ass next to my face. I'd have to turn and take a bite out of your luscious curves."

A shiver ran down Ari's spine at the image he was placing in her mind. She wouldn't have minded having him nibble on her derrière, either. Guilt seized her at having such a thought when her mom was still in surgery. One more reason to hate Rafe.

She ignored his comment as she moved through the various displays of food. Nothing looked remotely appealing, so she finally just grabbed an item. This didn't seem to please Rafe because he threw several more items on her tray, then shuttled her along to the cashier.

She didn't even attempt to pull money from her purse. She hadn't asked for the meal, so she wasn't offering to buy it. Rafe paid the cashier, then led Ari to a table in the back corner of the cafeteria.

She was less than thrilled to share another private moment with him. There were about ten other people sitting around the room, but they weren't close enough to be able to hear any conversation.

After Ari and Rafe had been sitting in silence for several minutes, he suddenly sighed as he gazed from her to her untouched plate.

"Please eat." His softer tone startled her.

She didn't understand his sudden fascination with her eating. What was the big deal? It didn't affect *him* in the least.

"Why do you care?" she asked, completely baffled.

"I normally couldn't care less what you eat or how much sleep you're getting. You're a grown woman and should be perfectly capable of making basic health decisions. But when I see that you are literally starving yourself and about to pass out from exhaustion, I feel it's time to step in. You may not have signed on with me, but believe it or not, Ari, I would be this hard on one of my sisters, too. My father taught me from a young age that when a woman needs to be taken care of, men are always supposed to step up to the plate. I'm calling a truce for the next couple of hours while your mother finishes her surgery. When it's all over and she's back on her feet, I'll throw down the gauntlet again," he answered with a warm smile and a flirtatious wink.

Ari could see the truth in his eyes. Her stomach clenched as he let down his ever-present guard and she saw the man behind the mask. She automatically sat back — the power of her attraction to him was so intense in that moment. Talk about Dr. Jekyll and Mr. Hyde. He was the modern version of the nineteenth-century classic.

Her defenses went up when she realized how easy it would be for her to fall for this kind and caring Rafe. She could put up something of a fight against Rafe the bully, but Rafe the White Knight was too much to handle. She was sorely tempted to run straight into his arms.

"Take a bite, Ari," Rafe commanded when she was motionless for too long.

"I'm getting to it," she said as she picked up the turkey sandwich. She bit into it and chewed the soft bread a few extra times in hopes that she could get the lump of food down her throat.

"Good girl."

Ari was almost grateful that his mocking tone had returned. She could handle him like this.

"I am nobody's *good girl*," she snapped, feeling relief as a surge of irritation began filling her once more.

After several minutes, she was surprised to find the sandwich gone. In her annoyance with Rafe, she hadn't even realized she'd been taking bites and swallowing.

"If angering you gets you to eat, then your wrath is worth it," he said in response to her surprise.

"Then I shall grow nice and fat with you around because I'm always angry."

"Mmm, I can picture you growing a bit more ripe. You have stunning curves, but a few pounds would make them even more luscious. I have already enjoyed the view of your supple breasts spilling from my hands."

Ari gasped and looked around, praying no one had overheard his vulgar comment.

Rafe leaned forward, inches from her face, "Are you embarrassed, Ari? Everyone has sex. It doesn't have to be a shameful experience."

"I thought you'd called a truce," she reminded him. "Besides, sex with you is beyond shameful and leaves me feeling dirty," she finished as she speared a piece of cantaloupe and bit down on it too hard, causing its juice to squirt out and land on Rafe's face.

The sight of him with cantaloupe juice running down his cheeks gave her the giggles. She didn't know whether it was stress, depression, or what, but she started to laugh, and then couldn't seem to stop.

Several people turned her way as Rafe's expression darkened and he reached in his pocket to grab his monogrammed handkerchief, which only made her hilarity intensify. Her stomach cramped as the laughter kept bubbling up. Was she having a breakdown? No matter how hard she tried to stop, she couldn't. The giggles just kept on coming. Soon, tears began to crawl down her cheeks.

"It seems our truce was short-lived. However, I'm so glad I entertain you," Rafe growled as he rubbed the juice off his face, sending her into a whole new fit of laughter.

She wasn't sure if she would have continued laughing until the hospital staff took mercy on her and knocked her out with a sedative, but a splintering sound echoing through the halls stunned her into stopping.

Several loud explosions filled the air, followed by the sound of people screaming. Rafe was on his feet in seconds, and he pulled Ari along with him.

"What was that?"

"Someone has a gun!" a woman shouted as she ran into the room, then went flying forward as red began spreading across her shoulder.

Just as Rafe was lifting Ari into his arms, a large man carrying a semiautomatic weapon marched through the cafeteria doors. Ari's frightened eyes met his before he turned the gun in her direction. He pulled the trigger. Rafe swore and tried to shield her body, but it was too late.

Ari felt as if she'd been punched in the chest, thinking maybe Rafe had dropped her. She looked down at herself and was fascinated as to see red begin to spread out across her T-shirt.

"That's too bad. This was my favorite shirt," she gargled before the world went black.

Chapter Twenty-Three

Fury engulfed Rafe as Ari's blood spread, soaking her soft cotton tee. Gently setting Ari down, he flew through the cafeteria. He felt a blow in his arm, but nothing was going to stop him from killing the man who'd dared to shoot Ari.

The gunman pulled the trigger again as Rafe rushed toward him, but was either out of bullets or his weapon was jammed. Either way, he had about two seconds before Rafe took him down.

The man's eyes widened as Rafe flew into the air and came barreling down. He tried pulling out another weapon from his belt, but he didn't have time before Rafe's body connected with his.

The man gasped when Rafe's fist found his jaw and dislocated it with one punch. The next hit sent blood spurting from the man's nose as a satisfying crunch echoed in Rafe's ears, even through the room of screaming people.

Rafe swung again, intent on finishing the worthless scum off. Who would dare to say the man was worthy of living after shooting people down in cold blood? he thought in his rage.

"Mr. Palazzo, we have him. Mr. Palazzo, you can stop. Stop now or you'll kill him!"

"I intend to," Rafe shouted as his fist flew downward again.

Suddenly, a couple of men grabbed him and hauled him backward. He turned, ready to fight off the men who had the gall to interfere, but then he felt a pinch in his arm and everything became fuzzy.

"No…" he called out before he faded.

When Rafe came to, it took a moment for him to remember what had happened. He heard monitors start sounding off as his heart picked up speed.

"Ari," he called.

"Mr. Palazzo, I'm Dr. Bruce. Everything is going to be all right. You were shot in your left shoulder, but we successfully removed the bullet and you'll recover quickly."

"I don't give a damn who you are. Where's Ari?"

"Ari?"

"Yes, the woman I was with, who was shot in the cafeteria!"

"Are you related to her, Mr. Palazzo?" Rafe was the one asking questions, and his fear and temper escalated as the doctor said nothing more.

"We both know I'm not married, and you know who my siblings are, so it's pretty obvious I'm not related to her. You will tell me how she's doing, though, right now!"

"Mr. Palazzo, under the HIPAA regulations, I can't —"

"Don't make me remind you how much money I give this hospital! I want information now. If you can't give it to me, then I guess I'll have to donate somewhere else."

Rafe wasn't in the mood to play around with hospital rules. He wanted to see Ari, and he needed to assure himself she was OK. The last thing he could remember was her bleeding in his arms. He glared at the doctor, as he watched the man struggle to decide what he was going to say.

"Ari was shot in the chest. It was dangerously close to her heart, and surgery was touch and go for a while, but she made it through. The next forty-eight hours are critical. She has a fifty percent chance of survival at this point."

Rafe sat up in the bed and started ripping out the lines attached to his arm. There was no way in hell he was lying in this cold hospital bed while Ari was somewhere else fighting for her life.

"Mr. Palazzo, I highly recommend you stop now. There's still a chance of infection setting in if you don't stay here to be monitored."

"I don't give a damn about infection. Take me to Arianna Harlow this instant or I'll make sure you never work another day as a doctor in this town or anywhere else," Rafe shouted.

The doctor looked at him for a moment, then shrugged his shoulders as if to say *it's your funeral, buddy*. "Fine. Follow me."

Rafe rose from the bed and had to pause for a moment as the room started spinning. The doctor didn't dare advise him on his weak condition, but just stood in the doorway waiting for Rafe to orient himself.

When his world stood still again, Rafe took one slow step in front of the other. He wasn't happy at all with the hospital gown they'd placed him in — he was a man who valued his dignity, and the loose tie at the back made dignity impossible.

"Once you get me to her, have a nurse fetch my clothes," he commanded. The doctor simply nodded.

They walked down the hallway and reached the elevators. Once inside, the doctor pushed the button for the fifth floor, and the rising car made Rafe nauseated. He fought it down, but only felt relief when the car stopped moving and he was able to step out on an unmoving floor again.

He followed the doctor through double doors and around a corner, then felt his heart nearly stop when he saw Ari lying helplessly in a small bed with all kinds of wires sticking from her pale skin.

"She's stable for the moment," the doctor said as he looked at her charts. "I'll have your clothing sent up right away."

Rafe didn't acknowledge the doctor as he collapsed in a chair and gripped Ari's warm hand. He tried telling himself he was only concerned because he was the one who'd led her to the cafeteria in the first place, but he knew it was a lie.

Somewhere along the line he'd developed feelings for this woman. Once the emergency was over, he would push those feelings far away and lock them up. He had no room for emotions in his life. This was about control. He needed to own her so he could gain control back in his life. That was all it was. Nothing more.

He leaned his head on her bed and fell asleep while still clasping her hand. Without the stream of painkillers entering his IV, his arm was throbbing and his head felt as if a construction worker were remodeling his brain. But because of the extreme amount of stress he'd been under lately, exhaustion was pulling him under — sleep was a welcome relief.

"Rafe. Where am I? What happened?"

Rafe snapped awake at the scratchy sound of Ari's fear-filled voice.

"Ari. How do you feel?" he asked as he tried to wipe the fog from his brain.

"As if I was run over by a train. What happened? Why am I hooked up to these monitors? Why does my chest hurt so badly?" she asked with frightened eyes trained on him.

"You were shot. I don't know any details yet because I haven't left your room, but I'm damn well going to find out who the man was and why the hell the hospital didn't stop him before he got to you."

"And my mom?" she asked as tears filled her eyes.

"She's fine, Ari. The nurse came in a few hours ago and said she made it through surgery without a hitch. They didn't want to frighten her right after her surgery, so she thinks you're just catching up on some much-needed sleep right now. I will personally go to see her in a few minutes. I just wanted to make sure you were OK first."

"Thank you. You didn't need to stay here with me; I know how busy you are. When can I see her?"

"It will be a little while because you're in in the ICU right now, and you can't leave for at least another day. You were shot in the chest and had major surgery. It's amazing how well you're doing."

"Please, I need to see her," Ari begged.

"Ari, you won't do her any good if you collapse at her feet. You need to rest and take care of yourself before you can possibly take care of her."

"Then please go to her. Please tell her that I'm OK and I'll come to her as soon as they'll let me."

"OK, I'll go now." Rafe leaned over and gently kissed her lips before he stood up and walked from the room.

It didn't take him long to find Ari's mother's room. She was lying in the bed with her eyes open when he stepped through the doorway. At least he had his clothes back on and wasn't entering the woman's room with nothing but a paper thin-gown.

"Ms. Sandra Harlow?"

"Yes, that's me. Can I help you?" It was almost eerie how much the woman looked like Arianna. They both had the same delicate high cheek bones, straight nose, and petite frame. They even had the same hazel eyes. But Ari had long brown curls, and

Sandra had short blond hair with the beginning streaks of gray running through it. Sandra was still a stunning woman.

"I'm sorry to be the one to tell you this, but there's been an accident with your daughter. I want to assure you that she's doing fine, but it will be a couple of days before you're able to see her," he said, making sure to keep his tone reassuring.

"My Ari? What happened? I need to see her now," Sandra said as her monitors indicated her increased heart rate.

"Ms. Harlow, Ari is fine, but both of you just came out of surgery, and neither of you can move right now. You need to focus on getting better because Ari will need you to be strong," Rafe said as he sat down and took her hand.

Her frightened eyes met his, and he was relieved when the monitors indicated that her heart rate starting to slow.

"Who are you?"

"I'm Ari's friend," he lied. He couldn't exactly tell Ari's mother the truth — that he planned to use her daughter and then dump her when he grew bored. He somehow didn't think that would go over very well...

"What's your name?" she asked with the same suspicious tone as her daughter used. It was so similar that it made him smile.

"Raffaello Palazzo. It's a pleasure to meet you, Ms. Harlow."

She looked at him with confusion for a few moments and then her eyes widened.

"I've heard that name before. Some of the nurses have spoken about you. Are you the same gentleman that has done so much for this hospital?"

"None of that matters, Ms. Harlow. What matters is that you and Ari both get better."

"I see you like to avoid questions about yourself." Rafe smiled again at her direct tone. He had a feeling that his mother and Sandra would get along wonderfully. He'd have to make sure the two of them never met — their getting together would be a lot of headaches for him waiting to happen.

He only wanted Ari to satisfy his needs. He didn't need anyone's family members trying to make it anything other than that. Rafe didn't need them to know one another at all.

"I just wanted to let you know what happened to Ari, but I need to get back to her now," Rafe said uncomfortably.

"You didn't say what happened. You only told me that she was doing fine after surgery," Sandra pointed out. Rafe didn't want to be the one to tell the woman that her daughter had been shot, but he didn't see a way to get out of it.

He took a deep breath and explained the shooting incident in the cafeteria. Sandra's eyes widened, and her pale skin turned even whiter, but she managed to keep herself under control as he explained the events of the day before.

"It's a good thing you were there," she finally said after a long pause.

"I was the one who insisted she go there in the first place," he replied guiltily. Self-recrimination ate at him.

"I'd say that's a good thing, as well, Mr. Palazzo. My daughter hasn't been taking the best care of herself lately. I'm grateful you were there and amazed you managed to get her to eat. I've been trying to force food into her all weekend. If you've known Ari for any length of time, you must know how stubborn she is."

Rafe smiled at Sandra. He agreed fully with her on that point — her daughter was beyond stubborn and a downright pain in the ass. It was unfortunate that he enjoyed that quirk in her personality.

"She certainly is, but I've managed to bend her to my will on occasion," he said with a wink.

"Hmm. That's interesting, Mr. Palazzo. Will you keep me updated on how she's doing until the doctor lets me see her?"

Rafe shifted in his seat. He wanted to spend as little time as possible with Sandra. For one thing, he found himself enjoying her company, and that wasn't good. For another, it would be far harder for him to have the type of relationship he wanted with Ari if her mother was involved.

He'd been taught to respect family, and if he knew Sandra, and then bind her daughter in as his mistress, it would gnaw at him. The situation continued to become more complicated with each passing day. He wished he could cut all ties — he wasn't ready to do that just yet.

"I can make sure the nurses keep you informed."

"Oh, I'd much rather hear from you personally since you'll be with my daughter," she said as she looked at him with hurt eyes.

Damn it!

"I'll keep you informed, Ms. Harlow," he conceded.

"Thank you, dear, and you can call me Sandra. We'll be seeing each other often over the next few days."

Rafe looked at her in surprise. There was a spine of steel beneath her weakened body. She was clearly letting him know that he'd better update her more often than he'd been planning.

"Well then, get some rest, Sandra, and please call me, Rafe," he said before standing and walking out her door.

Instead of heading right back to Ari's room, he stepped outside the hospital and let the cool breeze slap him in the face. What in the hell was he doing? He was starting to get in way too deep.

What he should do was call his driver and leave right now. It was time to cut ties with Ari *and her mother*. It was time to hire a new mistress — *one with no family* — and get his life back to normal. He shook his head as he stood there undecided.

"Raffaello Palazzo, you are in so much trouble."

Rafe groaned as he turned toward his sister, who was tapping her foot and staring at him with fire blazing in her eyes.

"Hi, Lia. How are you?" he said with resignation.

"I'm pissed. That's how I am. I can't believe you were shot and you didn't bother to call us!"

"Mom's going to have your head on a platter, you know?" Rachel piped in as she walked up and threw her arms around his waist. "We've been so worried."

"I'm fine," he promised, feeling guilt consume him.

"Well, we'd better go find Mom. She's furious with you," Rachel warned.

"Where is she?"

"In Ari's room with Dad. That's where the staff said you'd been all night. When you weren't there, Lia and I came searching for you, but Mom was sure you'd return, so they waited there. I think she just wanted to be with Ari. She seems to like her." Rafe didn't like implication of his sister's words. He in no way wanted his family trying to turn this arrangement he was planning with Ari into more than it was.

Rafe's heart picked up speed as he turned back to the door. He *really* didn't want his mom and dad spending more time with Ari. This was quickly spinning out of control and he felt as if he were free-falling.

Chapter Twenty-Four

"Oh, Arianna, you poor little thing."

Ari turned to find Rafe's mother and father walking through her doorway. What were they doing in her room?

"I'm fine," she automatically responded.

"You are far from fine, darling. I simply can't believe that such a thing happened to you. I am furious with my son for not calling us at once. Poor Rafe was shot, you were shot, and he doesn't even bother to call his own mother," she said as she sank down in the chair next to Ari's bed and grabbed her hand.

"Rafe was shot?" Ari gasped.

"You didn't know?"

"No. He didn't say anything. I really don't know a whole lot. The last thing I remember was feeling like I had been punched in the chest and then seeing blood on my shirt. Everything went dark after that. The doctor said I was very lucky the shot didn't enter an inch to the left or I would have been dead. I'm incredibly grateful that if I had to be shot, at least it happened in a hospital, where they were able to operate immediately."

"You little darling. I'd be a lot more grateful if neither of you had been shot in the first place. How terribly tragic this all is. A brand-new mother was killed — her new baby left in this world without a mama. Two others were taken too soon from this world, as well. I know it's selfish of me, but I've been so worried. The thought of losing my Rafe tears at my heart. It would be unimaginable. I've been so worried about you, too. I know we don't know each other well, but you're such a sweet little thing, and knowing you were hurt just breaks my heart."

Ari's eyes filled at Rosabella's kind words. How could the apple have fallen so far from the tree? Rosabella was kind, caring, compassionate — all the things Rafe wasn't. Of course, that wasn't entirely true. Rafe had his moments of unbelievable kindness, but he quickly pushed them away and hid behind his mask of coldness.

"Where was Rafe shot?" Ari needed to know.

"He went after the gunman, and that madman managed to shoot him in the arm before Rafe took him down."

"Rafe ran toward the guy?" Ari gasped.

"Well, of course he did, dear. The man had just shot you," Rafe's father said as if it was the most natural thing in the world for Rafe to attack a man aiming a weapon at his head.

"I…I didn't know." Ari felt terrible about how selfish she'd been. All she'd been doing was worrying about her mother. She hadn't even noticed that Rafe was wearing a bandage. Maybe she really was a self-absorbed person.

"Mom. Dad. What are you doing here?" Ari turned her head to find Rafe looming in the doorway, looking none too happy. She cringed involuntarily.

"Raffaello Palazzo, don't you dare use that tone of voice with me. You are in *huge* trouble. I can't believe that I had to find out from a doctor that my only son was nearly killed. You should have called your father and me immediately," Rosabella stormed.

She squeezed Ari's hand before getting up from her chair and rushing over to Rafe to throw her arms around him. Even though she was reading him the riot act, the love in her actions shone forth. So like a mother — terror made her yell when she felt more like crying.

"I'm fine, Mom. I wasn't almost killed. The guy barely nicked me," he said as his uninjured arm came around her, his tone gentle.

"You aren't speaking the truth. I thought I taught you better than that, Rafe. The doctor told me the shot had to be removed. I don't care if it's merely a flesh wound. If you're shot, then you need to call your mother," she scolded.

"I was a bit busy, Mom," he said, though his voice carried a gentler tone as he noticed the tears streaming down his mother's cheeks.

"Of course you were, son. Poor Ari. I can't believe anyone would fire a weapon at this sweet little girl," she said, her voice softening.

"He will pay." The menace was clear in Rafe's tone.

"Yes he will, son. They have him under lock and key on another floor," Martin said as he came over and patted Rafe on the back.

"Yes, the staff have been quite secretive about his location," Rafe growled.

"Son, you need to let the law take care of him. You stopped him and now he will go to prison, where hopefully they'll execute the worthless scum. Before he made the mistake of entering the same room as you, he killed several people."

"Their poor families," Ari gasped.

"Yes, although money can't make a difference to a child losing a mother, Rafe is making sure the victims' families are well taken care of," Rosabella said with pride as she turned back toward Ari.

Ari turned quickly and met Rafe's eyes. He wasn't responsible for the shooting. Why did he feel accountable to take care of the victims and their loved ones? Her curiosity was piqued as Rafe showed yet another side of himself. He wasn't as one-dimensional as she'd first thought.

"Mom," Rafe said in a warning tone.

"Oh, Rafe. You're always so modest about how much good you do in the community. Don't get me wrong, you can be quite arrogant at times, but underneath it all you really are quite the softy. I don't know why you're so worried that the world might find that out."

"That's enough, Mom," he said, his tone very quiet. It sent a shiver down Ari's spine.

"Rosabella, you're embarrassing him," Martin warned.

"Oh, hush," Rosabella said, but she stopped.

"We should leave and let Ari rest," Rafe said, looking at his parents.

"I'm so sorry, dear. We're just talking away when you need to get sleep. I'll come back tomorrow and visit with you. I'll leave the rest of the family at home so they don't causing all kinds of ruckus," Rosabella said as she let go of Rafe and walked back over to Ari.

Ari was shocked when the woman bent down and very gently hugged her. She felt a lump in her throat at the motherly gesture. The woman barely knew her, and yet she was so concerned. Ari couldn't help but compare Rosabella to her own mother, both of them compassionate with a natural ability to draw others to them.

What had happened in Rafe's life to turn him into the control freak that he was? In his defense, it seemed he was only that way when it came to relationships — or business. Apparently, he was a saint when it came to everything else. Ari found herself wanting to know more about him.

But she was smart enough to realize that was a road best not taken.

"I'll be back later," Rafe said. The look in his eyes left no doubt that arguing would do her no good. Fear seized her as she realized, once again, she could actually fall for this man. Under no circumstance could she allow that to happen. It was completely unacceptable.

Chapter Twenty-Five

Rafe was silent as he walked from Ari's room alongside his family. For once in their lives even his sisters were quiet as they made their way down the hallway. This situation had gone from out of control to radioactive levels.

Rafe didn't know whether it was stubborn pride, or obsession, but he knew he wasn't letting Ari go just yet, no matter what difficulties she presented to him and his settled way of life. So it looked as if the only option was to smooth out the waters, convince his family to return to their home, and put things back on the right path.

"Let's have dinner," Rafe said as they entered the parking lot.

"That's a good idea, son," his father said in a serious voice. "Then you can explain to us why you wouldn't call us immediately after being shot. I'd also like to know what's really going on with this Ari you seem so fond of."

Rafe had to hold in the retort that was fighting to burst forth from his mouth. He'd never been disrespectful to his parents and he wasn't about to start.

"Isn't it obvious, Dad? Rafe's in love," Rachel said in a singsong voice.

"Rachel, for once in your life you need to keep your mouth shut. Ari is…she's just a potential employee."

"Ha!" Lia muttered.

Rafe glared at both of his siblings.

"Well, well, if it isn't the man of the hour — the hero of San Francisco, who swoops in and takes down an armed man while saving the princess from certain death."

Rafe turned to find his best friend approaching them. He wasn't thrilled to see the amused smile on Shane's face, and braced himself for an even longer evening — he loved the guy, but there was nothing Shane liked more than to find a weakness and then dig in.

"I thought you were out of the country, Shane."

"I flew all night to make sure your sorry butt was OK. Thanks for calling, by the way."

"Everyone is simply overreacting to the whole situation. I'm fine, thank you. Go back to South America, or wherever it is you've been saving the world."

"Raffaello, you're being so rude," Rosabella scolded as she approached Shane and gave him a welcoming hug.

"Yeah, buddy, very rude," Shane said with a wounded look. But he winked at Rafe as Rosabella released him. His friend knew how to make Rafe look like an ass and he enjoyed doing it.

"Would you like to join us for dinner? We were just leaving," Martin asked.

"Of course I would. I haven't seen my favorite family in over six months now. How are *you*, beautiful?" he said while rubbing Rachel's head.

"I'm not ten years old anymore, Shane. You no longer get to do that," she snapped.

"Sorry, squirt; you'll always be twelve in my eyes."

"What about Lia? Will she also always be just a small child?" Rachel goaded, causing both Lia and Shane to squirm.

Rafe's eyes narrowed as he saw the tension between his best friend and little sister. What the hell was going on?

"Shane?" he questioned. Rafe knew there was a problem when Shane wouldn't look Lia —and now him — in the eye.

"Hey. I thought we were getting some grub. I just flew halfway across the planet and I'm starving," Shane said with a laugh.

Rafe noticed that Shane still wasn't making eye contact with Lia. No question — he was going to have to have a chat with his best friend before the night was out.

"Yes, with all the stress today, I haven't been able to eat a thing. Knowing that you're going to be OK has returned my appetite. Let's find a restaurant with a view," Rosabella said as they approached Rafe's waiting ride.

The family climbed in the back of the limo, and Rafe was watchful as Lia scooted all the way to the far side, while Shane sat as far away as possible on the opposite seat. He just hoped he didn't explode before he was able to get Shane alone.

"Where have you been and what have you been up to?" Rosabella asked.

"Oh, nothing much. I've just been down in South America," he answered, squirming a bit.

"Nothing much! You're building houses for families who would otherwise sleep in tents if they are lucky, and with your own money, too. Not only that, but you've managed to gather a group of other investors to jump in and donate not only their funds but their time. That takes some heavy lifting," Lia said.

"Why is it that you and my son are so overconfident in business and yet so awkward when talking about volunteer work and the beautiful things you do for people? Those are the things you should be shouting from the rooftops."

"First off, it's really not that big a deal. I spent a lot of time as a teenager and in my twenties being selfish, taking whatever I wanted and not even thinking of giving back anything. Plus, if someone is doing community service for a pat on the back, then they're wasting their time. Giving of yourself or your money is meaningless if you're only doing it because you want to be seen or praised. The reason I like doing volunteer projects out of the country is because I don't have the news hounding me every five seconds. If nobody knows where I am, I finally get a bit of peace. Your son's been on a few projects with me. He says it's to get away, but he works his behind off," Shane answered, nodding at Rafe with respect.

"Speaking of my secretive son, do you know what's going on between Rafe and this lovely Ari?"

Shane's head whipped around and he finally met Rafe's eyes. Rafe sent him the slightest shake of his head, asking his friend not to question him in front of the parents. When he saw the gleam enter Shane's eyes, he knew he was screwed.

"Well, I haven't heard of Ari before, which tells me that Rafe may actually be interested in this woman."

"If you haven't heard about her, then it can't be that serious," Martin said with some confusion.

"Ah, but that's where you're wrong. You see, Rafe and I share everything with each other. I know all about his conquests within days of their meeting. If he's keeping her from me, then it's because he doesn't know what he's doing. Rafe always knows what he's doing, so it looks as if a woman may have finally come along that is able to knock him off of his perfectly projected life," Shane answered with a smile.

Enough was enough!

"I haven't mentioned Ari because we hardly know each other. Yes, I'm dating her, or at least considering it. She's a little brash, contrary to my usual taste, but she has her qualities," Rafe started when he heard his mother gasp in shock at his rudeness.

"However," he continued. "My dating life is none of your business, Shane. Mom, if I were to ever get that serious about a woman, I would tell you. The bottom line is that no woman has gained much of my interest in a long time — Ari included," he finished.

"That is a horrible thing to say, Rafe," Rosabella scolded.

"I think it's best if we just drop this subject. Besides, I'm far more interested in learning why

Shane and Lia can't even seem to look at each other."

All heads turned to Lia first, whose face was flaming red, and then to Shane, who seemed to be breaking out in a sweat.

"There's nothing to tell," Shane said awkwardly as he fiddled with his cuffs.

"Nothing to tell! How about a few months ago when you spent the night together," Rachel piped in with a wicked smile.

"What!" Rafe thundered as he glared at his best friend.

"Before you attempt to kill me, let me explain. We didn't exactly spend the night together .." he hedged.

"You have about five seconds to explain before I toss you from a moving vehicle, then have the driver run you over."

"Look, Lia and I were at the same fundraiser a few months ago and we got together for dinner and drinks. We both ended up drinking a few too many glasses of the exquisite wine and then decided to have a couple of glasses more in my room before calling it a night. We passed out. Nothing happened." When a deathly silence filled the car, he added, "I swear!"

"Dad, open the door — I think I'll throw Shane out anyway," Rafe thundered.

"You're such a damn hypocrite. I didn't even touch your sister — I treated her with nothing but respect. I love your family too much to violate Lia. You, however, treat women like they're nothing more than used gum on the bottom of your shoe and *you're* going to sit back and judge *me*? I love you, Rafe, but when it comes to women, you're a certified asshole," Shane said with a glare.

"Ha! Talk about the pot calling the kettle black. When's the last time you've spent two nights in a row with the same woman? At least I'm responsible in my affairs. I stay with the same person for a minimum of three months," Rafe countered.

"You think you deserve sainthood because you treat your relationships like another business merger?"

"There's nothing wrong with having strict guidelines."

"I think we should just drop this, Rafe."

"You're probably right. I'd rather we didn't say something that can't be taken back."

Rafe looked around — he'd forgotten for a moment that his parents were sitting across from him. He didn't like the look of censure in his mother's eyes or the thoughtful expression on his sisters' faces.

Rafe sat there brooding during the rest of the ride to the restaurant. The complications with Ari continued to pile up, and he wished he were alone to think everything over. Was he in over his head? Surely not.

When the limo stopped, Rafe nearly sighed with relief. Too much tension. It didn't help that his sisters seemed to be communicating silently with each other. The two of them had done that since they were little, and more often than not, it had led to trouble.

As his family was seated, Rafe noticed the continuing tension between Shane and Lia. He needed to take his friend aside soon and find out exactly what was going on. He and Shane were cut from the same cloth — both messed up when it came to women. Rafe didn't want Lia mixed up in that. He didn't think his friendship could survive it.

*****

"Are you going to refuse to meet my eyes now?"

Shane stood there trapped by the door of the men's restroom. He hadn't thought Lia would follow him there. Rafe had to be even more suspicious, and Shane knew a private confrontation was coming. *If Rafe finds out about the vivid dreams I'm having about his sister, I'm dead meat...*

After several awkward seconds, Shane finally looked at Lia. Her worried expression and defensive stance didn't improve his outlook on the situation.

"Lia, this is a mistake. I shouldn't have kissed you that night — Rafe's my best friend. I just don't know how it happened."

"I'm not a little girl anymore, Shane. I can kiss guys all I want without my big brother's permission. As a matter of fact, I can even have *sex* with them if I want," she said boldly.

Shane wanted to punch a wall. The last thing he wanted was to think about Lia having sex — unless it was with him.

"If you're trying to get a reaction, you are doing a damn fine job — and you're not going to like the results," he threatened.

"A reaction? Oh, that couldn't possibly happen. There can be nothing but stiff formality and indifferent looks from the mighty Shane. You know what? I don't care. I think I'll just head over to the bar and pick up someone who isn't ashamed to look at me," she stormed and turned away.

Like hell she would!

Frustration taking over his good sense, Shane gripped Lia's arm and swung her back around to face him. The surprise in her eyes quickly gave way to desire as he pulled her up against him. Knowing it was a mistake, but unable to stop, Shane gripped her head while he captured her lips.

All thoughts fled as he tasted the sweet honey of her kiss. There was no slow exploration. He felt like a starving man finally finding food. Pushing Lia up against the wall, pinning her body with his own, his hand moved down her neck, then roamed over the front of her shirt while he plundered her mouth.

When she cried out as his hand brushed her breast, his body hardened and he pressed his arousal against her, trying to seek relief.

She greedily accepted all he was giving, encouraging him to take her right there. His hand slid beneath her shirt as he reached for her bra. He needed to feel her bare skin.

"Well, isn't this interesting? I can see there's *nothing* going on between the two of you."

Shane froze at the sound of Rachel's voice. He pulled back from a very flushed Lia, horrified at the way he'd been virtually ravishing her in public.

"I'm sorry," he said before turning and making a quick exit from the back hall of the restaurant.

"That was one great bathroom break" was the last thing he heard Rachel say before he went straight outside. He'd call Rafe later to invent an excuse for his early departure. Rafe would take one look at him right now and have no doubt about what he'd just been up to.

Guilt ate at him as he hailed a cab and fled. And when his phone rang five minutes later, he ignored it. Shane knew he'd have to face the music sooner or later, but he wasn't ready to go there yet. Rafe was his best friend — his family. If he lost that friendship, he didn't know what he'd do.

The situation was hopeless. Even running off to a Third World country hadn't rid his mind of Lia. He was falling hard, but a relationship with her was impossible.

In the long run, he knew he'd just hurt her because he wasn't capable of having a long-term relationship. An affair with her wasn't worth it because in the end he'd hurt her and lose his best friend. Now, if he could only convince certain parts of his anatomy of that, he'd be just fine.

Chapter Twenty-Six

"If you don't get a wheelchair and take me to see my daughter right now, I swear I'll find a sharp object and the first person who touches me gets stabbed through the eye."

"It's OK, Sandra; I'll take you to see Ari."

Rafe couldn't hide his smile of amusement as Ari's tiny mother threatened the two-hundred-pound orderly. What was even more comical was that the man actually looked intimidated.

"Finally, somebody's saying what I want to hear," she snapped as she started shifting her legs over the side of the bed.

"Let me help you so you can save your energy for as much visiting time as possible with Ari. She too has been threatening the hospital staff the last few days. I can see where she gets her temper."

"I'm happy now that you're taking me to see my daughter, but don't push your luck. My body hurts like the dickens, my baby girl has been shot, and these moronic doctors keep telling me I need to stay in bed for my own good. I have no room left for anyone humoring me. I want my daughter and I want her now!" Sandra snapped as she held Rafe's gaze.

He admired Sandra — and that was a problem. He had no doubt she'd follow through on her threat if she didn't get what she wanted, just as he knew that his mom would slice anyone in half who stood between her and her children. The two women were disconcertingly alike.

"Do you have some Italian in you, Ms. Harlow?" he asked as he helped her into the wheelchair.

"I have no idea. Why do you ask?"

He placed each of her feet into the straps of the footrests, then grabbed a blanket and covered her lap.

"You have a lot of passion inside of you. That speaks of a strong heritage," he said as he began wheeling her through the hallways. He knew no one would dare stop him, even if the doctors felt that Sandra should wait another day before getting out of bed. If Rafe said it was fine, then in this hospital, it *was* fine.

"Ah, Rafe, passion is in all of us, though we rarely feel the need to express it. I'm normally a very happy and quiet person, but the people on staff here should know better than to try to keep a mother and her child separated. I grew her inside of me, protected her fragile body as it formed, and then gave birth to the perfect baby. I may not always be able to keep her safe in this world, but I dang well won't lie around when she's been hurt. Cancer or not, my daughter comes first. A bit of discomfort won't kill me. Heck, I'm beginning to think nothing will."

"I agree with you there. You've been through more than most people could endure and you're still fighting strong. Keep up the battle and never lose the fight," he advised as they reached Ari's floor.

"You know something, Rafe? I look forward to our little chats. You hide behind that expressionless mask of a face most of the time, but I see fire underneath the surface. I don't know if you know this or not, but you're a good man."

Rafe nearly stopped at her words. If she knew what he had planned for her daughter, she wouldn't feel quite the same way. Mothers like her tended to steer their daughters clear of men like him. For that matter, he never employed women with mothers like Ari's. An upbringing like that could instill silly, idealistic ideas about love.

An ironic smile fell upon his lips as they entered Ari's room. She stiffened until she saw her mother and beamed with the first smile she'd shown since the shooting. Maybe he *didn't* have to worry about Ari falling for him. She was as antagonistic in his company now as she had been from the beginning.

So he had nothing to feel guilty over. When she agreed to be his, she'd have absolutely no illusions on what kind of man he was.

He wheeled Sandra to the bed, then quietly stepped from the room. Mother and daughter needed time alone together, and he certainly didn't want to witness their happy reunion. He needed to harden his heart to prepare for the upcoming battle of wits with Ari.

*****

"I'm glad you're here, Mom. I've been so incredibly worried about you."

"That goes double for me. How are you feeling?"

"I'm much better. My chest still hurts, but it's nothing I can't live with. What's more important is how *you* are doing. The doctor told me that your surgery was a success, but I want to know how you feel, not the technical stuff he was spouting off to me."

"There's not a whole lot to tell. They were able to get control of the infection and they said no new cancer has been spotted. I'm going to be more weak than normal for another month or so, but the staff is sure I'll be going home before we know it. I can't tell you how badly I just want to sleep in my own bed again. I'm sure all the plants have died, but planting new ones will give me something to do until I can get back to the flower shop and begin working again."

Ari's heart raced as her mother spoke. She should tell her right now that the house and shop were gone. She'd been protecting her mom since she woke from the coma, but wasn't it worse to leave her with her hopes up? Ari opened her mouth, but no sound came out. She just couldn't break my mother's heart now.

"I'm glad to hear you speaking so positively, Mom," she finally whispered, tears choking her throat.

"Oh, baby, I'm sorry. Here I am rattling on and on about my big plans and you're lying here miserable. I'm a terrible mother," she said as she reached up to brush Ari's hair back, just as she'd been doing since Ari could remember. The gesture made Ari's tears overflow.

"No, Mom. I love hearing you speak about the future. I was so scared that we wouldn't have one, and it was the worst feeling in the world. I can't make it through this world without you," she cried.

"Arianna Lynn Harlow, I don't ever want to hear you say that again. You're a precious gift, entrusted to me to raise. You're the reason I love life. The rest of the world could crumble around us, even take me with it, and I'd be just fine with that as long as I knew that you were OK. Parents should never *ever* outlast their children. It's just wrong. When my time comes, promise me that you'll keep on dancing," Sandra demanded.

"I can't —"

"Of course you can! I raised you to be strong, and no matter what life throws at us, we can dodge it and then get back on our feet. I've never been more frightened in my life than when I found out you'd been shot. I can't believe anyone would dare hurt you. You are my life. I've thanked God for you every single day since the day I found out I was pregnant."

"Mom, if you keep on saying all that stuff, I'm never going to quit crying. I love you, too, more than you could imagine. It's been a hard year, but we're coming up on the other side."

This would be the perfect moment for Ari to tell her mother about the house and the floral shop. She knew she'd be sad, but she'd understand that Ari had no choice. She again opened her mouth to speak, and again the words refused to come. While she seethed in frustration, there was a knock on the door.

"Is this a bad time?"

Ari and Sandra both turned toward the door to find Rosabella, Lia and Rachel standing there with flowers and a giant box of chocolates.

"Anyone bringing chocolate is welcome in my room day or night," Ari replied with a watery smile.

"A girl after my own heart. How are you feeling today, Ari?" Rosabella asked as she set the chocolates on Ari's table.

"I'm feeling a lot stronger right now. The doctor said my iron levels are too low, and my blood pressure needs to go up, but I think he's just trying to torment me. A good dose of chocolate is the cure," she answered as she opened the box and pulled out a piece, popping it right into her mouth and sighing as the creamy confection melted on her tongue.

"I'm so rude. I apologize, but I see chocolate and the rest of the world goes hazy. Mom, I'd like you to meet Rosabella, Rachel and Lia, Rafe's family. Everyone, this is my mother, Sandra," Ari said sheepishly as she finished chewing and swallowed her chocolate.

"It's very nice to meet you all. I appreciate your being so kind to my daughter."

"It's a pleasure to meet you, as well. You have a beautiful little girl," Rosabella replied as she shook Sandra's hand.

After they all said hello and conversed for a moment, Sandra turned to Ari with a grin before leaning toward her table.

"You could be polite and offer to share," Sandra said as she swatted Ari's hand away and grabbed her own piece of candy. As Sandra bit down on the delicacy, her face wore the same expression of delight as her daughter's had.

"We brought a really big box so you'd share with us all," Rachel said as she sat on the edge of the bed and grabbed a piece.

"Rachel, that's not for you," Rosabella scolded her daughter.

"If I eat all of this," Ari broke in, "they'll have to find me a bigger bed. Thank you for such a thoughtful gift. Please, share it with me and let's all enjoy it together."

"Well, you talked me into it," Lia said as she sat on the foot of the bed and leaned forward to grab a piece. "Your color looks a lot better today. I'll bet you can go home soon."

"I sure hope so. I think your brother is bribing the staff to keep me here against my will as punishment for not obeying him," Ari said offhandedly, not thinking about her words.

"Not obeying him? What did he want you to do?" Rachel asked with a smile.

"Ooh, I bet it was something kinky," Lia joined in with a laugh.

"Girls, you're terrible," Rosabella scolded.

Ari's face flamed crimson as she looked from her mother to Rafe's mom, and then his sisters. There was no way she'd reveal their relative's kinky after-hours activities.

"This hospital doesn't get very many TV channels, so someone please tell me that you watch *Supernatural*, and fill me in on what Sam and Dean have been up to. I would so totally turn into an evil vampire just so I could get in a tangle with the two of them. Yummy!"

Ari's tactic worked. Her uncharacteristic sentiments shocked everyone into forgetting all about what she'd said about Rafe.

"Well, Dean got into another scrape…"

Ari sat back as Lia caught her up on the adventures of the Winchester boys. The show was her one weakness. She had a thing for the sexy brothers, and who could blame her?

Chapter Twenty-Seven

"That's four kings. Read 'em and weep!" Ari shouted as she did a victory wiggle on the bed and waved her arms.

Rafe's body instantly hardened as her breasts swayed and her face flushed. It had been a month since he'd felt her tight core gripping him while he was buried deep inside her. He was on edge and it seemed that even a small draft of air made him turn hard as a rock these days.

"Oh, quit being a sore loser. You're not concentrating at all today, and I'm way up in winnings," Ari said with glee.

The comment distracted him from his sexual frustration. When he'd demanded that be a prize when they played cards, she'd insisted on playing for nickels. The really funny part was that she got excited when she won a humongous jackpot of…two dollars! Even more comical was his own enthusiasm when he won. Somehow being in Ari's presence brought out the kid in him.

Ari was messing with his head, and it frightened him most that he found joy in playing simple card games with her. Never had he taken an afternoon off of work to play poker. He had to put a stop to this, and the only way to do that was to get her out of the hospital and into his bed.

"Are you going to brood all day about your loss or are you going to deal again?"

"Hasn't anyone ever told you that patience is a virtue?"

"Once or twice. Now, deal. I'm on a winning streak," she commanded as she rubbed her hands together.

Rafe found himself laughing as he shuffled the cards, not a fake humor-a-person laugh, but a real deep-from-the-gut one. Ari had a way of knocking him off his feet.

When he looked up, she was staring at him in wonder, her eyes dilated as they moved down to gaze at his lips. Just when his body had started to behave, she had to look at him like that. His erection came back in full force and more painful than ever.

"If you're going to look at me with that come-hither expression, I'm going to forget that you're injured and take you right now," he warned, then began moving the table aside.

Her mouth opened in a shocked gasp, but she didn't tell him *no*. Rafe stood up, and shut the door and locked it. He'd be gentle, he assured himself as he reached for the button on his pants.

"Knock, knock. Time to take your vital signs."

Rafe quickly unlocked the door again, but he nearly growled when the nurse walked in. He was on the verge of telling the woman to get the hell out, but he caught himself. And without turning back to look at Ari, he fled. His body was on fire and it looked as if he wasn't going to find relief anytime soon. He knew the moment was over and Ari would be back on guard when he got back.

A stiff drink, or ten, was about all that would help him until he got her in private. He left the hospital, having decided it best not to return that night.

*****

"You're doing much better today. The doctor said that if your vitals remain stable, you can return home."

Ari glared at Rafe as he invited himself into her room. She'd been in the hospital for two weeks, and each day Rafe had been there. He'd been kind and considerate, and had played games with her, brought her amazing food, and generally treated her like royalty.

His hands were constantly touching her, rubbing her feet, brushing her arm, pushing back strands of her hair. Her nerves were shot, and this news was some of the best she'd ever heard. She had to get away from him before she did something stupid like agreeing to work for him.

"Good. I'm ready to go home. I can't believe I still have a job after missing work for weeks, but

I'm counting my blessings. I just want my life to return to normal."

"Of course you still have your job, Ari. Would your boss really fire the woman splashed all over the papers for assisting in taking down a killer?"

Rafe sat on the edge of her bed and she automatically scooted away. Each time their bodies brushed, heat surged through her, and resisting him kept getting harder.

"I didn't assist you in taking down the shooter. I was shot and I passed out. The press just likes to put a good spin on things so it can sell more papers. Do you realize how many magazines have called wanting the latest scoop? When I tell them what really happened, they quickly grow bored and move on to the next story."

"Ah, that's just because they don't know you the way I do. If they were to take the time to delve into your head, they'd be down here panting to hear your story," he said as he picked up her hand and brought it to his lips.

"Why do you keep pursuing me? I'm not a match for you. I will never be obedient. I will never do the things you ask of me. And why are you so human one minute, and then a complete jerk the next? Do you realize that if you turned off the jerk buttons in your brain, you would actually make an excellent boyfriend?" she asked.

Instantly, shutters came down over his eyes and he took on the cold expression for which he was well-known. How hot and cold the man could run, she reflected. One moment he was a white knight, rushing in to rescue the frightened maiden, and then the next, he was every superhero's worst villain.

After getting to know his parents a little more, she really couldn't understand him. He'd been raised in a loving home; so what if his wife had betrayed him and wounded his pride? Normal people got over such things.

"I'm your ride home. I'll be back in two hours," he said in a clipped tone and left.

Ari rolled her eyes and silently wished him good riddance. Still, she resigned herself to the fact that he'd be taking her home — Rafe was determined, and she saw no way out of it.

Once she was out of the hospital, her life would return to normal and she could go back to being just plain old boring Ari. She liked her uninteresting self. With her new friends, she allowed her adventurous side to appear a little more often, but her everyday life was humdrum — and she was happy with that.

Sure, she didn't have love and excitement, but the offset to that was she didn't have pain and heartbreak, either. Being with Rafe would be one huge roller coaster of emotion, and most of the time she'd be coming down, not going up. She didn't need that in her life.

*****

Rafe spoke to the doctor before heading back to Ari's room. She was good to go. And *he* was ready for the hospital visits to end. He had desires that needed to be taken care of, and playing a game of cards with her wasn't doing it.

Rafe made plans for the next chapter in their adventure. Today had been a good day, for he'd acquired what he needed to seal the deal with Ari. All it would take was the perfect moment for him to lay his cards on the table. Every good gambler knew finesse was half the game. "I see you got the clothes. How are you feeling?"

"I'm fine, Mr. Palazzo. Thank you for your kindness," she grumbled, not thrilled with having to use one more item he'd given her.

"Ari, do we have to go through this again? I've heard you say *Rafe*, so I know you're capable of doing it. Every time from here on out that you call me Mr. Palazzo, I'll remind you why I'm the one in charge. Do you understand? When you answer me, say my first name."

He was smiling, but he could see by her expression that she knew he wasn't bluffing. He hoped she defied him because he was more than ready to teach her a few new games. He'd thought about satisfying his needs with another woman, but somehow the idea just didn't appeal. It was a problem he knew he'd be able to solve once he broke his little Arianna.

"Your time is running out," he warned as the muscles in his jaw twitched.

"Yes. I understand...Rafe," she said through clenched teeth.

The sound of his name on her lips caused his pulse to skip. She was a spitfire, a true gem that he would worship...for a short amount of time.

"I have to admit that I'm a bit disappointed, Ari, but I'm not too worried. You can't help but defy me. I look forward to the next time," he said with a wicked smile.

She glared at him with murder in her eyes. He had no doubt that she desired him, but she also despised him. That was good. She needed to remember who he was and what he wanted.

Women had an agenda. Some admitted it, others didn't, but they all wanted something — no, a long list of things — from a man, whether it was riches, fame, security, whatever. Men were simple creatures who wanted only one thing from their women: that they fill their needs, satisfy them. Why should he be ashamed of his one-track mind? It was natural; love wasn't.

He wasn't a bad guy — not at all. He was actually being kind to women by letting them know up front how he felt and what he expected. A small voice in his head called him a fool, but he quickly pushed his conscience down, and he escorted Ari from the room. He had a couple of stops on the way to her apartment. If he could help it, she wouldn't be in that dump for long.

Chapter Twenty-Eight

"Where are we?" Ari asked as Rafe parked the car in an underground garage. He'd had to use a card to enter and there were cameras everywhere. Rafe was a lot of things, but she hadn't really figured him for a kidnapper.

Maybe he'd grown tired of waiting for her and decided to lock her away until she finally consented. Her stomach knotted as he climbed from the car and walked around to open her door.

She warily stepped from the vehicle and waited for an explanation. He simply smiled at her as if he had everything under control, then held out his arm. She was too worn out to fight him, especially when she knew she'd lose anyway, so she allowed him to lead her to a set of elevators. He did all of this without saying a word.

Rafe swiped a card against a black box and the elevator doors instantly opened. Ari threw him a questioning glance as she stepped inside; he ignored the look and pushed a button. The two of them began climbing floor after floor in a smooth ascent that seemed interminable to Ari. At long last, a small chime announced their arrival. Relieved, she glanced at the number highlighted on the elevator buttons and learned that they were on the sixteenth floor.

"This way, please."

Now wasn't the time for Ari to defy him, in what looked to be an apartment complex. Even though he always promised her that all she had to do was say *no* and he'd stop, she was afraid not of him, but of her reaction to his touch.

She didn't think she'd be able to tell him *no*, and she almost hated herself each time she detonated in his arms. She didn't feel like the woman her mother had raised her to be.

He pulled out another card and slid it where a doorknob should have been, and the door opened easily. Whatever had happened to keys and knobs? It was doubtless too ordinary for Rafe to enter a building that used good old-fashioned deadbolts. She wouldn't be surprised to discover laser beams ready to strike down trespassers.

"Are you ever going to tell me where we are?" she snapped as she walked inside and found herself entering a large living area.

"This could be your home. I've owned it for months," he responded as she turned to look at him. She was appalled at how confident he was that she'd cave to him.

"You're wasting both *your* money and *my* time. I don't want your apartment. Please take me home now," she said and turned back toward the door.

"Look around, Ari. What have you got to lose?" Though he spoke softly, the tone in his voice told her he wasn't making a request. It was a command.

"So, this is where you chain your whores up and do unspeakable things to them. It looks a bit too home and garden. I was expecting a dungeon with whips and chains hanging on the walls. Of course, I haven't seen the rest of the place, so that might just be through a secret passage," she said as she began moving toward the hallway.

"I don't need whips and chains, Ari. I'm quite convincing," he whispered in her ear, making her jump. She hadn't realized he was right on her heels.

"Yes, you're a macho god whom all should fear and bow to. Whatever was I thinking?" she said as she turned back to bat her eyes at him.

Rafe glared at her. "One of these days that tongue will get you in more trouble than you know how to deal with."

"Is that a threat, Rafe? For a man who doesn't punish his women, you sure use a lot of intimidation."

Rafe pushed her hard against the wall, his body blocking her from moving as he gazed down at her, his eye color almost fully purple. Her heart rate quickened and her breathing became shallow at the hunger mixed with rage that shone through his dark depths.

"I never once said I don't punish, Ari. I do punish, and I will delight in teaching you obedience.

What I've said is that I don't cause pain," he growled before his head bent and he took control of her lips.

She pushed against his chest, knowing that within a few minutes she'd be a goner if he continued ravishing her mouth. Just as her knees began to grow weak, he pulled back, his breathing ragged.

"Finish your tour," he commanded, then he turned and walked away. Ari leaned against the wall for several more seconds as she heard him open a cupboard. When she felt confident that her legs wouldn't fail her and she could move without sinking to the floor, she progressed down the hall and walked through an open doorway.

Her eyes widened at the stunning four-poster bed in the center of the room. Its posts were thick and intricately carved; a deep purple comforter spread over it caught and held her eyes. Was there any way he could have known that purple was her favorite color? No, it was surely a coincidence. She wanted to run her fingers over the gleaming fabric and see whether it was as soft as it looked, but since she'd never sleep in that bed, there was no point in torturing herself. She'd never attain such a life of luxury.

That isn't true, she snapped at herself. When she finally finished college and got the job of her dreams, she'd earn an excellent salary. She'd treat herself to those things that made life a little easier, and she'd also treat her mother and make up for all the years of sacrifice.

Ari turned to leave, not daring to look into the bathroom, where she knew there would be a large tub calling her name, and that's when something caught her eye. She turned back to the bed and looked up.

Her eyes widened as she realized what it was. Her hand came up and covered her mouth; she took a step closer. Yes, it really unsettled her, but only because it wasn't horror she was feeling — it was the first stirrings of excitement.

"I can see by the way your body is tensing that you won't be as opposed to my lifestyle as you so vehemently insist. Just the thought of the things I want to do to you appears to turn you on, and you're just too afraid to admit it — to me or yourself."

The sound of Rafe's seductive voice whispering in her ear while the sight of his bondage straps floating before her made her knees weak. His hands snaked around her stomach and slid beneath her shirt.

His fingers slowly moved up and over her breasts, lightly brushing against her nipples through the thin cotton of her bra as his breath whispered across her neck. When his tongue slid out and tenderly trailed across her skin, heat surged through her, demanding that her body respond — and it did; her core instantly grew moist and ready.

"Yes, Ari. You want this. You want this so badly that you're trembling. You want to play all kinds of games with me. Admit it. Stop fighting me and let me make the decisions. I've never once had a woman regret it."

Ari's entire body tensed as her passion evaporated. He might as well have slapped her in the face. How many other women had he screwed in this same bed? How many others had he run his fingers across, then thrown out like yesterday's garbage?

"I'm ready to go home now," she said as she wrenched herself away and walked out the door. She didn't stop until she was clear of the condo and standing before the elevator. She was grateful he didn't try to stop her. At least he was keeping his word of taking *no* for an answer.

Chapter Twenty-Nine

Utter silence marked the ride to Ari's apartment. Why her sudden change of heart? Rafe wondered. He'd handpicked that condo for her, chosen every single item in it.

He always treated his mistresses well. But with Ari, he'd gone above and beyond what he normally did and had taken extra time to get to know her. He knew which scents were her favorites, knew that she preferred a luxurious bath to a diamond necklace, and most importantly, knew that she was trapped in a prison, just waiting for someone to free her.

She might think she's won in our battle of wills, but she's only delayed the inevitable. At the moment Rafe was too angry for further discussion. Besides, he wasn't fighting on a fair battlefield — she was still recovering from surgery. So if he pushed and she gave in, how could he value her surrender? The delay was all for the best. He preferred his victories when his opponent was at full strength.

He pulled up outside her dilapidated apartment complex and stepped from his vehicle. Annoyance flashed through him when she opened her car door and stepped out before he made it around to her side, but he said nothing, just followed her up the sagging steps.

Should the next item on his to-do list be to get the complex condemned? It wasn't up to code, so he'd be doing the tenants a favor. Rafe loathed slumlords, those worthless bottom-feeders who preyed on the weak and helpless. Maybe he'd buy the property and fix it up. He made a mental note to look into it.

"Thank you for the ride," Ari said as she slipped her key in the rickety door lock and moved it around as Rafe stood silently by. When she finally opened the creaking door, she let out a breath of relief as she stepped inside.

"I'll see you soon, Ari."

"Don't bother. I think we've come to the end of our brief journey together. I hope you'll respect me and yourself enough to let this go," she replied while looking down at her feet.

Rafe backed her into the apartment, his meaning clear as they moved until she ran into the wall. He placed his fingers beneath her chin and tugged until she finally met his gaze.

"If all I saw was indifference on your face, then I *would* go away, Ari. Unfortunately for both of us, you're far more interested than you profess. There's fire burning in your eyes, and whether you like it or not, your body responds to me like a fiddle to its bow. When you stop the fight, I'll be there to release those inhibitions you hold on to so tightly and you'll have to hang on for the ride — because believe me, it will be wild."

Ari's breathing deepened and Rafe knew he could take her right where she stood. He knew she wouldn't fight him — wouldn't do anything but cry out his name as the crescendo of her pleasure reached its peak.

"You have my number," were his parting words as he walked out her door.

Needing to burn off energy, Rafe drove straight to the gym and changed, then headed to the boxing ring. As he did his warm-up activities, adrenaline began pumping through him. He'd feel much better after a good battle.

"Rafe, it's been a while. You're in luck — Sam's here."

Rafe turned to find his favorite trainer, Mickey, leaning against the wall with a delighted smile on his face. Rafe just nodded his head. The man got a bit too excited at the prospect of blood spilling, and they both knew that was about to happen. Sam was a middleweight champion boxer, and Rafe's favorite sparring buddy.

They always got rough, and by the end, both of them would be hurting, but it was a good ache. Boxing was a perfect outlet for Rafe — it relieved his high levels of stress and calmed him. He was ready.

A crowd started to gather as Rafe climbed into the ring. They all enjoyed watching a good sparring match. Then Sam strode in and their eyes locked.

"I didn't think I was going to be able to kick some ass today," Sam said with a smile. "It's been a while since you've been down here. Are you sure you want to go a few rounds with me, pansy?"

"I think you're just too damn chicken to fight me. Did you leave your 'big boy' pants at home?" Rafe shot back.

"Nah, I left them at your mother's house when I snuck out the window this morning."

Rafe laughed as Sam stepped into the ring and came over to give him a half-hug. They turned as Mickey joined them, holding out the headgear.

"No." Rafe pushed away the helmet. He wanted to feel a bit of pain — it would help ease his anger.

"It's your funeral," Sam said with a wicked grin.

"All right, boys. You know the rules. No groin shots or any of that sissy hugging. If I have to pull you apart, I'm going to get cranky. Keep it clean and knock the crap out of each other," the trainer said as he patted them each on the shoulder.

Rafe and Sam hit gloves, then went to their corners. The bell rang and they came out fighting...

"Rafe! What happened to you?" his mother exclaimed when he walked in the house. His family members were all supposed to be gone already, but they'd delayed their departure. As much as he loved them, he was ready for their meddling visit to be over.

"I'm fine, Mom. I was just sparring at the gym."

"You have a black eye and swollen lip," she exclaimed.

"Yeah, that tends to happen when I spar with Sam," he said with a chuckle. "You should see what his face looks like. It's never pretty, but it looks even worse now."

"That's terrible. I didn't know you were still into that awful boxing. I could just kill your father for introducing you to the sport."

"Yeah, you have to say that as my mother, but it looks a lot worse than it feels. As a matter of fact, I haven't felt this good in a while," he answered as he walked into his den and moved behind the bar.

He grabbed a cold bottle of craft beer and took a long swallow. He wouldn't admit it, but he was a lot more sore than he should be. It really had been a while since he'd sparred.

"We were planning to leave tomorrow morning, but we can stay until you're better."

"No! I mean, thanks for the offer, but I'll be working night and day over the next few weeks, so you'd be wasting your time hanging out here," he added quickly, hoping he hadn't hurt her feelings.

"OK, I get it. You want your space back. We'll take off, but you'd better call us if there's anything at all that you need. Do you understand?"

"Yes, of course, Mom. I'm going to head up to bed. Let me know when you get back home, OK?"

He gave his mother a hug, then managed to walk up the stairs without flinching. As he tugged off his shirt, he winced. His shoulder felt like it was on fire. Sam hadn't realized he'd been shot a couple of weeks ago, and had landed a punch in the exact wrong place. Rafe had seen stars for a moment, and Mickey had called the fight, then proceeded to lecture Rafe for the next fifteen minutes about being a stupid idiot.

Rafe didn't allow many people to call him an idiot, but he made an exception for Mickey. He'd known the guy since he was in grade school.

After a hot shower he felt far more human and decided he'd survive. He also had his appetite back, so he made his way downstairs again to grab a sandwich. After he'd finished, the doorbell rang. His staff had already turned in for the night and he didn't want his parents to be woken up, so he rushed to the door to find out who could be rude enough to come calling at almost midnight.

Rage filled him when he saw who his unwelcome visitor was.

"Good evening, lover. It looks like I got here just in time. You seem to be in need of some tender loving care."

Chapter Thirty

"What in the hell are you doing here, Sharron?"

"Now is that any way to talk to your wife?"

"You haven't been my wife for several years. Get the hell off my property before I have you arrested."

"But, baby, I miss you so much." She dropped her coat, revealing a skimpy red teddy, and not much else. Before he could slam the door in her face, she grabbed ahold of him.

Rafe quickly gripped her arms and pushed her away in disgust.

When she realized seduction wasn't getting her what she wanted, the waterworks began.

"Oh, Rafe, I need you. I thought I wanted something different in my life, but I just can't seem to live without you. Please don't be so cruel," she sobbed as she reached for him again.

"So for the past three years you've done nothing except cry over our broken marriage? Was that before or after my former best friend dumped you?" he mocked.

"No, of course not. I tried to live my life, attend parties, smile for the cameras, but all of that was nothing but a show. Once a woman's been with a man like you, there's ultimately no moving on. I need you, Rafe. Please. You used to love me so much. I know you still do," she wailed.

She was a great little actress. She'd really missed her calling in life. Rafe didn't know whether it was vindictiveness or just because he'd had a hell of a day, but he invited her in by opening the door wide.

"Oh, thank you, baby. I knew you'd missed me, too," she said as she once again threw herself at him. He brushed her off and started moving down the hallway.

"Follow me."

Her five-inch heels clicked on the hardwood as she practically ran to keep up. He imagined her modified breasts were about to spill from her lingerie. Nothing about her manufactured body did a thing for him. When he'd met her, she'd been real, not some plastic Barbie Doll.

He really should have known what she was. She hadn't tried to hide her greediness all that carefully, Rafe reminded himself. But he'd just assumed she appreciated the finer things in life — nothing wrong with that — but he hadn't realized that the finer things were the only things she appreciated from him.

"Sit down," he commanded.

She sauntered over to his office couch and sat, arranging herself in the most appealing way she could. He gazed at her, wondering if there would be even the slightest spark inside him. After all, he was *incredibly* sexually frustrated.

As his gaze traveled from her expertly made-up face, over her breasts, and then across the top of her thighs — he felt nothing, not even the barest twinge. Interesting.

"Why don't you sit with me, Rafe? Better yet, why don't you take me to your bedroom — I've learned a few things over the years that I think will make you a *very* happy man," she promised.

"I have a better idea," he said as he reached for the file he was looking for and slowly approached her. Triumph sparked in her eyes when he leaned down. She really thought she had him fooled.

"What's that, lover?"

"Why don't we talk about you," he said, his tone not giving anything away.

"Mmm, what do you want to know? I'm an open book,' she said seductively.

"Well…" He paused, wanting to fully enjoy the devastation on her face when she heard what he was about to say.

"Why don't we talk about the fact that you're broke, you're about to be homeless, and you've been banished from the high-society circles from here to New York?"

It took a moment, but his words finally registered. Sharron stiffened; her satisfied smile fell away and hatred glowed in her eyes before she managed to control it. She plastered on a devastated expression in its place.

Rafe didn't feel the victory he'd planned on. To his surprise, he almost pitied the woman — almost. She had reaped what she'd sown. He was done with his small game. When he walked to the phone and lifted it to call his security, she flew off the couch toward him.

"What are you doing? Please! Let me explain. I was trying to be happy again after you threw me out. I lost all joy in life and wandered around like an empty shell. Then I met Antonio. I thought he was a good man. He was so nice to me at first. That's why I got the new breasts and nose — I wanted to please him. But then he turned out to be a real jerk. I thought he'd take care of me, so I wasn't careful with the divorce settlement, and then, out of nowhere, he kicked me out of his house, wouldn't even let me have the jewelry he'd bought for me. I didn't do anything to deserve that. Now I have nothing, no money, no home — nothing. You can't just leave me like this, Rafe. You love me."

Rafe listened to her speech without feeling a single emotion.

"According to my sources, he kicked you out because he found you in bed with the pool boy. Isn't that a bit clichéd, Sharron? The pool boy — *really*?"

"That's a lie. I would never do that."

"Tell it to someone who cares. I honestly don't. I thought I'd enjoy seeing you like this, but you matter so little to me that I've already grown bored with this conversation."

"You were never so cold before. What in the hell has happened to you?" she screamed.

"I'm who I always should have been."

"But what am I supposed to do?" she wailed.

"It looks as if you'll have to figure it out. I want you to leave my home, Sharron. Don't come back."

With that, Rafe lifted the phone and called security. They were there within seconds and Sharron didn't stop screaming the entire time they hauled her from his office. If she came back again, he wouldn't hesitate to have her thrown into jail.

Chapter Thirty-One

"It's so good to have you back, Ari!"

Ari braced for impact as her three friends engulfed her in a group hug. The embrace caused a modicum of pain to her still-healing wound, but it was worth any discomfort to feel so loved.

"I've missed you girls. What crazy adventures were you up to while I was gone?"

"We filled you in on everything when we went to visit you in the hospital. Now it's *so* your turn to spill. Who the heck was that complete hunk who was in your room the last time we were there? It's been killing us waiting all weekend to find out."

"Oh, he's nobody, really," Ari said, unwilling to discuss Rafe. With the messages she'd been receiving from him, she'd been on pins and needles. She knew the other shoe would drop; she just didn't know when. If he'd only stop playing games, at least then she would know what his next plans were. As things were, she was jumping at every shadow, listening through her thin apartment walls to every door that opened or closed.

Ari was grateful finally to be back at work — he wouldn't be showing up here. He had too much class to storm her building and carry her off. Darn! The thought of him doing just that stirred up the beginning flames of excitement. Shudders, yes, but not of fear...

What was she thinking? The man was screwing with her head whether he was around or not. All this stress couldn't be good for her health.

"You are such a liar — and a very bad one, at that. From the second he walked into your room, the temperature rose fast and furiously. The heat in his eyes alone was enough to melt the skin from my bones. After leaving your hospital room, I went home and jumped my husband. He was so thankful, he told me to go back and do whatever it was I was doing before getting home," Amber said as she fanned her face.

"Amber!" Ari cried with mortification as she looked around.

"Oh, come on, Ari. We all do the down and dirty. I just need a pic of your guy hanging above my bed so I can have red-hot sex with my hubby while fantasizing about your sex god."

"How cute. You're actually embarrassing her," Miley said with a laugh.

"Come on. We've known Ari for months now. You know she blushes at even the mention of the *S-E-X* word," Shelly said.

"You are terrible, monstrous friends. I can't believe I'm still standing here taking this abuse," Ari said with a smile.

"Yes, we're horrible. I'm expecting a chariot of fire to show up to escort me to the gates of hell at any moment. For now, I'm still here, so spill the beans before we try Chinese water torture on you," Amber threatened.

"I just want to say that I truly feel sorry for your husbands. Living with any of you has got to be like being married to an FBI agent — all this constant interrogation. Geesh."

"Yeah, yeah. Now spill," Shelly said, tapping her toe impatiently on the floor.

"He was…just a friend. I refuse to spill anything further. I've been away from work for a couple of weeks now, and I don't want to give them any excuses to fire me. If you promise to leave me alone for the entire day, then maybe, just maybe, I'll share something with you after work," Ari said, making sure to look each of them in the eye.

"Fine, but I want you to know that I'm not very happy about this," Miley pouted.

"You can grumble and call me names behind my back."

"OK. That makes it a little better," Shelly said with a forgiving smile.

"We really have missed you, Ari. No one has managed to enter this friendship circle before you came along. You've turned us from the three musketeers to the Foursketeers."

"Foursketeers? That's not a real word," Ari said with a laugh.

"Yeah, well, it sounded good in my head," Amber responded.

"Are you ladies planning on working anytime soon, or do you think chatting around the water cooler is in your job description?"

"We're going. Keep your pants on," Miley said as she turned toward her office.

"Miley," Ari hissed and then glanced apologetically at her boss. "I'm sorry, sir. I'm coming now."

"It's good to have you back, Ari," he replied before smiling and heading back to his office.

Amber hugged her again, and they all went to their desks. As Ari sat down, she took a relieved breath. The job was hardly exciting, but her friends made it worth being there. She truly hoped they never ended up going their separate ways. She'd found laughter again, and she didn't want to lose it.

Ari managed to avoid telling her friends much of anything about Rafe, but she didn't know *why* they didn't pump her for information. They had got ahold of her cell phone while she was in the bathroom and found several steamy text messages from him from the week before. Even though his parting words had left her to believe he'd wait for her to contact him, that hadn't lasted long. The things he said to her were unacceptable – and yet they made her ache in ways she absolutely didn't want to ache.

Since the girls were determined to hook her up — she needed it! — they decided to use this opportunity for some matchmaking. The messages they'd read were all about what he wanted to do to her…all night long, but Ari's replies were less than enthusiastic.

Her friends wanted to see a show, and they were about to get their money's worth.

Chapter Thirty-Two

"I won't take no for an answer; do you understand?"

Ari stood frozen, as if trapped, knowing there was no way out. She either said *yes* and did this the easy way, or she said *no* and was kidnapped and had all sorts of tortures inflicted upon her. She wanted to run, but she knew there was no way out.

"Fine, *yes*. I want you to know that I'm not going willingly and I'm *very* upset with you."

"I can live with that."

Ari watched as Amber sauntered away, obviously pleased to have gotten her way. Ari was stuck going out dancing with the girls. At least Amber had promised that they'd go a classy Latin club where her brother was a bouncer. Ari had threatened their lives if there were any more roofie incidents.

"Let's go. Miley and Shelly are already in the car. My husband took the kids to a movie, so my house is where we're getting ready. I have the perfect outfit for you."

"No way are you dressing me 'slutty,' Amber," Ari yelled as she chased after her friend. She had to protest even though she knew she would lose in the end. It seemed to be the story of her life.

For the entire half-hour's drive to Amber's place, the girls chattered on about how amazing this club was. Ari had to admit, if only to herself, that it did sound rather fun. She'd ignored the messages from Rafe all week, and tonight was a good time to see whether she could find a man who'd spark her interest as much as he did.

Heck, for that matter, she'd be satisfied if she could find a man who sparked even half that much interest. She refused to believe he was the only man alive who could turn her knees to gelatin.

"I'm on hair duty," Miley called as she walked in the bathroom and grabbed the curling iron, flatiron and several bottles of hairspray. Ari cringed, knowing how long it was going to take her to get her hair back to normal.

"Cool. I'll do makeup," Shelly said as she grabbed the beauty bag.

"That leaves me to pick out the outfits," Amber said with far too much enthusiasm.

"Sit," Miley ordered as she led Ari to the table. Within seconds she was twisting Ari's hair into a series of tight loops and pinning them to her head. Once her hair was off her face, Shelly started applying makeup.

"Don't make me look like a hooker," Ari insisted.

"We're just trying to help you get laid. Be grateful." Miley snapped as she tugged on a strand of her hair.

"I don't need help," Ari grumbled.

"That's where you are so wrong. If anyone has a stick higher up her ass, I don't know where to find her. Relax. We'll have fun tonight."

"Why does it seem to be your mission to hook me up?"

"Isn't it obvious? We're all in marital bliss and we want to spread the joy," Amber said as she joined them. The three women burst out laughing at her joke.

"It's more like we're trapped in suburbia and we get to live vicariously through you," Miley admitted.

"Are your marriages that bad?" Ari asked with concern.

"Oh, honey, you know we're just kidding around We all love our husbands and our kics, but honestly, each of us got married too young and didn't get to play as much as we wanted, so it's fun to have a single friend we can pimp out. Not one of us would cheat on her husband, though. I promise you that," Amber said solemnly.

"OK, fine. You win. Do what you want, but I'm warning you that I have two left feet. No matter how good you try to make me look, it won't matter when I step all over some poor schmuck's toes."

"Ari, you'll look so smoking hot, he won't care what part of his body you're stepping all over, just as long as he can touch you," Amber said with a whistle.

By the time they left the house, Ari was almost too embarrassed to be out in public. The dress she was wearing hugged her curves like a second skin, from her cleavage-showing top to her hips. There, the bright red material flared out until it ended at mid-thigh. As if that weren't bad enough, there was a slit in the side that would show the world too much of her goodies if she turned wrong.

"Quit fidgeting. It ruins the siren effect," Miley snapped.

Ari did feel sexy, she had to admit. Never had she owned anything so daring. Her feminine assets were on display, but since the other women were dressed almost as sexily, she didn't feel out of place. Besides, they had connections at the club, a personal bodyguard, so what could go wrong? Nothing. That was, nothing could go wrong unless your friends advised the bodyguard to let you get a little action on the dance floor.

"OK, we got here early enough for the dance lesson. I hope it's a good one tonight," Shelly announced as she climbed from the vehicle.

"No one said we were taking dance lessons. I'm afraid even to move in this dress, let alone swing about," Ari gasped in horror.

"Ari, you promised to be a good sport. If you go back on your word, then we won't lay off you all month. If you just go with the flow tonight, we'll leave you alone forever," Amber said, with her fingers crossed behind her back.

"You swear?"

"Of course. I just want to add that I'm hurt you even asked," Amber said as she turned and walked away.

"I'm sorry. I'll quit griping and just enjoy myself," Ari called out. She caught up to the other three.

"Good. That's what we want to hear," Shelly said as the club door was held open for them.

Ari was a little suspicious of their instant forgiveness, but the low, smoky lights of the club caught her attention and she forgot all about their little tiff.

"Darlings, you got here just in time. Pierre is about to start the lesson, so hurry on over. You know how he hates to be kept waiting. Tonight it's the cha-cha-cha."

Ari turned to find a small man wearing way-too-tight pants, who seemed to be herding them toward the back of the room.

"Donnie, it's been too long. We've missed you," Miley said as she kissed him on the cheek.

"That's because I'm a one of a kind, gorgeous. Now go," he commanded as he smacked her on the butt. Ari quickly followed them, not wanting to get left behind.

"Hurry. Hurry. You four are holding me up. If Donnie hadn't insisted his friends were coming, we could have been well into our lesson by now."

Ari was rendered motionless at the sight of the stunning dance instructor. His pants were also too tight, but that was a blessing for every female in the room.

"Are you going to stand there gawking all night, princess, or are you here to learn?"

Ari was mortified as her friends laughed while dragging her to the front of the room.

"Don't worry, Ari. The first time I saw Pierre, I had a minor orgasm. When he touched my ass during a lesson, I had a major one. Don't get too excited, though, 'cause he and Donnie are a couple. It's probably a good thing, 'cause I think I'd forget my husband's name if that man wanted to heat the sheets with me for a night," Amber said with a giggle.

"The cha-cha is a teasing, sexy and fun dance. You want to move toward your partner and then entice him to come back for you. The more you use your ass, the better. God gave you those luscious, beautiful behinds, so don't be afraid to shake them. If you can't shake your backside, then get out of my club because Latin dances without a shaking derrière are useless."

Ari was stunned to see that Pierre spoke with a completely serious face. She might actually be kicked out of the club. She'd never wiggled her butt before. She didn't know how to. With sweat breaking out on her forehead, she looked on in fear while he demonstrated the steps they'd be learning. She'd never pick that up in half an hour.

"*You*, come here."

Ari gazed at Pierre in complete terror. Was he kicking her out before they'd even begun? Could he tell by just looking at her that she was a fraud?

"*Go.* You do *not* want to keep Pierre waiting," Miley urged as she pushed Ari forward.

"Take my hands," he commanded. Luckily, her brain was working because somehow her arms came up and she found herself clasping the stunning man's hands.

"There are two basic steps to the cha-cha. The first is a rocking step. Basically, you're going to shift your weight from one foot to the other as you slowly move backward and forward. Remember to use the ass, always use that luscious booty. Don't just stand there. *Shift!*"

Ari looked at his legs and copied what he was doing. This wasn't so bad —just shifting her weight. She gained a smidgeon of confidence as the two of them moved.

"Good job, Ari. Nice butt wiggles," Amber called out.

Ari was going to kill her.

"Now, you add in a little bit of cha-cha-cha," Pierre said as he did a sort of wiggle with his knees while his hips shook back and forth. She stumbled a few times while trying to mimic him, and just when she thought he was going to lead her straight to the door, her body seemed to absorb the information.

"Good. You're doing well for a first-timer," Pierre told her.

"How do you know it's my first time?" she asked, feeling more confident.

"Ha. That's amusing. If it's not your first time, then just give up now," he said with a smile to take away the sting. He wasn't as scary as he'd first appeared.

Pierre placed Ari back in the line, then went through the group, helping each person until they got the basic moves down.

"Now, partner up. Yes, it's mostly women — don't be such prudes. I'm not asking you to strip down naked and get jiggy. You need to learn how to do the dance with a partner. Dancing is a prequel to lovemaking. If you want to make your man sweat on the dance floor, ladies, then tease him with your bodies. The dance should be a chase, and you don't allow him to catch you until you're good and ready. Do you understand?"

"Yes!" several of the women shouted out excitedly.

"Good. That's very good."

The time flew by, and too soon, Ari's dance lesson was over. She felt good as she walked from the back of the club. She might not be able to swing her butt as well as some of those women, but she could certainly cha-cha.

"Let's order a drink and then get to dancing," Amber said as they moved toward a table Donnie had saved for them.

The next few hours flew past and Ari danced with so many men, she couldn't keep track of them all. If she'd known what her friends were doing while she was on the dance floor, she'd have been on her way to prison for homicide.

Chapter Thirty-Three

Rafe's phone buzzed. He decided to ignore it —
he was tired, irritated and not in the mood for
whoever it was at the other end of the line. But
when the damned thing buzzed again, he sighed and
pulled it from his pocket. He would check quickly
and then turn the device off. Time to sleep, or else
to try to.

When he saw it was a message from Ari, his
pulse picked up a beat. She'd been ignoring his texts
all week. His first thought now was that she was in
trouble. As he clicked the button to open the
message, his heart stalled for a single beat.

When he looked at the two pictures that came in,
any thought of sleep evaporated. Who the hell had
sent him the pictures? Clearly not Ari. At the bottom
of the images was the club name. He knew exactly
where that was.

Rafe threw on his jacket and grabbed his keys. It looked as if Ari hadn't learned her lesson. She was out on the town again, attempting to get abducted for a second time. Rage simmered inside him.

She continued to deny *him* when all he wanted to do was offer her security. Well, offer her security and have her at his beck and call.

Rafe made it to the large Latin club in record time, walking to the front of the huge line outside its doors. Pulling a wad of hundreds from his pocket, he approached the bouncer.

"Welcome" was all the man said as he opened the rope for Rafe to enter while the people standing in line grumbled.

"*Shut up* or none of you are getting in," Rafe heard before the loud music drowned out the outside world.

He made his way to the dance floor and spotted Ari almost immediately. She was locked tightly in the arms of some heathen while the damned man ran his hands down her ass. Rafe saw red as he pushed forward.

"I'm cutting in," Rafe commanded.

The man turned, glaring at Rafe, until he saw Rafe's face — then he immediately backed down.

"Rafe. What are you doing here?" Ari asked as she grinned drunkenly at him.

"Apparently, I'm saving you again," he growled as he went to grab her hand. She was leaving with him *now*. "Let's go!"

"I don't want to go. Let's dance. I learned the cha-cha-cha tonight and I'm very good at it. John, Paul and Tiger… no…Trevor — oh heck, I can't remember his name — all said that I can move my ass just fine." she spouted happily.

Rafe stared at her incredulously. What in the hell was she talking about?

"Ari, I said, *let's go*," he repeated.

"I want to dance," she pouted. She then lifted her arms in the air and started doing the steps of the cha-cha. When she circled around and shook her backside with the slit of her dress exposing the side of her very thin black panties, Rafe forgot all about leaving.

He tugged her into his arms as the music shifted to a more sensual number. His hands slid down her back to tug her flush against him, and he began shifting his feet, one foot sliding between her legs, giving her no choice but to arch into him.

"I don't know this dance," she murmured huskily.

"Just follow my lead," he said as he began circling her around the dance floor.

"Mmm, I think I like this dance, too," she whispered as he moved his head down and inhaled her sweet scent.

He hadn't taken her in such a long time. Yes, it was wrong to seduce an inebriated woman, but wasn't alcohol just a social lubricant? Didn't a few glasses of courage only allow a person to do what they truly wanted to do in the first place? It wasn't as if he and Ari hadn't already had sex before.

"I'm taking you home and stripping that dress —if you can call it that — from your body."

"I like this dress. I was mortified to wear it at first, but Amber insisted. And when she gets her mind stuck on something, there's no talking her out of it. I think she secretly works for the government as a master torturer." Ari giggled at the thought.

"Amber? Is that one of the women who came to see you in the hospital?" The pieces of the puzzle were still hazy.

"Yes. I came with Amber, Shelly and Miley. They insisted on making me as slutty as possible because they're determined to get me laid. They said I'm too repressed and I need to let loose. Since sex was so incredibly hot with you, I figure, *why not*?"

Rafe didn't know whether to thank his lucky stars her friends liked to meddle, or put a leash on Ari. He now knew who'd sent the pictures. Her friends must have gotten into her phone, seen his messages and decided to stoke the fires. He groped back through his mind to recall what he'd texted her. Surely it was nothing too bad. Hell, at that moment, he really didn't care.

"So, what you're telling me is that you want to go out and have sex with strangers, but you won't sign on as my mistress."

He knew it was the alcohol talking, but still there had to be *some* truth to her words. Had he read her wrong all along? Did she really not desire him more than she would anyone? It was unlike him to feel doubt, but he didn't know what to think right then.

"I didn't know I liked sex until I had it with you, but it was good, *really* good, and I've decided I want to do that again and again. I can't do it with you though, 'cause you're a control freak who wants to rule my life."

"No, Ari, I want you to submit to me."

She looked at him with a furrowed brow for a minute as her booze-soaked brain tried to comprehend his words. He took the opportunity to caress her neck with his mouth and felt her low groan all the way to his toes. His manhood jumped painfully as she ground her hips against him.

"Isn't that the same thing?" she panted.

"Not at all. Let's go home and I'll show you the difference."

She looked at him as if she were trying to solve a difficult math problem. His body throbbed while he waited for her response. If she said *no*, he'd stay at the club until her friends took her home — but he hoped she'd just say *yes*.

"OK. I'd better tell my friends, though."

It took almost a full minute for her words to sink through to his brain. When it registered, he wasted no time in pulling her from the dance floor.

"Where are they?"

"Over there." she said with a drunken gesture.

He spotted the women he'd seen in her hospital room and made a beeline for their table. The three of them were staring at him as if he were their next meal. He had to admit they frightened him just a tad. He'd have to check for hex bags beneath his bed.

"The mysterious Rafe arrives. I vaguely remember seeing you at the hospital," one of the women said.

"Yes, somehow I received a message from Ari's phone with a picture and her location. I'm taking her home now."

"Is that OK with you, Ari?" one of the women asked.

"Oh, yes. Rafe is going to show me the difference between control and submission."

Rafe nearly groaned as he watched the three women's eyes pop out of their sockets at Ari's words. He and Ari were going to have to have another talk about privacy. Her friends suddenly seemed unsure whether they should allow Ari to leave with him.

He didn't care. Let them just *try* to stop him.

"Goodbye," he said firmly as he wrapped his arm around Ari's waist and grabbed her purse. Before the women could even think about standing up, he was hauling Ari through the club. He got her into his car and floored the gas pedal.

Just as he reached home, he looked over at her, anticipation burning hot. A groan escaped him. Ari was completely unconscious in the passenger seat. He might like a submissive woman, but he certainly didn't want a corpse.

He wondered whether a man could die from sexual frustration. He was beginning to think so. After he carried Ari into his home and laid her on his bed, he decided it was time for a stiff drink and an ice bath.

Chapter Thirty-Four

Ari turned over and felt a small ache in her temple — nothing too unbearable, but enough to make her realize she'd had one too many drinks the night before.

The blackness that surrounded her let her know it was sometime in the middle of the night. Her mouth felt parched; she was desperate for a glass of water. While she started to move the covers, her arm landed against something solid.

Tentatively, she wiggled her fingers and realized there was a man next to her. She froze, then tried to assess her situation.

The first thing she needed to figure out was *who* it was she'd gone home with. Very carefully, she reached inside the covers — she had some clothes on! That was a good sign! Ari let out a relieved breath.

Now, she just needed to figure out who was next to her in bed. To think that she'd decided to have a one-night stand, and she didn't even remember with whom. Horror filled her at the thought. Yes, she talked big, and she'd even thought she was capable of having casual affairs, but the reality of it was beyond mortifying. How could she respect herself when she treated sex like nothing more than a game? She felt bad enough that she fell apart each time Rafe so much as looked at her.

As soon as her thoughts touched on Rafe, Ari's memories came flooding back. She remembered dancing until her feet were screaming. There had been so many men, and it had all been nothing more than innocent flirting, and a whole lot of hip action. *Cha-cha-cha.*

One minute she'd been dancing with a stranger, then the next she'd been in Rafe's arms — right where she'd pictured being all night. He'd swept her across the dance floor, turning her excited body on in ways none of the other men could come close to doing.

Oh, the things she'd said to him. It was bad — so very bad. She'd practically begged him to make love to her. Ari felt her cheeks flaming in shame. *OK, if I can sneak away successfully, I'll never drink again,* she promised.

Very carefully, she slithered from beneath the covers and started edging herself off the bed. She started to smile as her feet touched the ground. She was almost there.

Just as she started to stand, his voice stopped her.

"Where are you off to, Ari? I've been waiting for hours for you to wake."

Oh, crap! Deal's off. I'm having a drink right now, she thought.

"I have to use the bathroom," she said as she rose to her feet and rushed across the room. She thankfully entered the correct door, and she found herself in his large bathroom, not his closet. Feeling trapped, nonetheless, she took her time, washing her face, guzzling some water, and using his facilities.

When she reached her hand up to push back her hair, a groan escaped. It was one giant rats' nest and it would take her forever to undo it. She spent twenty minutes fighting a losing battle before she gave up. The only thing that would help was an expensive bottle of conditioner applied about three or four times.

Knowing she'd wasted as much time as possible, she had to leave the bathroom. Though she didn't give it much of a chance, she was hoping he might be fast asleep as she turned the doorknob. Miracles could happen. She opened the door slowly…and the bedside lamp was on. Darn.

"That took a while. I hope everything's OK."

How rude was that? Was she on a timetable now? It didn't matter. She was going to be rational, not get into another futile sparring match.

"Um…well, thanks for the ride, but I need to be going now. I was a little drunk last night and said some things that I didn't really mean. You know how that goes. See ya," she muttered as she made an attempt to reach his bedroom door. He was there to block her path before she advanced three steps.

"Why in such a hurry? We made plans before you passed out on me."

"Look, I just said that I didn't really mean any of it. I do not want to stay, so I'll be leaving now," she said with false bravado. She was lying and they both knew it. She did want to stay. She was so tired of fighting him.

It didn't matter, though. They could come together like this a thousand times, but the bottom line was that she couldn't be the woman he wanted her to be. She decided that the only way to get out of this situation with him for good was to piss him off so badly that he wouldn't want to see her face ever again.

"You meant it, Ari — every last word you spoke on that dance floor."

"You know what, Mr. Palazzo? I'll tell you. I think you're a pig. I think you just want everything you can't have. Because I've told you that you can't have me, it's been your new mission to acquire me like any of your other possessions. I am not for sale. I am not your new shiny toy, and I think you're actually rather pathetic. Deal with the fact that this is one game you can't win."

Ari was proud of the strong tone of her voice. She was facing a giant and appeared to be winning. Ha, she'd go fight Goliath next! The slight flaring of Rafe's eyes as she used his last name again caused a tremor of fear, but she repressed the feeling.

"Do you want to know why I always win? I *always* win because I hold all the cards. I never go into anything without a guaranteed outcome. I've let you think you have a choice in all of this, but there's never been a choice. The only decision you've actually had was in controlling the time frame. Even that has been relative. Now, my patience has worn thin. It's time for you to accept that you're mine."

"You're so used to having everyone jump to do whatever you want that you don't see what an unmitigated tyrant you are. Does this kind of talk motivate people? Do you really think that you command respect? Fear and respect are two *very* different things, and you may inspire fear in those around you, but none of your people respect you."

"I could disagree with you, but I don't care enough to do so. I've tired of your self-righteousness, Ari. Why don't you just concede defeat and show me the appreciation that I deserve? I've saved you now on more than one occasion. You need to show your gratefulness to me. A good start would be by dropping to your knees and demonstrating your loyalty," he said with a smirk.

Fire raged in Ari's stomach. Never before had she wanted so badly to strike someone. She stepped closer to him, ready to show him exactly what she thought of his idea of controlling her.

"Undo my pants," he commanded. She froze at the arrogance emanating from him. Did he honestly think she was about to satisfy him? Maybe he was actually insane. Her arm rose involuntarily, and then the only sound that could be heard in the dark room was the sharp tone of flesh against flesh as her hand connected with his chiseled jaw.

His eyes widened with incredulity, and he raised his hand, his fingers gliding over his jaw.

"I must say I wasn't expecting that. You are quite full of surprises, Arianna," he murmured, flexing his jaw.

Her unplanned action still left Ari stunned.

"I'm leaving now," she finally gasped as she turned to run away.

"Oh, you're not going *anywhere*, Ari. You've asked me about punishment before. Well, you'll find out about it right now."

Ari screamed as he quickly picked her up and threw her over his shoulder. Fear, and yet a strange excitement, overtook her body as his hand came up and smacked her on the ass.

"Stop wiggling. The more you fight me, the more intense your punishment will be," Rafe said with eager anticipation running through his voice. When he stopped to pick up a few silk ties, Ari's eyes rounded with nerves. What was he planning to do?

Chapter Thirty-Five

Ari's stomach trembled as Rafe set her down on the cold tile floor. She immediately tugged against his hold on her arm, but she wasn't going anywhere.

"Rafe, stop. This is insane. We both said some things, did some stuff. All's forgiven. Let's just pretend this never happened," she pleaded with him as he turned a knob inside the shower and a forceful jet of water began flowing.

"Too late, Ari. You did two things wrong. Calling me by my first name now doesn't help you."

"Fine. How about I call you asshole, or demon spawn!"

"You're not helping," he said, an obvious smile in his voice. He was enjoying himself.

He picked her back up, and though she struggled against him, it made not a bit of difference He far outpowered her. Much too quickly, he had her hands secured together and then the soft sash he'd grabbed was holding her prisoner against the wall of the shower. He'd tied it to what looked like a bar on his shower wall.

Water cascaded over her still-clothed body as he stepped back and stripped off his own clothes. She couldn't turn her gaze away as he stepped inside the large space and his growing erection brushed against her hip.

"You fight this the whole way, but your body doesn't lie, Ari. That's unadulterated desire burning in your eyes. The pinch in your nipples means they are reaching out for me to take hold of them. The wet heat dripping from your body is you preparing for me to slam myself deep inside you. You're ready for this — for me. Let yourself go," he whispered as his thick staff leapt against her hip.

She shook her head, refusing to cave. She couldn't give him all the power. He'd never stop taking from her if she did.

"Time for you to learn why it's not a good idea to defy me," he whispered next to her ear before he took the lobe between his teeth and softly bit down.

Shudders racked her body as his mouth traveled down her neck. So far she wasn't seeing a downside to defying him. If it always ended like this, maybe she'd call him names more often. Then again, she knew regrets would come later — so there was a negative.

Suddenly his mouth left her and she heard a ripping sound as he tore off the shirt she was wearing. He tossed the saturated material to the back of the shower, and he ripped off her panties next, leaving her naked and trapped before him.

She moved forward, scooting to the wall as his hands reached for her ankles. Soon, her feet were spread apart and he had them secured, effectively trapping her with her body wide open to him.

"You think pain comes in just one form, Ari?"

"Yes," she trembled.

"You'd be wrong. You see, I've learned how to get what I want without beating a woman. I've learned how to gain control without being — what was it you called me? — demon spawn? I know I can hurt you if I want. I'm obviously bigger — stronger. There are many forms of torture in the world."

"What are you going to do?" she asked as he circled around her. She wished he would just get it over with; her dread of the unknown was surely worse.

"Do you like how your body feels as it builds up to an earth-shattering orgasm? What about the feeling as you glide over that edge into sweet bliss? Does that make you tremble, Ari? Can you feel your body growing hotter — wetter — tighter?" he asked as his hand slid down the curve of her hip, then slid around and glided inside her.

"Rafe..." she groaned.

"What, Ari?"

"Please. I was wrong. I want to have sex with you," she pleaded.

"We will, Ari, but you don't get to come."

"What?" she gasped as his finger moved in and out of her. She couldn't understand what he was saying. She strained to take his fingers deeper, but he pulled out, leaving her panting.

Rafe grabbed the shower head and started moving it across her body, the pulsing stream of water massaging her, sharpening her desire. He ran the jets across her protruding nipples, the sensation more intense than if he were sucking them into his mouth.

"Ohh, please," she groaned as he moved the strong jet down her torso and over her swollen core. As the water caressed her most sensitive area, she felt her orgasm building, felt release nearing. She strained to keep quiet, not wanting to alert him to how close she was.

"Do you think that will work, Ari? I can read your body. I can feel *everything* through your tense muscles," he whispered, pulling the spray away and moving it around to her back.

He continued massaging her body with the water, running the flow across every sensitive area she had until she was in tears. The agony of not feeling release was worse than anything she could imagine.

"Please, Rafe. I'll do anything," she cried. She needed him to take her over the edge.

He put the nozzle down as he pressed up behind her, his thick, pulsing staff resting on the crack of her butt. Grinding his hips against her, she tried to wiggle her behind, tried to tip her body so he'd slip down and slide deep inside her core.

"Not yet, Ari. This isn't about your pleasure; it's about mine. You told me you don't want this. You kept saying *no*. Well then, you don't get to feel satisfaction. When you say *yes*, I'll make you scream with pleasure," he promised as the head of his erection slid an inch inside her.

"I said *yes*," she cried.

"Not just *yes* for right now, Ari — *yes* for good."

"No," she moaned. She wouldn't give him that, even if she ended up expiring from frustration.

"Too bad for you," he said as he sunk into her. Oh, that's what she wanted. Yes! He felt so good, filled her so perfectly. She could dance with him like this for hours. He slid in and out several times, once again leading her toward the edge of oblivion, but then before she could reach her peak, he withdrew.

"No," she screamed, anger overtaking her at this game he was playing. He walked around in front of her, water still streaming over both of them, and untied her hands. Then, leaning against the wall, he pulled her forward and brought her head to his erection.

Without much thought, she did as he bade her, pulled him inside her mouth to taste his pleasure. She'd never before desired to suck a man, never thought she could enjoy the tang, but as her body burned with unfulfilled need, she devoured him, taking him deeper with each bob of her head.

"Yes, Ari, like that, *yes*!" he cried as his fingers tugged through her hair, holding her in place as his hips thrust forward. She couldn't take him all in, but her greed to taste him made her attempt to. She wanted him deep in her throat, wanted to feel his warm pleasure slide down, to know she'd sent him over the edge.

She was so close to her own completion. The burning inside her body made her movements faster as she rose up and down his staff.

"That's it. Yes!" he called out as she felt warm liquid hit her throat. His staff pulsed in her mouth as he poured himself across her tongue. She sucked greedily on the head of his erection — she didn't want to let him go. His groans of pleasure echoed through the shower.

Her body was throbbing as he pulled from her mouth and began untying her legs. Now, the torture was over. Now, it was her turn. She reached for him as her restraints were undone.

"Please, Rafe, please," she begged as he stepped back.

"No, Ari. That's your punishment. You get to burn all night. You don't get to feel the pleasure of release."

When Ari realized he was serious, she looked him in the eye as her hand moved down her body and she reached for the place that was pulsing with need. A few strokes and she could relieve the ache herself. There was no way she was going to leave her body aching like this.

"Ah, ah, ah," Rafe scolded as he snagged her hand. "I wouldn't make a very good monster — would I? — if I allowed you to be satisfied," he jeered as he carried her from the bathroom.

"Let's see what we can do about this." He laid her wet, naked body on the bed, then quickly tied her hands back together and secured them to the headboard.

"You can't do this. It's kidnapping," she screamed when he moved about the room.

"You told me *yes* in the shower, Ari," he reminded her.

"I've changed my mind. I want to leave now."

"Too bad. Don't cross me again, and we won't go through this."

"You won't have to worry about that as I plan on never seeing you again after tonight." Though she knew it was useless, she struggled against her ties.

Rafe walked from the room, and Ari's breathing was ragged. When he didn't return after several minutes, she began to panic. Did he really intend to leave her like this for the rest of the night?

She didn't know how long she lay there struggling against the restraints, her body burning, but soon the door opened again. She glared at him as he walked in. She wouldn't beg him anymore that night.

He said nothing as he came over and covered her up, then turned off the lamp and walked from the room again. Eventually, sweet oblivion came over her. Her last thought was of sweet revenge against Rafe.

Chapter Thirty-Six

Soon after she fell asleep, Rafe walked back into his room and found Ari moving on the bed, her sleeping form trying to find comfort. He'd left her for an hour, wanting to punish her, needing to reprimand her for her behavior.

Knowing she was so close, knowing she'd welcome the thrust of his hardening staff inside her heat made it impossible for him to stay away any longer. He could, of course, once again achieve his own pleasure without giving her satisfaction, but he didn't enjoy such an orgasm nearly as much.

He stripped off his robe as he made his way to the bed and slipped the covers down so he could admire the full softness of her beautiful breasts.

His fingers glided over her nipples, which instantly hardened beneath his touch. With just that light contact, his manhood stood up fully, ready to plunge deep inside her. He opened the nightstand

and sheathed himself before pulling the blankets the rest of the way off her gloriously naked body.

Spreading her thighs, he moved his head between her legs and woke her up with his mouth encircling her heated flesh.

"Oh, yes," she cried, her aroused body instantly waking, seeking the orgasm he'd withheld from her earlier. "Please don't stop," she sobbed. "Please…"

She struggled against the ropes as his tongue swirled around her swollen bud. When he brought her right to the edge, he pulled back, making her scream in frustration.

He slid up her body and gripped her head with his hands as his hips thrust forward and he buried himself inside her hot folds with one precise thrust.

Her cry of pleasure echoed in his mouth as one hand moved down to her hip and he gripped her, holding her securely in place so he could plunge quickly in and out.

He felt her walls convulse around him as she reached her peak, her scream filling the room. With a deep thrust, he buried himself so deeply that it seemed not a single place on their bodies remained unconnected.

Her body gripped his manhood, ripping a cry from him, pulling every bit of pleasure from him one pulse at a time. For the briefest of seconds, his hand caressed her flushed cheek and their eyes met. Hers were dreamy and satisfied, sucking him into their gaze. He started to bend forward to softly kiss her lips when he stopped himself.

As her eyes closed and she drifted back to sleep, Rafe jumped from the bed. He was getting too attached, turning sex into something it wasn't. He didn't believe in making love. It was sex — just sex.

He paced for several moments before he made his decision. He never let his mistresses stay with him. It was a solid rule. Because he wanted to break that rule with Ari, he forced himself to call his driver.

*****

"Ari, time to go."

Drifting between wakefulness and sleep, Ari struggled to open her eyes. Rafe? It sounded like him.

"Ari, you need to wake up. Your ride is here."

Finally Ari managed to get her eyes to open. She stretched her body and realized it was sore. As her foggy brain processed the moment, the night flooded back with the force of a tornado — the club, shower, and then the bed.

"Ride?" she asked, still not understanding.

"Yes, we're done for the night. I've arranged a ride home for you."

His cold tone of voice finally sank in, along with his words. He'd gotten what he wanted, so it was time for her to leave. Instant hurt filled her, but she immediately suppressed it. She had no right to be hurt — Rafe had never lied about what he expected.

He was clear from the beginning that he wanted only sex, nothing more. His paperwork stated specifically that his mistresses didn't sleep in his home. It was all laid out in black and white; she had no reason to be surprised.

True, she hadn't become his employee, but that didn't change the rules in Rafe's mind. She might have witnessed brief moments over the last few months when he acted more human, but the bottom line was that Rafe was what he was. He didn't put on a show, didn't pretend to want anything other than sex and control.

"Give me time to dress," she finally said and got up, grateful he'd undone her ties.

Neither of them said a word as she found her clothes from the night before lying on the foot of the bed. She didn't bother concealing herself as she put them on. What was the point? He'd seen her, all of her, gotten what he wanted, and was done for the night.

She needed to get out of there before she cried.

"I have the employment agreement if you're ready to work for me. I've even upped the wage to two hundred and fifty thousand."

Ari didn't allow her body to tense, didn't allow herself to show any emotion at his words. Rage and hurt were dancing around for dominance inside her, but she made sure her face remained blank as she slipped on her shoes.

She said nothing else as she made her way from his room. She heard the sound of his feet moving behind her, probably to make sure she left for the night — that she didn't try to hide somewhere and then sneak up and stab him through the heart.

It was actually a very real possibility.

"Think about it" were his parting words when she stepped out his front door and climbed into the backseat of his car. Ari's humiliation prevented her from meeting Mario's eyes. How many times had he taken Rafe's mistresses home? How many had he given the very last ride to? Ari was just one more in a long line of women.

There was no reason for her to feel the melancholy that had settled over her, but she couldn't seem to shake it. Rafe's torture had been effective. If she had been in a relationship with him, she wouldn't have wanted to defy him — wouldn't have wanted that buildup of pleasure to be for nothing.

As Mario pulled onto the street, Ari fought her tears. She wouldn't cry in front of Rafe's employee. Mario was obviously loyal to him and would report back that Ari had fallen apart. She would be home soon and then she could cry…though she didn't see what good it would do her.

Thankfully, Mario kept quiet, even showed her enough respect not to look at her in the rearview mirror. She liked Rafe's driver and normally would have tried to break the silence, ask him how his day was, but Ari couldn't speak. If one word slipped from her mouth, she knew she'd become a blubbering mess.

She managed to make it all the way home without a breakdown, then dealt with Mario's insistence on walking her to the door. She got inside without the key's giving her too much trouble, then calmly walked to her bed. Only when she knew it was safe to do so did she allow her knees to buckle and her heart to break.

Somewhere along the way she'd developed feelings for Rafe. She wouldn't say she was in love with him, but she'd grown to anticipate his arrival, look forward to their sparring matches, and desire his touch. She'd been stupid enough to begin falling for a man who made it more than clear he wasn't available for anything but what *he* wanted.

It wasn't enough for her. She would lose herself in him if she kept seeing him. So she would give herself this one morning to cry over Raffaello Palazzo, and then she'd make sure to avoid him no matter what it took. If she kept seeing him, she'd end up having sex with him. If she slept with him again, she wouldn't recover.

Sleep finally separated her from her misery, and when Ar woke up in the late afternoon, she had a firm resolve to listen to herself and not fall back into Rafe's twisted world. No matter how he pursued her, she wouldn't cave in to him or her own desires. She'd just have to take it one step, and one day, at a time for now

Chapter Thirty-Seven

Rafe slammed down the receiver — Ari had disconnected her phone. He'd given her a week to cool off before he'd begun calling again. She'd ignored his calls, messages, and e-mails.

Enough. He was finished giving her time. She could do this the easy way or the hard way, but the bottom line was that she would be his by tomorrow. He was finished waiting.

"Cancel my meetings," Rafe announced to his stunned assistant, then walked past her and straight through the offices to the elevators.

He was supposed to meet with a congressman in an hour. He didn't care. There was nothing more important on his agenda than getting his life back in order. Did he have a problem? Of course not. For some strange reason, Arianna Harlow had gotten under his skin, but it was temporary, nothing more. No feelings for the woman had grown in his heart, he told himself. It was about sex and only sex. What more could it be?

He wanted her all the time, night and day, but what angered him was he missed their daily interactions. His time with her in the hospital had been…surprisingly pleasant. He'd looked forward to hearing the sound of her laughter, seeing her victorious smile when she bested him at a game of poker, and witnessing the way she always had a kind word to say to the staff treating her.

There was so much more to Ari than he'd seen with any woman he'd been in a mutually pleasurable relationship with. He thrust that feeling aside. She desired him — that's all either of them needed to make this arrangement work.

Rafe called his driver on his way down the elevator, then glanced at his watch. It looked as if he was going to have a meeting with Ari at her place of employment. The thought made him smile. She wouldn't be able to fight him, because she didn't like public scenes.

The drive didn't take long, and soon he was outside the front doors. Rafe didn't hesitate as he strode inside.

"Mr. Palazzo, it's great to see you," the guard said as he jumped from his desk.

"Thank you, Dean. Don't announce me. This is a personal visit."

"Yes, sir," the man replied with a confused frown. Rafe wasn't known to simply drop in at the businesses he owned. He didn't like to be kept waiting, so it was much smarter for him to let the management staff know of his plans for arrival and be there to greet him.

He headed straight for the elevator and pushed the button for Ari's floor. Anticipation mounted as the car moved upward. When the doors opened, he stepped out and looked around at the staff, all of them hard at work. The manager seemed to be running a tight ship, and Rafe was pleased.

He turned a corner and spotted Ari at her desk — his gut instantly clenching. It had been a little over a week since their last encounter. He wasn't thrilled by the fact that he'd felt her absence. He'd often gone two weeks, sometimes a month, without seeing one of his mistresses when he was traveling. It had never bothered him. But now...

It must be only because their relationship wasn't official — still left up in the air. He didn't like the waiting — the uncertainty.

"Ari." He said nothing else as she stiffened before slowly lifting her head. He could see she'd rather be anywhere else at that moment than trapped into a conversation with him with her co-workers within hearing range.

"Mr. Palazzo, what are you doing here?" she asked between clenched teeth.

"We have unfinished business. Since you've refused to answer my calls, you've left me no choice but to seek you out."

"There is no unfinished business. We've said all there is to be said. Now, I'm at work, so I'll kindly ask you to leave. This is highly unprofessional," she scolded.

Damn, he really did like her fire — loved the fact that she wasn't afraid of him. That didn't mean he wouldn't break her; it just meant that it would take much longer for him to grow bored with their relationship.

He grabbed her arm and pulled her from the chair, not saying anything else as he led her to an empty conference room. Rafe had no doubt that the only reason she was coming along without a fight was her fear of causing a scene. But it worked for him at that moment.

Once inside with the door shut, she turned to him with fire in her eyes.

"Seriously, who in the hell do you think you are? This is where I work. If you think I'll come willingly to you if you get me fired, you're wrong."

"I have a trip tomorrow and I want you to go with me, so I don't have time to wait for you to figure things out. I've come to expedite the situation."

"Then you're going to be very unhappy with what I have to say. I'm done with you. No more games, no more drunken nights of sex. Nothing. Nada. Zip. Do you comprehend?"

"You are still refusing me?"

"That's what I've just said!"

"Then you've left me no choice." He walked away. Let her think what she wanted. She'd be his tomorrow.

*****

Ari watched Rafe walk out. She stayed where she was like a caged animal. Was it a trick? Was he going to turn around at any moment and pounce? She didn't know what to think right then. She waited for several minutes inside the conference room, and her body tensed when she saw the door handle begin to turn.

He was back.

"Ari, what the heck was that all about? Mr. Gorgeous stormed by my desk looking like he was pissed."

"Honestly, I have no idea, Amber," said Ari, still rattled but relieved that Rafe wasn't the one who'd walked through the door. "He wants to be in a relationship, but I've repeatedly told him it's not going to happen. He basically told me this was my last chance, and when I still refused, he left. It's not like him. I'm a bit afraid of the other shoe dropping."

"I get that I don't know him — but he's gorgeous, has a drool-worthy body and buttloads of cash. Why would you not want to go out with him?"

"It's complicated and I just want to get back to work. I promise to tell you all about it when I'm not so freaking ticked off," Ari said, hoping to appease her friend.

"I'll respect your privacy, but I hope you know this is taking years off my life. I'm dying to know what the big mystery is."

When Ari didn't say anything else, Amber let her be. Ari walked from the room and went straight to the bathroom, where she could splash cold water on her face and freshen up her make-up. She was in the middle of her shift and didn't have time to fall apart.

If Rafe had other plans, there was absolutely nothing she could do about it, so it wouldn't do her any good to fret. She'd been away from her desk for a good fifteen minutes now and it was time to get back to work.

When nothing else had happened by the end of the day, she decided that maybe he'd just given up. What Ari didn't understand was the slight disappointment she felt. With all the stress she'd been through in the last months, she wouldn't be surprised if she was having a nervous breakdown.

Her mother was getting out of the hospital any day now and Ari still hadn't found the courage to tell her about the house or her mother's business. Rafe's chasing her had been one wild ride after the other. Not having work — and then managing to land a great job.

"Just place one foot in front of the other and remember that tomorrow is a new day." That was what Ari told herself at least twice a day — that day she had to repeat it about twenty times. Being with Rafe was like finding herself inside a fast-moving tornado. Ari wasn't sure she even understood what a calm, normal life felt like anymore.

Chapter Thirty-Eight

"Can I see you in my office?"

"Yes. Let me finish this e-mail and I'll be right there," Ari said as she pressed the intercom speaker and replied to her boss. With a few keystrokes she finished her work and sent the document.

Rising from her seat, she stretched her arms and smiled. Although her job was boring and mundane, and it made her want to rush back into the classroom so she could do what she truly loved, she liked where she worked.

She had amazing benefits, worked with good people and made enough money to take care of her mother and still have some left over for savings. She thought she might even be able to get back to school within the year. That was the best-case scenario.

She walked down the long hallway and knocked on her boss's open door.

"Come in, Ari. How soon can you get home and pack a bag?"

"Sir?" She'd been told that she might have to travel, but she'd assumed she'd get a lot more notice than *go pack a bag*. She wasn't upset about going somewhere — just the opposite, in fact. She thought it would be nice to get out of town, *anywhere* other than the Bay area. She soon had to face picking up her mother at the hospital, telling the poor woman how much her beloved daughter had messed everything up, and then, with luck, gathering up the pieces of her mom's shattered heart.

"The CEO requested you for a business trip to New York. The jet leaves in two hours. A car is waiting out front to take you back to your place and then get you to the airport. Will that give you enough time?"

"Yes, of course, but I don't understand," she hedged. "How long will I be gone? Why would the CEO have requested me? I really don't think I'm qualified for…" She trailed off at the smile on her boss's face.

"Don't look so frightened, Ari. This is a good thing. It means that you do such an excellent job here that the corporate officers have taken notice of you. This could end up being a big promotion for you. I don't want to lose you here, but I'd never hold you back. If advancement is on the horizon, then you need to reach out and grasp it," he said with sincerity. "Headquarters didn't say how long you'd be gone, but I think it's a quick trip. Normally, they give a lot more notice than two hours if it's anything longer than a couple days."

"I guess I can go, then — I don't know what to say," she answered hesitantly as shock filled her.

She wasn't sure that she wanted advancement. What if the job ended up being wonderful and then she never went back to school? She didn't want to settle for a job just because it paid well. She wanted to finish her education and do what she was always meant to do.

"You say a heartfelt thanks and then rush home to get ready," he replied with a chuckle.

"Thank you, Mr. Avery. I appreciate your confidence in me," she replied automatically.

He waved her off and she turned around and went back to her desk, where she gathered her coat and purse and then made her way to the bank of elevators. It didn't take long for her to reach the lobby, and then to step outside.

A nice Bentley was parked at the curb with a driver waiting at the back door. He immediately opened the door when he spotted her and Ari slid inside without saying a word. She hoped it was the company car and not a kidnapper — not that she'd be worth kidnapping. She didn't have a wealthy family that could post ransom. She certainly didn't have any kind of influence with the rich and famous. She was just Ari.

"Good afternoon, ma'am. I have your address here. Do you need to make any other stops before we arrive there?"

"No, but thank you."

The conversation ceased during the drive to her apartment. It was nice not having to fight the busy city traffic or take public transportation. She could seriously get used to being chauffeured around.

They reached her apartment in about fifteen minutes, and she ran up the stairs to throw a few items together. She hadn't been told anything about the trip and thus was unsure what to pack. She didn't have any dinner dresses, so that was out. She hoped she wasn't expected to attend anything formal. But if she were, she'd just have to buy something.

She wouldn't like cutting into her savings, but she *would* be in New York, and it would almost be a shame for her not to do at least a little bit of shopping. Her optimism rose as she took a moment to think about it.

This could be a great trip. She'd probably be sitting in on meetings during the day, taking notes, and then typing things up. She was certainly good at that. Her nights would most likely be her own to do with as she pleased. If they were going to be there several days, maybe she'd even be able to take in a Broadway show. The best part of all was that she'd be on the other side of the country — far from Rafe. She was still unsure what his surprise visit was about yesterday.

Ari made sure she had her ID and a few changes of clothing, and then she double-checked all her windows, making sure they were locked. Her next task of business was to call the hospital. Her fears were assuaged when the doctor assured her that her mother wouldn't be released until least Tuesday. She'd have plenty of time to get home. Luckily, she didn't have any pets to worry about, so she was back down to the car within twenty minutes.

"That was much faster than I'm used to," the driver said with a smile as he again held open her door.

"I don't like to waste time. There was only so much to pack," she said as she handed him her bag and then slid into the back seat. He stowed her luggage in the back, then came around, and the car was back on the road.

Ari wanted to fill the silence with conversation, but she didn't know what to talk about, so she just sat back and enjoyed the ride. It was a beautiful and sunny day, perfect for seeing the view out the jet's windows as they took off.

When the driver skirted the main airport, Ari grew concerned. As worse-case scenarios began to play out in her mind, he turned down a connecting road and approached a private facility next door.

"Why are we here?"

"This is where the corporate jets are stored. They use a separate runway."

"Oh, that makes sense."

"Right this way, please," he said as he helped her from the car and then led her to the building, straight through and out the back door.

Ari gasped at the size of the jet in front of her. It was as large as a commercial aircraft. This had to be the wrong one. Private jets were small and sleek.

"Is something wrong?" the driver asked.

"Is that what I'm traveling in?"

"I know, it's a bit large. I've always wanted to ride in her. It's a 747, picked up right from the factory and converted into a beautiful private jet. It has a large master bedroom, two other sleeping quarters, a conference room, general meeting area, kitchen and two more bathrooms. If you're going to travel, this is the way to do it."

"Wow. I had no idea the company I work for had this kind of wealth. The offices are nice, but they're not *that* nice," she said with a whistle as she started to move forward again.

She missed the incredulous look he gave her. Had she stopped and listened to him a few more moments, she never would have stepped inside the jet, and then never been thrown the hardest choice of her life.

Chapter Thirty-Nine

Rafe stayed where he was like a panther preparing to leap. What amazed him were the nerves coursing through his body. He didn't succumb to such weakness — he was Rafe Palazzo and nothing could affect him.

He sat back in his comfortable lounge chair and watched Ari's shadow edge into the jet, showing him she was now walking up the stairs.

He waited.

Taking a sip of his bourbon, he leaned farther back in his seat, casually placing one foot across the top of his opposite knee. He was the picture of cool confidence, though the fire raging in his eyes could certainly quash the rumors that he was a man of ice.

Finally, Ari stepped inside. His eyes never left her face as she glanced around at her surroundings with some dismay, apparently intimidated by all the luxury and expense. It wasn't surprising that Ari, having grown up in a lower-middle-class neighborhood, might have a difficult time adapting to his world. He didn't even blink when he lost millions in the stock market, but then that was nothing to him, not when he had billions more to secure his future. She could hardly have the same reactions.

Ari's eyes adjusted to the light, and that's when she turned and spotted him sitting there. His first instinct was to stand up and haul her to the back of the jet, where his luxurious suite was available for him to devour her. Still, he didn't allow even so much as a single muscle to twitch.

This was a game — and his ultimate victory would come when she surrendered herself totally to him. He would let her speak first — if she did so at all. By the look in her panicked eyes, it was obvious she hadn't expected to see him. Had she honestly thought he would allow her to leave him so easily? He was soon to find out.

*****

Ari was frozen to the spot as she looked into Rafe's now frosty purple eyes. How could she not have put the pieces together? Of course she hadn't been so lucky as to get her current job on her own. The minute that call had come in, she should have researched the company, found out all there was to know.

It wouldn't do her any good to kick herself now. She felt as if she'd been run over by a herd of animals. She was trapped against the ground and the line of mammals continued to keep her locked down, with pain radiating from every single inch of her body.

"You own Sunstream Electronics." She wasn't asking, but merely making a statement. She refused to play the victim or ask senseless questions.

"Obviously." He wasn't going to make any of this easier on her. But then again, when had he really made things easier? Yes, there'd been some moments. A few brief flashes in time when he'd actually seemed to be human, but those times were quickly fading in light of how manipulative he'd actually been the entire time she'd known him.

To be honest, Rafe had said he always played to win. He'd let her know in no uncertain terms that she was nothing more than a plaything, another trophy for his shelf. She thought the two of them had played every game, with her always losing the battles, but apparently there was still one game left to play.

It looked as if she were losing her job.

His last hand was being dealt and her only question right then was how bad the damage would be to her. If he felt confident enough to reveal himself as her true boss, then one of two things had happened.

He was either bored with her and ready to purge her from his life, or he had an offer he felt was too good for her to refuse. If the latter was the case, he had underestimated her. One thing she'd learned in the last few months was that she could survive on her own.

It wasn't always easy, and she knew there were plenty of speed bumps ahead in her long journey, but her confidence had grown. She was managing to take care of herself and her mother. She might have been working for Rafe all along, but she took it as a huge victory that it hadn't been as his personal call girl.

With a surge of confidence, she threw her shoulders back and stepped farther into the jet, walking up to him and looking impassively down into his once again burning eyes.

"Mr. Palazzo, we've been cleared for departure. Would you like us to shut the doors now?"

Before Rafe could respond to his attendant, Ari spoke, staring straight into Rafe's eyes the entire time, making sure he knew she wasn't afraid of him.

"No. I'll be getting off the aircraft in just a moment."

She nearly stumbled back a step, away from the flames leaping in Rafe's dark depths. If looks could kill, she'd be nothing but ashes. But instead of revealing her slight moment of weakness, she decided to push his buttons a bit harder, and she smirked.

"Hold the doors for a moment and leave us," Rafe commanded. The attendant almost scampered away.

"It seems we've finally arrived where I knew we'd end up all along. You've just made an increasingly long ordeal out of something that should have been taken care of that day in the restaurant."

"I told you then that I wouldn't be your whore, Mr. Palazzo. That decision still stands. That you were able to trick me into your employment anyway doesn't mean that you own me. I will find other employment."

He paused with a knowing look on his face. Her stomach fluttered as she waited for him to hit her with whatever it was he had to say. Nothing could make her change her mind…

The longer he waited, the more her agitation grew, which he could obviously read in her eyes, for his own face reflected his confidence in victory.

"Your mother gets released from the hospital on Tuesday, Ari. I happen to own your childhood home now. It's your decision whether your mother discovers you sold off everything and she has no place to go, or whether she can heal in the comfort of her home. I also happen to own her floral shop. Do you give her back her life, or do you remain as self-serving as you've always been and take all you can at the expense of the woman who raised you?"

Ari stood frozen. The one thing that had been eating her alive when her mom talked about returning home and getting back to work was what he held against her. She'd underestimated his desire to win.

Rage filled her as she looked into Rafe's burning eyes. He wasn't even human. How dare he put her in this position! How could he live with himself! It might kill her mother to find out that she had nothing left after surviving a car crash that should have taken her life, and then beating all odds and surviving the cancer that had tried to finish her off.

"It looks like you have a choice to make, Ari? Do you choose love or callous self-respect?"

"You're a bastard, Rafe. Do you care for no one other than yourself?"

"Ah, I hope you choose love, because it will be a great pleasure for me to break your spirit — and leave no doubt about it, Ari — I will break you."

Her stomach lurched as she looked into the eyes of a stranger. This wasn't the same man who'd rescued her, laughed with her, and adored his family. This was indeed a monster — one who wanted nothing less than everything — her pride, her self-respect, her very soul.

"If you choose self-pity, you're free to go, with no one to worry about but yourself. You can feel sorry for yourself about the situation you're in and try to put back the pieces of your shattered life, or you can choose love — love for the mother who raised you. I neither want nor need your love, so don't ever get the idea that this will lead to more than what it is. You will be my mistress and nothing more. I tried love once, and got nothing but affliction for my efforts. Make your decision quickly because I have a long flight ahead of me and work to do."

"I need time…"

"Your time is up. You can exit the way you came in. *Or* you can take yourself back to my bedroom and strip. Your training will begin immediately."

Ari held back the tears of anger as she turned away from him. She was faced with an impossible choice. She couldn't sign her life over to him — but she couldn't leave her mother to die.

Maybe he was bluffing. She could walk out the door and find out. She retreated a step while still looking into his eyes. He showed absolutely no emotion as she wrestled with the hardest decision she'd ever had to make. He really didn't seem to care one way or the other what she would decide.

With a firm resolve, Ari turned from him and took a step toward the aircraft's open door...

THE END

Book Two: Submit, *Expected May 31st of 2013*

Go to http://www.melodyanne.com and sign up for Mel's mailing list to receive an e-mail when the second book becomes available.

You can find Melody Anne's other romance and young-adult series at all major retailers.

ABOUT THE AUTHOR

Melody Anne is the author of the popular series, Billionaire Bachelors, and Baby for the Billionaire. She also has a Young Adult Series in high demand; Midnight Fire and Midnight Moon - Rise of the Dark Angel with a third book in the works called Midnight Storm.

As an aspiring author, she wrote for years, then became published in 2011. Holding a Bachelor's Degree in business, she loves to write about strong, powerful, businessmen and the corporate world.

When Melody isn't writing, she cultivates strong bonds with her family and relatives and enjoys time spent with them as well as her friends, and beloved pets. A country girl at heart, she loves the small town and strong community she lives in and is involved in many community projects.

See Melody's Website at: **www.melodyanne.com.** She makes it a point to respond to all her fans. You can also join her on facebook at: www.facebook.com/authormelodyanne, or at twitter: @authmelodyanne.

She looks forward to hearing from you and thanks you for your continued interest in her stories.